BEYOND ABSOLUTE LOVE

Beyond Absolute Love

LUCRETIA BINGHAM

Rand-Smith LLC

Print ISBN: 978-1-950544-30-1
Digital ISBN: 978-1-950544-31-8

First Printing, 2021

Rand-Smith Books
www.Rand-Smith.com

CONTENTS

| 1 |

Those first weeks in New York were a blur of physical details, many of them painful. Cornelia was trotted about. People grabbed her chin, twisting her face from side to side. They ran their fingers over her body, pinching her stomach to see if there was any excess flesh.

There was not.

Other people painted her face then rubbed it off. They washed her hair, yanked it free of tangles, jerked it up into high, backcombed madness, then brushed it back out. People barked at her to take off her clothes, yelled at her when she squirmed, pushed her to stand taller, jump higher, project better. Lights flashed, so bright they made her squint. Voices shouted to arch her back, open her eyes, angle her face, thrust out her pelvis. The only thing she would not do was smile. Whenever they asked, she scowled.

Geraldine Dodge, who, it turned out, was a bit of a comic nightmare, orchestrated everything. She was a parody of an aging fashion model - all bony angles and paper-thin. Her lips had thinned, but their ghost was still sharply outlined in crimson. She yelled at Cornelia to be grateful, poked at her posture, and kept track of every little penny she, Geraldine, was spending, so that one day, when the "dollink gull," as she called her, was earning her keep, Cornelia could pay her back in triple.

Her mother Nevin fluttered around, her face creased with worry. "Why *won't* you smile?" she begged Cornelia.

Cornelia had no answer. She hated the fittings and cuttings, the posing and reposing, and the endless rounds of makeup and hair pulls. She felt invaded, attacked, silenced, made fun of, and talked down to--anything but herself, whoever that was.

After an endless series of taxi rides to midtown offices, downtown lofts, and Seventh Avenue dressing rooms, at the end of each day, a final taxi ride took them back to their tiny room at the Barbizon. Cornelia would collapse face down, spread-eagle onto the bed, and fall fast asleep, only waking briefly to devour whatever take-out Nevin brought back to the hotel.

One day, several weeks into this madness, Geraldine summoned them to her office high up on the twenty-sixth floor of a midtown Madison Avenue skyscraper. In the taxi on the way there, Nevin chittered such a string of what-ifs that Cornelia snapped at her to be quiet. When Nevin cringed, an increasingly familiar frown tugged at Cornelia's forehead. "Sorry," she said. Nevin bridled.

With Cornelia slouching behind, Nevin nodded at the security guard, told the giraffe-like models in the elevator that they looked lovely, then chatted with the receptionist as they waited for Geraldine to call them in. People were always telling Cornelia how lucky she was to have such a sweet mother, but Nevin's cheerfulness toward strangers just made Cornelia want to sink through the floor.

Finally, Geraldine's heavily made-up assistant, teetering on sky-high platforms, waved them in. "Quickly now," she clicked her fingers, "Geraldine's cleared out a whole fifteen minutes for you. Make it good."

What does that mean, Cornelia thought *Make what good?* Later, she was to understand that in the world of the success-driven, you had to grab those fifteen minutes and fill them with your presence. But at the time, slumping in behind a chirpy Nevin, she hadn't a clue.

Geraldine didn't look up as they came in. She was studying a row of proof sheets on her desk, magnifying glass in hand, hunched so low that with her severely drawn-back chignon and the perennial slash of red across her lips, she looked like a vulture pecking at a carcass.

Cornelia slouched down into a green leather chair and tried to erase the vulture image from her brain. She studied all the framed magazine covers on the wall. There were cover pictures of Geraldine's "dollinks" stretching back to the 1940s. An awkward silence ensued. Nevin dealt with it by snapping her clutch open and then closing it. When Cornelia leaned over to make her stop, Nevin flinched and tried to smile, but her eyes drooped with anxiety. "What if she doesn't like your pictures?" she whispered.

"Well," Geraldine finally drawled, "you're certainly not *Seventeen* material." She peered at them over her half-moon spectacles.

"That's bad, isn't it?" Nevin asked.

"Well now, I didn't say that now did I?"

"No, no, I guess not," said Nevin.

"What do you think?" Geraldine's eyes pivoted to Cornelia.

"What do I think?" she said.

"That's what I said, didn't I? Don't tell me you don't understand such a simple question." Her eyebrows shot up and she drew off her glasses with a dismissive wave.

Anger flared in Cornelia. "Well now, thinking depends on being given something to consider, doesn't it now? You've stated I'm certainly *not* 'Seventeen' material but given no reason why. What does that mean, I'm 'not *Seventeen* material?' I'm too young? Too skinny? Too tall? Too what? So, what do I think? I think I need to know more than you're giving me; that's what *I* think."

"*Cornelia*," said Nevin. Both Geraldine and Cornelia ignored her.

"Well now," Geraldine smiled, "the gull speaks. I was beginning to wonder whether you had a voice at all. I wasn't sure whether letting your mother do all the talking for you meant that you were too stupid to say anything or were just too used to letting her do all the talking."

Nevin pitched forward to the edge of her seat, "Let me just say..."

Geraldine held up just one hand, "We've had enough of that for now. For one moment, for God's sake, stop being a stupid little woman."

Nevin clamped her mouth shut.

Though she agreed with Geraldine, a reptilian part of her wasn't going to let this pass. Cornelia jumped to her feet. "Don't you dare speak to her like that."

"Ah ha. So the gull has fierceness as well." Her lips stretched out and up in what passed for a smile. "I was wondering when the person in front of me was going to match what I'm seeing here." She tapped at the proof sheets with a red talon fingernail. "Or whether she was just another sullen spoiled brat." She cocked her head down at the proof sheets, "Here," she said, "come take a look."

Cornelia walked around to stand next to Geraldine behind her big oval desk. She smelled like musky fruit. The skin on her forehead was stretched taut.

Cornelia looked down at the proof sheets. Everything about her was angular. Her thighs were rangy, her shoulders hunched, her pelvic thrust extreme. The bony face was fraught, the scowl ferocious. Her eyes seared the camera. "They're awful. Bad." she whispered.

"You think so?" Geraldine peered up at her. There were milky rings around her irises, contrasting strangely with the smudge of black kohl around the rims. "Awful? Maybe. *Bad?* Not at all." She poked at the shots with her index finger. "*Not* 'Seventeen,' *that's* for sure. But *editorial?* Yes indeed."

"Editorial?" said Nevin, in so low a tone as to be obsequious. "Is that good?"

Geraldine glared but answered her. "That means *Vogue.* And *Women's Wear Daily.* And *Harper's Bazaar.* It means Helmut Newton. After he shoots her, everyone will want her. That's what it means. They'll be fighting over the bones when we scatter them."

Cornelia shuddered.

"Oh my," said Nevin.

After that, the madness truly started.

Cornelia dashed from one photographer's loft to another, all a bewildering haze of lights and mostly men barking orders at her from behind the black hole of the camera lens.

Flashing by the windows of taxis, the city was a maze of claustrophobic canyons, clogged with traffic, writhing with gray pedestrians, the homeless slumped over their despairing banners, whores flashing their sausage legs, and a constant cacophony of horns, engines, and squealing brakes stuffing the air.

And then the exotic locations started, preluded by long overnight plane rides and an endless series of airports that all looked the same. She was photographed leaping out of a carved dugout in Papua New Guinea. She writhed on a beach in Cabo San Lucas. She jumped out of a window in Mexico City. She climbed the ramparts of Machu Picchu and posed with a llama.

But she never stopped long enough to walk or enjoy or to look, much less think. And of course, because she was still so young, Nevin went with her everywhere, charming the crews and flittering around Cornelia as if she were a mindless fairy godmother. "Isn't this just wonderful?" she clapped her hands, "It's a dream come true." She smiled, and they all smiled with her. And the frown between Cornelia's eyes became as fixed as if it were set in concrete.

"Ain't you jest a fierce liddle spider monkey noaw?" quipped one South London photographer. And the moniker stuck. *Fierce liddle spider monkey* or *sulky liddle rich girl?* blared a *Women's Wear Daily* headline. And finally, it was just spider monkey, and then monkey, and she no longer even had her own name.

"Monkey!" The photographers would call out, and she would turn, and scowl, and they would flash their lights at her in response.

The money started flowing in.

Geraldine took out her triple payback and still there was money left over. Nevin found a soulless apartment on the Upper East Side. Bloomingdales delivered two single box-spring beds. Nevin swore that when they had time, she would furnish it and make it a home. But for now, the rooms rang with emptiness. What difference did it make, Cornelia thought, she only needed a shower and a bed after all.

At night, scrunched up tight at the bottom of the box-spring mattress, she could just see a sliver of the full moon slicing the East River into silvery ribbons. Grateful for the dark and silence, she would lie awake for hours and wonder.

She allowed herself to wonder about Rudy and Nathan. Nevin had found an article on page 11 of the *Sunday Times Arts and Leisure* section about the new Moral Absolutes musical called *Up with Youth*. It was touring Cincinnati, Cleveland, and then on to Pittsburgh and points farther west in the heartland. Rudy was described as the only lyrical breath of fresh air in an otherwise turgid mess of a propaganda production. "Absolutely Banal" was the title of the review. And there was no mention of Nathan. Nevin and Cornelia pored over the fuzzy photograph above the review in which a radiant Rudy was front and center. She refused to give Nevin the satisfaction of agreeing that Nathan was the out-of-focus head behind her.

"Both my children, stars in the making," said Nevin.

"Hardly."

"But you are. Everyone says so."

Cornelia snorted.

"Why do you always have to be so negative? I should think you'd be happy about everyone fussing around you all the time. I know I would be."

As always, Cornelia felt guilty. She put her arm around her mother's shoulders and cooed, "Poor liddle Mummy, does she want her own hair and makeup people?"

Nevin shrugged off the embrace. "It doesn't matter at all what I want. It's all about you now."

Cornelia also wondered about her father.

He was ensconced, he wrote, in the European headquarters of the Moral Absolutes, now legally separate from the American group. The center was housed in a wonderful old grand hotel, set high up in the Alps above Lake Geneva in Switzerland.

You are always welcome. It might be good for you to take time to think about where your life is heading. Frankly, this new twist in your life bewilders me and I fear its superficiality. Though several friends disagree, my clear guidance is to trust that God has a plan for you. It is no surprise to me that your mother seems delighted by this strange turn of events. I know she always dreamed of fame for herself. And now she'll have a chance to live out that dream through you, it seems.

She was not comforted by his words.

Cornelia Nevin Woodstock was just a child when she left the isolation of her mother's goat farm to live within the confines of her father's "group," the Moral Absolutes, where purity and honesty were championed, but predatory leaders were not punished. Years later, when she was known only as Cornelia, she was often asked how she had grown up. Her bony face would grimace. "That's not an easy answer. First it was life on a desert island. And then it was the cult. Both had good and evil. It took a while to figure it all out." The one good thing, she always told people, was that she had met Hadji there.

She longed for Hadji. Her father wrote that he was back in India, trying to raise money for a forced march that would start at the ocean near Mumbai, then wind its way across India to Madras. The march was to be an effort to raise consciousness about healing the rift between the Hindus and Muslims. That letter stayed crunched up in the trash for less time than the others. "Tell him to write me," she finally wrote, feeling very daring.

And occasionally she also wondered about Hall Hamden, though these thoughts were full of shame and anger and guilt. Once, she had called the DA's office in Michigan but hung up when they asked how to direct her call. Her bites had faded to a row of silver crescent moons along her shoulder, but the memories still ached.

In the meantime, the endless round of fittings and posing and shooting whirled by until the past and any semblance of a family outside her mother seemed a far-off dream. Instead of school, she had tutors who quizzed her while her hair was up in curlers. Instead of boyfriends, she had hairdressers and makeup artists. And instead of girlfriends, she had Nevin.

The many long weeks turned into many long months, until suddenly she was seventeen and the stalk of runways, the blur of long plane rides, the flash of the lights began to obscure any other sense of reality. And, as her image grew in fame in the outside world, she faded into obscurity inside herself.

In the taxi on their way over to the Plaza, Nevin clutched her hand. "I'm so nervous, Nee, how do I look?" She fluffed her hair, hiding the still-pink scars that curved in a shell arc just in front of her ears.

They were on their way to meet Rudy and Nathan for afternoon tea in the Palm Court. It had been almost a year and a half since Nathan had seen Nevin and indeed her appearance had changed. First, she had chopped off her waist-long grey hair. "After all, it was only grown long for Ray", she had chirped, "Never my thing at all, *I* always liked my hair in a bob!" And so instead of having a silver bun pulled back up off her face, she now had short waves that spun like shiny doll hair all around her new face.

Nevin had first started off with buying clothes. She came home from shopping excursions, her arms piled high with bags, her face all flushed and pretty. Nevin's closet gradually filled with tailored suits, cinched in at the waist, ruffled silk blouses, and lovely dresses that showed off her full figure to its best advantage. Cornelia didn't begrudge her the buying because she was happy to see a smile on her face. Anything was better than her suicidal blues. And, she had to admit, Nevin was always careful to buy on sale or at discount stores.

Then Nevin started signing up for "free, don't you know" makeup consultations at various department stores. And she would come home laden with all the makeup they used. "It's not that I'm vain, I just need a little pick-me-up. You don't begrudge me that, do you?" She shot a look at Cornelia from under her eyebrows, sensitive, as always, to any disapproval. Cornelia tried to look as bland as she could, but she could feel the rictus frown setting like cement along her forehead.

Then she started talking about plastic surgery. "You don't want your mother looking like a hag, do you now?" When Cornelia scowled, she faltered. "Oh no, I won't do anything then. You'd rather me dragging behind you like some sad sack, wouldn't you? That would suit you just fine." Then Nevin would give her the silent treatment. Once they had gone a week without talking.

When she couldn't stand the loneliness any longer, Cornelia sighed and said, "Whatever you want, Mummy, I don't mind."

"Well, it's your money, don't you know. So I need you to approve. Of course, if I hadn't arranged for all of this to happen, we'd still be stuck in Nassau, wouldn't we now? But of course I'll do whatever *you* want!"

"Mummy, don't make this about *me* wanting you to have a facelift. It's you having the facelift. Not me."

"Well, you don't have to be cruel about it. I can't help it if I'm not young anymore. I should think you would want me to be pretty again."

"I do. I do."

"But your tone of voice is so awful!"

"Please, Mummy, just *go* get whatever you want done and stop talking about it."

So finally, Nevin had arranged to take several weeks off from her "work" of supervising Cornelia. She was going away for a *much-needed* rest, she told people. Only Cornelia knew Nevin had done her research and found out that the most highly acclaimed plastic surgeon was at John's Hopkins in Baltimore.

Cornelia snuck a look at her now in the taxicab, and she had to admit the result was good. Nevin looked well-rested and attractive. The sags and pouches on her face were gone; her skin was smooth and her eyes wide open. While not as pretty as she had been in her thirties, she was a beauty of a fifty-year-old, with a new firm chin line, carefully applied makeup, and a stunning new pants suit with a jacket that showed off her waist and cupped her full breasts.

"Isn't it a shame you didn't get my figure?" she said as she smoothed down her clothes over her hourglass body. Her eyes narrowed as she turned to study Cornelia. "Honestly, can't you even brush your hair these days? And those baggy jeans." Her hand reached out to push the hair off Cornelia's forehead.

Cornelia shrugged off the touch. "Stop it. Leave me alone." She raked her fingers through her hair and shook it out until it lay unfettered and wild all around her face and shoulders and down over, according to Nevin, her small breasts.

As Nevin prattled on in the taxi, obsessing about the upcoming reunion with Nathan, Cornelia stroked her jeans, as soft and faded blue as denim could get without fraying. Her groin throbbed. Nevin didn't know these latest jeans actually belonged to Alexander Chester. In fact, her mother knew nothing at all about Alexander.

When she travelled with her mother, Nevin always kept her on a tight leash. "You need your beauty sleep, Cornelia, you know you do." And so they always were in bed by nine.

While she was having her "rest" in Maryland, Nevin had arranged for one of Cornelia's makeup artists to chaperone her while in California for a shoot for Paris *Vogue*. They had stayed at the Chateau Marmont in Hollywood. Maisy, it turned out, hadn't cared what Cornelia did so long as she showed up for her bookings on time.

"Toodle-oo," Maisy waved her fingers as she headed out the door. "Don't do anything I wouldn't do," she winked.

That first night, Cornelia had stayed in her room and watched television. But the following day, she wasn't scheduled to shoot until the afternoon. Maisy asked her to go shopping on Melrose, but she refused. While Cornelia quite liked foreign markets and medinas, she found shopping in the United States exhausting. When people recognized her, it just made her want to sink into the ground.

An hour after Maisy had left, Cornelia felt restless, so she covered up a bathing suit with a man's white shirt, put on huge Italian sunglasses and went down to the courtyard pool. She lay down and basked. New York had been gloomy and gray for months, so she relinquished herself to the scorching embrace of the noonday Los Angeles sun. She fell asleep and awoke to Alexander Chester leaning down over her. He was only a boy, she thought, and lovely at that. She didn't get to meet many boys.

Despite Nevin's careful vigilance, men pursued her with brutal carnality. Photographers would grab her hand and then, when Nevin's eyes slipped away, quickly move it to their crotch. Agents cornered her at press parties, bragging about how they could make her even more famous, but only if she liked to suck cock. During those times, she was very glad to have Nevin nearby.

And yet sometimes, Nevin failed her. The worst had been the fat billionaire who asked them to spend the weekend on his massive yacht. Cornelia didn't want to go but Nevin insisted. "Don't you want me to have just a little bit of happiness?"

He sent his private jet to pick them up and flew them down to Miami where his one-hundred-and-twenty-foot boat was docked.

At dinner, flashing his capped teeth, he had plied Nevin with wine and compliments, until, flushed, she stumbled back to their cabin. Sometime before, Cornelia, sickened by her mother's flirting, had fled the dining room and was ensconced on a chaise looking out at the moon. He had hunted her down and before she could stop him, had rolled his rotund body on top of her, his fingers thrusting between her legs. "Take this as your first lesson in listening, let me just undo your jeans here, you won't feel a thing."

He grunted as she struggled to get out from under him.

He flopped her back.

She jabbed him in the groin with her thigh.

As he was groaning "bitch," she ran back to their cabin and bolted the door, then held a pillow over her head to blot out the sound of his fingernail scratch on the door. When he bantered with Nevin over the breakfast table, Cornelia stalked off the boat.

Half an hour later, Nevin stomped down the gangway. "Honestly, Cornelia, that was just rude. When I was having such fun. You resent me having fun, don't you?"

Cornelia turned away from her, afraid that her rage would spit bile all over her mother. Nevin sulked all the way back to New York. And for weeks she chastised Cornelia about how she had ruined her one chance at happiness.

* * *

At 22, Alexander was much younger than most of the men Cornelia met. When he smiled down at her, reflections from the pool danced across his face, literally dazzling her.

He held up his hands in apology. "I hope you don't mind; I took pictures of you while you were sleeping. I know I should have asked first. I'm sorry." He smiled, and his teeth flashed clean and white. His eyes were the cobalt of the morning sky before it bleaches white. Above his bushy black eyebrows, his hair waved up into a mass of streaked platinum curls. He started each day by surfing, he said, and he never rinsed out the salt or combed his hair. He smelled of mint and salt and all things fresh and clean.

A 35mm camera hung around his neck. She blushed to notice that, below the massive camera, his faded blue denim shirt opened to a nest of black curls. To her surprise, she wanted to touch him there to see whether the hairs were soft or springy. It had been a long time since she had wanted to touch somebody.

"You were just so beautiful lying there. I couldn't help myself. Do you forgive me?"

The opposite of cunning or predatory, he appeared more like a child asking another to play. When she nodded, a look of wonderful relief crossed his face. "Oh, I'm so glad. Listen, how would you like to go surfing? Have you been to Santa Monica?"

She shook her head.

"You do surf, don't you? You look like you surf."

She blushed and shook her head again.

"Body surf?" he asked.

She nodded. "I learned as a child."

"Oh good! Let's go then. Station 26. Best lifeguard station on the beach. Come on." He held out his hand.

"Now? Shouldn't I get something?" He pulled her to her feet.

"What could you possibly need?" he laughed. "You've already got on a bathing suit, here are your flip-flops. Let's go." As if he were The Pied Piper, she followed him without a qualm.

His Volkswagen van was filled with surfboards, a panting Golden lab, a pile of faded blue jeans, a stack of carefully folded white T-shirts, a rolled-up sleeping bag, a camp stove, and a box full of Ramen noodles and cans of beans. "Here, listen to this!" he said, putting a tape into the player on the dashboard. "It's the Beach Boys! Don't you love them?" He didn't seem to notice that the songs were fresh to her. They didn't play the Beach Boys in New York. There, it was all hard rock.

As they drove down the Santa Monica freeway with the windows open, her hair lifted with the breeze and her feet naturally hitched up onto the shelf below the windshield.

At the beach, they tumbled out, including the dog, and ran down across the sand at full speed. They splashed into the water, dove under the incoming waves, then swam out past the break to the calm outside.

"At first, the lifeguards gave me a hard time about Rex here," he nodded at the dog who was swimming in close circles around them, "but then they could see he didn't bother anybody, and when they saw he could surf, they didn't bother us at all." He threw back his head and laughed with abandon and she laughed with him.

They swam for hours, shrieking with glee when the big waves didn't tumble them but sent them scudding out in front of the break like wild screeching dolphins. They swam and swam until her muscles tired, and all the scowls faded away and she found her face aching with the unfamiliar stretch of a smile.

Finally, exhausted, they swam ashore and fell into the sand, and she curled up like a baby in the sun and napped for five minutes. And again, when she awoke, he was smiling down at her and held up his camera, lifting his eyebrows for permission. She smiled back, and he snapped the camera.

He drove her to her shoot, which was out at Zuma beach. Maisy cocked an eyebrow at her messy hair, and burned cheekbones, but smiled knowingly when she saw Alex, as he liked to be called. He stalked around the edges of the shoot, studying the lights and equipment and then, without saying goodbye, slipped away. When she saw his van driving out of the parking lot, her heart skipped a beat and she felt bereft.

But she needn't have worried. He seemed to have an almost magic sense of her schedule and would show up just when she was alone, and they would career around in his van. He took her out to the Antelope desert, where they wandered among fields of orange poppies, and then farther out to the Mojave where twisted Joshua trees waved their arms at the huge blue bowl of a sky. And she felt the tension ebbing away while once more being surrounded by beauty. And she smiled. And she hardly noticed that he always snapped pictures.

He hardly touched her at first, just once licking the crust of salt off her shoulder. Gradually he touched her more. He would grab her by the hand when he wanted to run. Or lift her up onto his shoulders when they walked through the evening along the Venice boardwalk. With her hands touching his warm, sunburned, muscular shoulders, and her legs hanging down around his neck, she experienced a mind-numbing sensual pleasure. When he lifted her down and his hands encircled her waist, she slumped against him, her legs as weak as a kitten's. He laughed and leaned down to quickly press his full lips against hers.

One night, in the parking lot of the Chateau Marmont, they lay in the back of his van on top of his sleeping bag, and he kissed her until she panted. But his fingers never strayed over her body. He let her come to him, until she climbed on top and rode his thigh and came like stars popping out all over heaven. She lay curled up in his arms and he stroked her hair and called her baby.

On the next day, when she and Maisy flew back to New York, she turned to the window and blinked back tears. She feared she would never see him again.

And so now, in the taxi on the way to the Plaza, a deep almost painful spasm of pleasure throbbed in her groin as she thought of Alex, or as she preferred to call him, Alexander. She hadn't told Nevin about him. Like a child stashing jewelry in a pink locked box, she was keeping him to herself. She knew Nevin would ask her who his family was, and what he did for a living, and she would have no answers for her.

| 2 |

A top-hatted doorman at the Plaza trotted down the steps to open the door of the taxi. Nevin flounced out as if she were a queen, passing him by with a curt nod. Cornelia slouched up the steps after her. A pair of joined-at-the-elbows matrons, dressed in matching pastel suits, swooped past, barely acknowledging Nevin but staring pointedly at Cornelia's clothes.

"Honestly, Cornelia, I don't know why you had to insist on wearing those awful jeans." Nevin hissed out of the side of her mouth. "You're obviously *not* dressed appropriately at *all*."

As another doorman swished open double-banked doors, Nevin lifted her chin and imperiously announced, "We're meeting my son in the Palm Court."

They swept past the bank of check-in desks, parading straight into the interior Palm Court. With a glass ceiling vaulting high above twelve-foot palms planted in massive porcelain pots, the tables in the Palm Court gleamed with silver and crystal, all set for afternoon tea. Nevin chose a prime table, pointed her chin in the direction of the elevators, her back held stiffly away from the back of her chair.

Cornelia sank down into the plush seat next to her, slumping down and stretching out her long legs beneath the table.

"Move *over*, Nee. I want Rudy on one side and Nathan on the other. After all, *I* haven't met her, and you know how much I want to see Nathan."

Though Cornelia sighed, she moved. It was easier just to do what her mother asked. Nothing much was worth upsetting the fragile equilibrium between them. As she once more settled in with her back to the bank of elevators, a sharp intake of breath and a hitch of her shoulders told her Nevin saw them coming. "Oh my, you didn't tell me she was *fat*. No, don't signal them. Pretend you don't see them. Let them come find us."

"*Mummy*. She's not fat. She's just got big boobs."

"Where'd you come *up* with a word like that?"

"Mom, everyone says boobs." She never told her mother about some of the cruder things the makeup and hair stylists told her. It would have made her head spin.

Nevin leaned in toward her as if she were confiding a secret. "Aunt Dee would *just* be spinning in her grave to see him with someone like that. She thought big breasts were vulgar, don't you know."

Cornelia didn't bother to remind Nevin that she was often comparing, with obvious self-satisfaction, her own full-breasted body to Cornelia's flat-chested one.

Cornelia swiveled her eyes sideways to watch them coming. Nathan ducked his head as he saw them. He looked pale and his hair was barbershop short. Beside him, Rudy minced along, sashaying so that the full skirt of her shirtdress swung like a bell. With a coy dip of her chin, her doll blue eyes cut up toward him. Even from a distance, her giggle projected out to her audience. As always, at least to Cornelia, her expression looked planned.

As they drew nearer, Nevin stood up and held out her arms. "Nathan, oh Nathan," her voice trilled.

He shambled toward her, flushing a vivid cerise as she pulled him into a full-body embrace, pressing against him, turning her face up toward him, begging him to love her. Cornelia was struck by how similar her look was to the one Rudy had been casting up at him just seconds before.

Over her shoulder, Nathan grinned at Cornelia, raising his eyebrows and rolling his eyes to show her how mortified he was by the intensity of Nevin's embrace. She finally let go of him and sank back into her chair, as if her legs could no longer hold her up. She patted the chair next to her. "Here. Sit here. I want to hear *everything*." Without looking at Rudy, she patted the seat on her other side. "Rudy, you must sit here. But forgive me if I take just a few minutes to talk to my son. After all, it's been *so* long since I've seen him. You've had him all to yourself for *such* a long time. You must forgive me for being selfish for *just* a few minutes." And with that, she turned briefly to Rudy, cocking her head, "I'm *sure* you understand."

Rudy nodded but the skin around her eyes tightened, and her jaw clenched. She turned to Cornelia and made the best of being dismissed. "So, Cornelia, how *are* you? I hear you've taken up modeling. Certainly, you have to be tall. And, how should I say it, a little unusual in your looks. Am I right? Not like acting where talent is needed. Speaking of that, have you kept up your acting? You showed so much *promise*." Her eyes went too wide.

Cornelia's lips tightened, but she said nothing. She wanted to see where Rudy was taking this.

"Course it takes years and *years* to be any good at acting," Rudy dimpled on cue. "I'm still learning of course, but I've been doing it for years now, haven't I? But then I suppose the world of modeling is just so glamorous. Jetting all over." She picked up her knife and scraped it back and forth along the starched linen tablecloth. She cocked her head, pointedly awaiting her response.

As the silence between them lengthened, Cornelia said, "Actually, airports look pretty much the same all over the world."

Rudy smiled but the smile didn't expose her teeth or reach her eyes. "I wouldn't know. I haven't had that opportunity yet. But did Nathan tell you I'm here for some readings?"

Rudy prattled on. After casting her eyes around the room, she raised her voice just enough for the occupants of the tables around them to hear her as well. "There's a Hollywood director who *may* want me for a movie, I'm not taking anything for granted. It's a wonderful opportunity. Of course I'd be *thrilled* beyond belief to get it. A career-making part, they tell me. Course I still don't have it. There are three other girls up for the part. But my agent tells me I'm the front-runner."

"What about the Absolute roadshow? The one you're doing with Nathan?" Cornelia managed to ask, wondering how Nathan would feel about being left behind. "I hear you've been playing in Cleveland."

Rudy snorted, "That's the problem. Cleveland, who cares about anything between the coasts these days?" Then as if she had divulged too much, she veered back to dulcet tones. "Well of course that's been *wonderful*. But Nathan will understand. If I get this part, it's just too good a chance to pass up. He cares about me way too much to hold me back. And of course, *I* don't have the Woodstock name like you do. I have to *make* my opportunities. Everyone says they would never have knocked on your door if you weren't a Woodstock."

Cornelia glared at her.

"My, my, guess *that* touched a sore spot. That was *so* thoughtless of me. So absolutely selfish. I *am* sorry." And she laid her hand sweetly across her full breast. "Will you forgive me?" she cooed.

Cornelia ground her teeth together to keep from saying something rude. The maître d's arrival came as a blessing in disguise.

With his suit straining at its buttons, he leaned down over his belly, not looking any of them in the eye and murmured to the center of the table, "I'm afraid I'm going to have to ask you to leave. Several of our diners have complained about the...," he cleared his throat, "the fact that one of your party is wearing blue jeans. We *do* have a strict dress policy here. Our clientele demands it of us."

Noting that Nevin looked stricken, and Nathan embarrassed, and only Rudy smiled behind the hands that flew to her mouth, Cornelia pushed back her chair and stood tall. "Clearly since I'm the one offending, I'll go. In fact, I'd be *happy* to go. The rest of you stay."

Nathan stood up and looked as if he wanted to go with her. She held up her hand. "No, Nathan, stay here. I'd actually prefer to go if you don't mind. I'll go for a walk in the park and meet you out front in an hour?"

She stalked out of the Palm Court as if she were on a runway, staring ahead with a blank expressionless face, thrusting out her long legs as if she hadn't a care in the world. She heard "that monkey girl" as she passed one table but didn't bother to turn.

As soon as she got outside, she bolted down the steps three at a time and raced across the street, veering through traffic as if she were a matador. One taxi honked, and she gave him the finger. She careened into the park and sprinted up under the long allée of trees. She didn't stop her full-out run until she came to the lake where lovers rowed out between ducks and floating debris. Though her heart pounded and sweat pricked at her neck, the anxiety and anger had faded, and she was glad to have escaped.

Besides, she looked down at the massive man's watch which hung low on her thin wrist, she had only five minutes before she was supposed to call Alexander out in California. She had been making calls at various public phone booths rather than having him call the apartment. Her heart raced with anticipation and anxiety as she loped back to a red phone booth at the corner of 59th and Central Park South.

At first, the phone calls had been full of promise. He had chattered on about his early-morning surfs far up past Malibu, where the waves were bigger and there were few locals to boot him off the surfing breaks. "You'd love it, Nee, yesterday a harbor seal rode the same wave as me. It was awesome, dude."

"Can't wait to see that."

"When are you coming?" His tone was eager. She could imagine his bushy eyebrows dancing up and down with enthusiasm below his salty blond curls.

"Soon I promise."

After sharing how much they missed each other, they hung up and the glow from that call lasted quite a few days. But the last phone call she'd had with him had been anything but satisfying. The tone of the conversation had abruptly changed when she asked if he could possibly come to New York for a visit. Her bookings made it impossible for her to leave right now, she explained.

"You don't seem to understand, Nee, I want to see you. I really do. But I've got a lot of irons in the fire right now. It's probably not a good time for me to leave."

"But just for a weekend?" she pleaded, hating herself for whining.

"The fact is I would, but I happen to be just a little bit strapped for cash right now."

"I could send you some?" She hated that her voice went up at the end.

There was a long pause. "Well, that might work. But I don't want you to get into the habit of it. When my ship comes in, I'll pay you back. I promise."

And so she had sent him money for the plane fare. And now today she was calling to find out when he was coming. She leaned against the glass, turning her back to the door of the phone booth, away from the view of the Plaza and the fountain in front of it. She dialed the number of his friend's apartment. Her heart skipped a beat when he answered the phone.

"Hello?"

"It's me, Nee."

His tone was cold. "What do you want?"

Her stomach clenched as if it had been kicked. "We arranged this time to call?"

"Oh yeah." She could hear several people talking in the background. Including the piping tones of a female.

"Is this a bad time to talk?" she asked.

"Maybe."

"Are you coming?"

"Coming where?"

"To New York, of course," she forced a giggle.

"Oh yeah, that." His voice was flat.

"You're not coming?" Her voice seemed tiny and far away, as if she were calling out for help from deep inside a canyon. The walls of the phone booth caved in around her and she hung onto the handle of the door for balance.

"Here's the thing, Nee, I need to know that you're going to let me...you know what I mean?" His tone was edgy.

"I think so," she stammered.

"Well, I need to know for sure before I fly all the way across the country. I don't want to waste my time if you know what I mean."

There was a long silence. "I know what you mean," she whispered.

"So, you know, are you going to or not?"

She had been grateful that he had not pawed at her as so many others had done. But now, much to her dismay, he sounded surly and demanding.

"So is the high and mighty monkey going to let me in? Or *not*?"

She blushed and said, "She will."

"She will?" And suddenly his tone was light again, and she could imagine his smile and the way his eyebrows pranced when he was pleased.

"Yes, please," she said.

And so they arranged for her to send more money since he had already spent what she had sent him, he explained, on a new guitar because his other one had been stolen and he couldn't live without making music, he said, and she told him she understood.

As she turned around after hanging up, Nathan was standing outside the phone booth, working the toe of his shoe down into a crack in the sidewalk, digging out an errant weed. He colored when he looked up, and his dear, speckled, bony face creased into a welcoming smile. She ran into his arms and hugged him as tight as she could, then released him quickly so as not to make him uncomfortable.

They walked up into Central Park together, swinging along in unison as they once had, falling into that same old long-limbed rhythm few people could match. He asked whether she was happy. She shrugged. And then, before she could stop herself, she was telling him about

Alexander. It was such a sweet relief to share her secret with someone that she babbled on for long minutes about body surfing and the van and Alexander's dog and the California beaches, before she had to acknowledge Nathan's rather grim silence and guarded look.

"Who is this guy?" he asked.

"I told you. His name is Alexander. He's a surfer. And a photographer. And a musician. He's taking time off to surf the world. He's saving up money. His next stop's going to be Hawaii, then on from there. He says he knows somewhere out there he's going to find the perfect wave. It's probably going to be on some remote outlying island like in Fiji that no one has ever surfed before. And he's going to surf it. And take pictures of it. Which then he'll sell. But only he will know where he took the picture, because he won't want anyone else to know where the perfect wave is. Doesn't it sound absolutely wonderful? Wouldn't you just love to go along with him?"

"Actually, Nee, it sounds wackadoodle if you want to know the truth."

"Wackadoodle? Where the hell did you get *that* expression?" She was stung and wanted to sting back.

"I'm just being honest."

"Oh yeah, I forgot, we must always tell the *absolute* truth now, mustn't we?"

"I just don't want you getting hurt," he protested.

"Oh, and so Rudy's never going to hurt you?" she said.

He stopped walking. His jaw dropped, and his lower lip swelled. "What makes you say that?"

"How are you going to feel if she gets this part and leaves you cold?"

"She wouldn't do that," he protested, but she could see the flicker of doubt, and she hated herself for having caused that. She patted his arm.

"I was just being mean. I'm sorry."

"I'm happy for her, you know. She really wants this." His eyes pleaded.

"I know she does. And you're so true blue, you want it for her," she blinked back tears at the thought he had once been that way with her.

"Come on. Let's stop talking and *go!*" And with that she skipped ahead of him, moving fast, letting him just catch up to her, then passing him by until he was forced into a full run to keep ahead of her and then she couldn't catch him, and they ended up breathless and laughing, totally pleased with each other.

They stopped to lean over a wall to look down at a lake where boys sailed toy boats alongside their fathers.

"How's Father?" he asked, and his expression was sad.

"Okay, I guess. I haven't seen him. He's at the Absolute headquarters in Switzerland."

"And Hadji? Do you ever hear from him? I always liked him."

"No." A deep sadness swelled in her chest, threatening to block off her breathing. She inhaled deeply trying to ease the sudden pain. "Not in a long time." These days, she was uncomfortable even thinking about Hadji. She knew he would disapprove of Alexander. But then she thought he might even be jealous and that thought pleased her.

"I guess we better get back," Nathan sighed. "They'll be looking for us."

"Yes, they will."

* * *

Even though Geraldine and Cornelia were at an inside table at a Third Avenue café, the traffic was deafening. Taxis honked. Buses spewed huge black clouds of diesel. Air conditioners dripped. Early spring in New York had morphed almost overnight from filthy gray snow into a smoggy summer nightmare. And Geraldine was not happy. She had called that morning demanding that they meet *immediately*, and not at the office. "What I have to say to you, young lady, should *not* be overheard by anyone."

Cornelia quailed and tried to put her off. But saying no to Geraldine was like trying to stave off the charge of a maddened rhino. And so here they were, perched at a table in a bow window with no other tables nearby. With her penciled eyebrows raised so high on her forehead that her eyes narrowed, Geraldine pushed a brown manila envelope across the table to her. "So perhaps you might explain the meaning of *this!*"

Her heart hammered as she looked at the handwriting on the front of the envelope. It was unmistakably Alexander's somewhat childish scrawl.

Some weeks previously, she had taken a taxi to the airport to pick up Alexander. Her subterfuges had been enormous but easy. She had lied to Nevin about having a long weekend shoot up in Rhinebeck on the Hudson. Maisy had called Nevin to say that she was going to be there so there was no need for Nevin to chaperone. Luckily, Nevin hadn't checked in with Geraldine about her schedule. "It's about time this happened anyway," said Nevin. "I need to start thinking about my own life now, you know."

"I know you do, Mummy."

Cornelia had found an out of the way, somewhat run-down hotel on the West Side overlooking the Natural History Museum. She figured she wouldn't run into anyone there who might recognize her. The seedy looking clerk had taken her cash without a blink of an eye and had booked a suite up on one of the higher floors.

When the taxi had pulled into the La Guardia terminal, she had bolted out the door and almost stumbled to her knees. She felt light-headed and nervous; her pulse raced. In anticipation of Alexander's arrival, she had been unable to eat for days. Her hands shook, every nerve-ending in her body fired with anxiety. In the taxi, she had almost come just by squeezing her thighs together.

She checked the board and raced down the concourse, sure that somehow, she would miss him at the gate, or that he would not have come at the last minute, or that his plane had crashed.

He was the first off of the plane.

When she saw his broad smile, the tousled mop of his platinum curls, the comfort of his oh-so-faded jeans and the scarlet slant of sunburn along the high edge of his cheekbones, she felt an electric jolt in her groin. His eyes were as blue as the ocean outside the reef, his smile as white as the froth on breaking waves. She felt such a surge of giddiness that she slumped against a column, literally too weak to stand. He had a guitar and a camera slung over his shoulder and he swept them both to one side and sprang across to her, lifting her up off her feet and swinging her around in circles. She threw back her head and laughed. He enfolded her in his arms and their hearts hammered against each other. She was grateful her feet weren't on the ground because she thought she might faint. Dots swirled in her peripheral vision. When he finally set her back down, for several minutes they just swayed together, thigh to thigh, chest to chest, heart to heart. She wept, a mixture of elation and relief. He gently wiped the tears away.

"I hope those are tears of happiness," he whispered.

She managed to nod.

They floated down the concourse, their arms wrapped around each other's waists. People seemed to magically part in front of them. She felt God-like.

"Do we need to get your suitcase?" she asked.

He laughed, "What do I need a suitcase for? I have you. Come, let's go."

He hailed a taxi and they tumbled inside and were all over each other, kissing and fumbling and panting. At one point, she broke away long enough to notice the cabby watching in the rear-view mirror.

Alexander followed her gaze then snorted, "I know! Get a room, right?"

By the time they got to the hotel, her nerves were exploding; her arms and legs pulsed with molten lava. They stumbled through the lobby and into the elevator where, even before the doors closed, he pushed her against the wall. His mouth came down to her throat and he sucked. Her head lolled back, and she swooned. He carried her across the hall to the door, growling for the key. She gave it to him, and he quickly unlocked the door. She nuzzled into his neck, inhaling deeply of his lemony salty flavor, suddenly feeling shy. He bolted the door but never put her down. Without another word, he carried her through the living room and into the bedroom where he lowered her down, carefully unhitching her arms from his neck. He unzipped her jeans and shucked them off her. He unbuttoned his shirt and threw it onto the floor. His chest and stomach muscles were firm and brown. A patch of curly black hair nestled down between his pectorals. Never taking his eyes off her, he yanked his jeans down.

With a moan, she reached up for him, then clung, pulling him toward her. He chuckled, and she could feel the reverberation deep inside his chest.

She awoke several hours later. The sheet lay draped over her body and Alexander was standing at the window, clad once more in jeans, but shirtless, staring out at the city lights. He turned as she whispered his name.

"Baby," he murmured as he came toward the bed, "Are you my baby girl, my sweet mighty monkey?" he sang.

"I am," she smiled.

"Stop," he held up his hand, "Stay right there! Hold that smile for me sweet baby." With one hand he reached for his camera and snapped away and she smiled up at him, as happy as she'd ever been. Finally, he dropped his camera to one side, climbed up on top of her, and entered her once more, rearing back so that he could watch her. He crooned as he rocked her once more to a wracking orgasm.

The next few days were magical. They drifted through the days and night, enamored of their bodies, enthralled by the ease with which they fit together and came together. "You're the best, baby, no one's ever loved me like this. Never," he chanted.

Occasionally, they left the hotel and, arm in arm, thigh to thigh, would scour the neighborhood for food. They found a Viennese restaurant on 72nd St. that served delicate and tender Wiener Schnitzel. They washed it down with vanilla egg creams. Then they rushed back to the hotel and made love again and again and again until she was raw and exhausted and mindless.

Finally, on his last day, he picked her up from the bed and took her to the bathroom where he had filled the tub with hot suds. He carefully laid her down in the water, and then washed her all over, as sweetly and carefully as if she were his baby. When he was finished, he picked her up, gently patted her dry, then took her back to bed where he tucked her in then slipped in beside her and wrapped himself around her from the back. His skin was hot and comforting and she fell sound asleep in his embrace.

When she awoke, some hours later, the room was empty and there was only a note in his childish scrawl, "I couldn't wake you, my sleeping baby. I couldn't bear the thought of saying goodbye. So, by the time you read this I'll be winging my way back to LA. Stay good. Stay well. No matter what, I love you."

The final three words had rung so loud that all else faded. But now, as Geraldine pushed the brown manila envelope across the table to her, intuitively she had the sudden and painful insight that this might be the "no matter what."

| 3 |

"Go on," snarled Geraldine. "Open it. I haven't got all day." Her red fingernails scraped the linen tablecloth as she pushed the manila envelope toward Cornelia. Outside the café, the traffic growled. Her head felt huge and heavy. A strange metallic taste in her mouth caused a constant flow of saliva, which made her swallow compulsively. Everything, even coffee, which she had recently started drinking, had lost its flavor.

She knew she was supposed to be grateful to Geraldine for her success. Everyone said so, particularly Nevin. But suddenly, and not for the first time, she hated everything about Geraldine. Hated the extra line of crimson etched above her shriveled mouth. When her lipstick was fresh, the illusion of full lips was fair at a distance. But after a glass of wine and a miniscule helping of fettuccine alfredo, all the color was gone. Her upper lip looked pleated, her lower lip non-existent. Once more, as she had done when Cornelia first met her, she reminded her of a vulture. The sudden forward hunch of her black silk-sheathed shoulders and the clang of solid gold bracelets thick above her claw-like arthritic hands did nothing to dispel the illusion. She hated the way Geraldine controlled her life. Choosing who would shoot her. Deciding where she went, and with whom she should be seen. But now, more than anything else, and this sharpened her hatred to a new keen level, she hated her for bursting the bubble of Alexander.

A sick feeling swept through her, and she pushed away her spaghetti Bolognese, nauseous at the sight of the slick olive oil that sheathed the upper edge of the bowl. Swallowing hard to quell a retch, she opened the manila envelope.

Inside, there was a sheaf of black-and-white 8x10 photos, and several pages of proof sheets. She flushed at the sight of the photographs.

"At least you have the grace to be embarrassed," Geraldine snapped.

Cornelia shot a quick look at her. Geraldine had misunderstood her flush. She was not embarrassed but pleased. For Alexander had captured her not only with a smile on her face, but a look of joy. Both of which were notably absent from the fierce, angry, dark postures Geraldine and the photographers worked to evoke.

The first blown-up 8x10 was a picture taken on the beach the day they had met. As always, her long hair waved in snake like tendrils, but her face was tilted up to the sun as if she were a flower, her eyes were downcast in what appeared to be a coy but pleased shyness, and, strangest of all, her lips were curled at the corners into a smile, a vivid contrast to the usual slash of monkey grimace the fashion photographers encouraged. She looked soft and feminine and very young. And pretty, she thought with a pang of delight. It seemed she was pretty after all.

Feeling elated, she shuffled through the other prints. Most captured that same combination of vulnerability and shy joy. There was one of her leaping across shallow waves, Alexander's dog bounding along next to her. What intrigued Cornelia was her blissful look of abandon, as if she were taking her first steps on the outside after being cooped up for many years. Which actually wasn't so far off from the truth, she thought.

Trying to ignore the impatient tap of Geraldine's fingernail, she reveled in the images. He must have loved her to capture what no one else had. Her favorite one by far was of her catapulting through the curve of a breaking wave, her arms outstretched as she looked full into the camera with a huge grin spreading across her face.

Geraldine, who claimed she looked best either in profile or at a three-quarter angle, prohibited this full-face pose. Geraldine's chosen poses emphasized Cornelia's bone structure. In full face, you could see the innate roundness of her youthful cheeks. And in this picture, she looked less a model than a romping child. Cornelia liked that her grin held none of the furtive sullenness she so often portrayed on the run-way or in front of a studio backdrop. She felt a huge matching smile crease her face as she looked up at Geraldine.

"*Stop* it. *Stop* it right there!" Geraldine's eyes darted around the room and out onto the sidewalk, then sighed with relief when she saw no one holding a camera. "What is *wrong* with you? Someone might see you like *that.* I've told you a thousand times your face goes all formless when you smile. It's awful. It should never, *ever* happen. We've worked too hard on your image to have it just busted apart by some cheap snap-shots of you smiling. *Never!*" She slashed her hand down as if she held a machete and were chopping the smile right off her face.

Cornelia began a spluttering response, but Geraldine quickly shushed her with a held-up hand of warning. "Have you *no* respect for how hard I've worked to build up your image? If these got out, it would cheapen your mystique. Are you so stupid you can't see that?"

Cornelia felt a familiar flash of anger rise in her at being called stu-pid. Geraldine forestalled her expressing it by snapping her fingers. "Don't you dare," she hissed. "After how hard I've worked, after we've been so careful to build you up as an angry icon, you want to abandon editorial for *this,*" she swept her hand out and grabbed up the pictures and jammed them back into the envelope, her long skinny hands trem-bling. "My, how to bite the hand that feeds you."

And then, just as she always did with Nevin, she saw the droop in Geraldine's face and the shuddering in her fingers and knew that the woman was old and scared. The childhood training of apologizing for being selfish struck her like the slap of a hand. She bowed her head. "I'm sorry," she whispered.

She could never, it seemed, go the distance to fight for her own identity. In the final rounds, despite putting up a good show of re-sistance, she always caved to everyone else's will. Her hatred toward Geraldine dissipated and she was filled, instead, with an old familiar self-loathing. The frown returned, and she scowled across the table at

Geraldine, who smiled at her and patted her hand. "There's my fierce little spider monkey. *There* she is."

As if she were sinking and the manila envelope was a proffered branch of rescue, she reached out to it, wanting that pretty vision of herself again, needing it in fact, to regain some kind of solid equilibrium.

"Oh no you don't," snipped Geraldine, snatching it back from her grasp. "Oh, I'll send this pathetic little guttersnipe money just like he asked for...." Her eyes narrowed as she saw Cornelia rock back in shock. "Oh, I see, he didn't tell you that, did he? Oh yes, this wretched creature wants dollars in return for the negatives."

She stumbled away from the table and out onto the street where she hailed a taxi, laid her head back against the plastic seat and resisted the urge to vomit all the way back to their barren apartment.

By the time she reached there, it was obvious Geraldine had called Nevin. She was sitting with her arms crossed, smoking a defiant cigarette, her legs all curled up beneath her, looking at Cornelia with big reproachful eyes as she let herself in the door.

"How could you?"

"How could I what?" Cornelia swallowed. The strange metallic taste and flood of saliva in her mouth was driving her crazy. All she wanted to do was close her eyes and give in to a dreadful bone-aching sense of ennui and fatigue.

"How could you so *jeopardize* our new life together? Doesn't our security mean anything to you? Answer me, Cornelia, what were you thinking? Who *is* this awful young man? How did you even meet him? Geraldine actually accused me of not watching you carefully enough when *all* I've been doing is watching you, *caring* for you. Do you think it's been easy having everyone fawn over you the way they do?"

Cornelia shook her head and headed for her bedroom. It might be empty of furniture and art and anything personal, but it did have a bed and that was all she wanted at the moment. That and to be left alone to pick at the scab of Alexander. For though she could not help but be pleased at his pretty vision of her, that he would try to extort money from Geraldine meant only one thing: that he was a predator as well as a charmer. That insight hurt too much to bear.

So she crawled under the covers, and though it was daytime and the sun fell heavy on the streets outside, she lay as quietly as black ice, as slick and fragile as if it were indeed midnight in winter, and she would fracture into a million shards if she so much as moved an inch.

Only when she awoke, many hours later, did she remember, with a sick lurch of her stomach, the naked photos he had taken of her in the hotel room. Those had not been in the stack Geraldine had showed her.

* * *

Between them, Geraldine and Nevin cooked up a plan of ever more stringent chaperonage. Before Cornelia could even say goodbye, Geraldine had Maisy blackballed from the fashion scene. Geraldine and Nevin also made sure Cornelia was not allowed to make any phone calls or go anywhere alone. Weeks passed before, on a restroom break at a restaurant shoot, she found a pay phone hanging in the hall and called Alexander.

A woman answered. Her tone turned suspicious when Cornelia asked for Alexander.

"Who is this?" she demanded.

"Mighty monkey," Cornelia whispered, not wanting to give her real name to a stranger.

"Well, I don't know about any mighty monkey. But if this happens to be Cornelia, he doesn't want to talk to you. Haven't you done enough damage as it is? Siccing that New York bat on him? She actually threatened to call the police. When he's done nothing at all."

Her heart skipped a few beats, then lurched into a gallop. Black spun in her peripheral vision, and she fell down a long dark tunnel. She hung up the phone.

When she wasn't working, she slept. In fact, she was sleeping between poses as well. When they combed her hair, her jaw slumped open, and she nodded off. When they adjusted the lighting, she leaned against a wall and closed her eyes. By the end of every afternoon the metallic taste in her mouth had turned to bile, and she hung over every toilet she could find, puking up bits of slimy yellow foam. The only thing she could bring herself to eat was an occasional saltine cracker. Though she had virtually stopped eating, not even Nevin seemed to notice. It was finally a photographer who called her out.

They were shooting her from the back. The dress was a creamy silk, falling in lovely folds all the way from her shoulders to the floor, scooped out in the rear with a swirl, exposing the whole of her back all the way down to the cleavage of her bum. She was supposed to turn and scowl back over her shoulder as if growling at the whole following world.

"Oferchrissake," shouted the Irish photographer. "She's nottin' but a bag of bones. They say they want sexy, well this effin' ain't sexy. Might as well be ridin' a skelltin'. No man in 'is right mind wants that." He stopped for a moment, sighed deeply, then shouted out to the whole crew. "'As no one friggin' noticed but meself that the child 'pears close to collapse? Coom off it, get off your effin' butts and fetch me a real woman." And with that, he stalked off the set.

Instead of being offended, Cornelia was grateful for the sudden flurry of whispered conferences. She slumped down onto a nearby chair, dropped her head across folded arms and fell asleep. She awoke to the inside of an ambulance. Instead of being worried, she was grateful for the warm blanket that the EMT draped across her. She fell back asleep. Hours later, when she awoke in a strange hospital room, she was grateful to be alone. She looked at the light streaming through the blinds and let the shadow and light dance her back to sleep. The next time she awoke, an officious but kind looking nurse with a tiny cap perched high on a bun was replacing one IV bag for another.

"What's that?" she ventured to whisper.

"Nothing but sugar water. You're dehydrated, that's what. Trying to get you strong again."

"Really," she murmured. "You'll make me strong again. I'd like that."

The nurse's lips narrowed., "You'll *have* to be strong to deal with those two harpies." She tipped her head in the direction of the hallway window and there, peering in, stood Geraldine and Nevin. "They're furious with me since I'm not letting them in to visit." She nodded again. "I let them in once and all they did was yammer at each other over your head. That wasn't going to do you any good, was it now? Figured you needed a rest. Besides, next time you wake up, I'm supposed to call your doctor. She wants to talk to you before those two get ahold of you."

"One of those harpies is my mother," she whispered.

"I know. I gathered that. But I don't care if she's the Queen of Sheba. She should know when to leave someone alone. I told her you needed to *rest*. And now you had better do just that. Prove me right, will ya?" She smiled out of the side of her mouth.

"Okay," she managed to say as she slipped back into a refreshing sleep.

When she next awoke, a handsome woman in her forties with close-cropped silver hair stood next to her, writing notes on a clipboard. "Hello there," she smiled. "Feeling better?"

She nodded.

"That usually happens a day or so after the IV drip. Hydration works miracles. And because we're feeding you at the same time, all is well."

Cornelia darted a look at the hallway window and to her relief the blinds were down and there was no sign of a perturbed Nevin and an angry Geraldine.

"Just in case you wondered, I'm Dr. Ruth Bergman. I'm your consulting OB/GYN, called in by the resident who admitted you to the ER two nights ago."

"Two nights ago?"

"Yes, that's right. Do you know why you're here?"

"The nurse said I was dehydrated..."

"Amongst other things. Have you been nauseous? Breasts swollen and tender? Tired all the time?"

"Yes," she whispered, the truth suddenly hitting her. "I'm pregnant?"

"That you are, eight weeks or so I'd say. Sound about right?"

She thought back to when Alexander and she had been together and nodded.

"Well, according to your chart, you turned 18 a few weeks ago and thus you're a legal adult. Which gives you the right to talk to me about all of this without the presence of your mother, you understand?"

She nodded again.

"Any idea what you want to do?"

She shook her head.

"I thought so. I thought you should have a chance to think about it before setting the wolves on you. So I've ordered no visitors for the rest of the day. I'll come back later, and we'll talk, okay?"

"Is everything okay with the baby?"

Her quick glance up from the chart was keen. "Interesting that you should ask about the baby first. To answer for both of you, everything looks fine. You were really debilitated, dangerously so I'd say. People die from dehydration, you know."

"Oh."

"Now, don't be alarmed, that's not what's happening to you. But, on the other hand, I'd say you were seriously malnourished. Still, the baby appears to be fine, probably been pulling all your reserves into himself. Embryos are a bit like that. Little vampires, they are. Take what they need without a worry to their host. It's my job to worry about you both."

"Thank you," she said.

She patted Cornelia's hand. "If you decide *not* to keep the baby, I'll call it a necessary D&C. If you decide to *keep* the baby, I'll take care of her and you, I promise."

"You said himself before."

"You don't miss much, do you? Truth is, we have no way of knowing just yet, so I use both he and she until we know for sure one way or another. Is there a father who should be part of this decision?"

"No!" She vehemently shook her head. "No, not that."

"I see." She looked sympathetic and the pat of her hand turned to a gentle squeeze. "You'll be okay. You're basically a strong, healthy young woman. You're going to be okay either way you go."

"Thank you," she said, thinking it might be the kindest thing anyone had said to her in a very long time.

After the doctor left, Cornelia lay there considering her dilemma, sinking into a mire of dread, only to be, moments later, buoyed up by a surging joy.

She had never been a girl who played much with dolls. Nor did she have any younger siblings, so the thought of a baby was like considering asking an alien to come live with her. Perhaps it would be charming, but perhaps monstrous and even life-threatening. Having spent her earliest years surrounded by animals, she knew that birthing and milking were bloody and painful and had an imperative to them that went way beyond free choice. And yet the thought of being absorbed in another person's needs above and beyond her own petty concerns was oddly exhilarating.

She rocked back and forth between dread and joy until finally, suddenly exhausted again, she closed her eyes and slipped into a half-waking sleep in which blond cherubs with ringlets, apple cheeks, and ravening teeth danced in her dreams.

A curse woke her. "Bloody hell!" Geraldine was sitting in a corner chair next to the window with her feet hiked up on the radiator. Her Chanel skirt was pulled too far up on her skinny but flaccid thighs. Her feet were jammed into pump stilettos. A bunion swelled to the right of her toe cleavage. To Cornelia's mortification, Geraldine was perusing her chart, so absorbed in her scrutiny of the paperwork that she hadn't noticed her awakening.

"What?" Nevin's hesitant voice came from her left. Cornelia quickly closed her eyes and did not roll toward that side of the room. "What does it say?"

"Bloody gull's pregnant."

"What?" Nevin's voice quavered. "She can't be. She would have told me."

Much to her chagrin, Cornelia felt a desperate need to pee. She squeezed her thighs together. To her relief, she was no longer attached to a plastic catheter. But the last thing she wanted to do was let them know she was awake. But neither did she want to wet the bed. To her infinite relief, Jackie stomped into the room and barked, "What is this?"

Cornelia narrowed her eyes to a slit to watch.

Jackie placed her fists on her hips and glowered at Geraldine and Nevin. "I suppose neither of you noticed the 'No Visitors' sign on the door?"

Geraldine waved her hand in dismissal.

She heard an intake of breath from Jackie as she realized Geraldine was reading the chart. "Just what the hell do you think you're doing?" She snatched the chart out of Geraldine's hands. "Give me that! You have no right...."

"I have every right," Geraldine uncurled her long lean body out of the chair and faced the small sturdy woman. She towered at least six inches above the nurse. Looking down her long nose, she spoke slowly as if Jackie was incapable of understanding. "This *child* is under my guidance and care. And this woman is her *mother*. We have *every* right to know *exactly* what is going on."

Much to Cornelia's delight, Jackie didn't back off an inch. "This *child* is anything but a child. In the eyes of New York state law, she is an adult and capable of making her own decisions. And no one, not even her mother," she turned to point her finger at Nevin, "has the right to read her chart without her permission."

Cornelia wanted to cheer.

"Hah!" snorted Geraldine.

Beneath lowered eyelids, Cornelia snuck a look at Nevin. Her eyes were round and sorrowful. She had her arms wrapped around herself as if she were the injured one. When she caught Cornelia looking at her, she rushed at her, throwing herself half up on the bed. "Why didn't you tell me?" she wailed. "How could you *do* this to me? Just when things were going so well. How *could* you?" She was working her way up into true hysterics. "This could *ruin* everything. When we've worked so *hard*."

"Stop it," squawked Geraldine, "This kind of thing happens all the time. Simple matter of taking care of it. Soon as it can be scheduled. Snip. Snap. All done. Finished!" She sliced her hand through the air.

The hairs on the back of Cornelia's neck rose up. Jackie saw her look of panic and clapped her hands to get their attention. "I'm going to have to ask you to leave. Both of you. This girl is just now waking back up to life. And I will not have the two of you creating a scene here. Out! Out now! Or I'll call security."

Nevin drew herself up. Her face twitched. "You can't be asking me to leave," she said. "I'm her mother." She turned a beseeching look on Cornelia. "Tell her Nee, tell her you don't want to be parted from your mother."

Cornelia was silent but looked over to Jackie and above Nevin's head nodded slightly toward the door.

As always, Geraldine missed nothing. "Ohferchrissake." She stood up and yanked her skirt smooth.

"Out!" said Jackie pointing her fat little finger at the door. "Out!" She stamped her foot.

Geraldine stalked to the door, studiously ignoring Jackie, but turning just before she exited to shake her finger at Cornelia. "Don't think young lady that you can hide out here much longer. You've got to face up to this and get *rid* of the problem. Too many people are counting on you to act like a grown-up and *just take care of it.* Nevin, are you coming?"

Nevin gave Cornelia her best forlorn expression. "You don't really want me to go, do you?"

Jackie looked straight at Cornelia and asked, "What do you want?"

Afraid she would lose her resolve, Cornelia couldn't look directly at Nevin. "I would like to be alone."

Nevin moaned. "Please don't do this. Please don't push me away. I love you so much. We're in this together. Geraldine says the procedure is nothing much. Doesn't hurt much more than a bad period. And I'll take care of you. Haven't I always taken care of you?" She wrung her hands together, and then gave Cornelia the beseeching look that usually worked.

Cornelia looked out the window, trying to hold back the sobs that were threatening. "Please go," she whimpered. "We'll talk later. I promise."

And so Nevin turned, cowering, as if she'd been kicked and slunk out of the room.

As soon as their footsteps faded, Cornelia rolled over to one side and let the sobs come. Jackie patted her on the shoulder. "Go ahead girl, let it out. You'll be okay. I can tell you're a fighter. Pay no attention to them. Only you know what's best for you."

"Really?" she managed to say between gulps. "I've got to pee."

"Really? Right then here we go." She folded the sheets back and nodded toward the bathroom. "Time to get up and get you peeing on your own. It'll hurt a bit, but you'll feel much better afterward. And a shower will do you good."

And she was right. It did hurt to pee. In fact, only a few drops leaked out, and she screamed as they came. But as she stood in the shower stall for a long time, letting the hot water swirl down over her head and shoulders, her muscles relaxed; and, though it hurt when the flow first started, cascades of urine sluiced down her legs and swirled down into the drain. After her bladder was empty, she soaped herself over and over, washing off the stink of three days in bed. It was only after she felt truly scrubbed raw that she cupped her still flat stomach with her hands and whispered, "Hello down there. Hope you're okay."

When she finally left the bathroom, Jackie was gone but her bed had been freshly made up with new sheets. A sudden burst of energy made her realize that the last thing she wanted to do was to get back into that bed. She found her jeans, T-shirt, and hoodie in the tiny closet, quickly got dressed, grabbed her messenger bag, which held her checkbook, an

American Express card that they had sent her when she turned eighteen, and her passport.

Head down, she walked quickly down the hall, hoping no one would notice she was going. She passed the nurse's station where she could see Jackie bowed down over charts. She felt badly that she wasn't saying goodbye, but she sensed she would understand. Without a backward look, she pushed open the door to the stairway, and bolted down the eight flights to the hospital lobby. With her heart hammering, she pushed through the revolving door, inhaled the night air, and loped down the street to where she could see taxis racing down Park Avenue.

She would hail one and have them take her to Times Square to some anonymous hotel where no one would find her. Then, she would go out and find herself a cheeseburger and a chocolate milkshake.

The pavement was slick from a recent shower. As the taxi swerved to pick her up, the reflection of its headlights dazzled, and the black rain puddle beneath her swirled with color. Oh, she thought with pleasure, as she splashed through it, only black ice shatters. Water is resilient.

| 4 |

After the euphoria of her escape faded, during that first night alone, she jerked and tossed from side to side, from back to belly, her thoughts tumbling and turning, worming their way into every half-conscious thought, and even into tortured dreams. The only clear thought that spiraled out was that she must not, *could* not, go back to her life with Nevin and Geraldine.

The next day, she met with her doctor from the hospital, and they went over her options. Because it was early in the pregnancy, the doctor assured her she still had a few weeks to think it all through.

That afternoon, she holed up in her dingy hotel room and tried to locate Nathan. She called the winter headquarters of the Moral Absolutes in Phoenix. The chipper receptionist said she believed he was somewhere in Oklahoma and promised absolutely to get a message to him.

She ordered room service, and devoured a cheeseburger, fries, and a chocolate milkshake. Whatever else the hospital stay had done, it had brought her an appetite. She patted her stuffed belly. "There, there, feeling better now?" She curled up and waited for him to call. Finally, at 10:03 p.m., the hotel phone rang.

He sounded impatient. "We just finished the show, Nee, can't this wait 'til the morning?"

"No, it can't wait."

"HH said you'd say it was urgent."

"Did you tell him I called?"

"I didn't have to," his voice was flat, "the operator told him."

"Are you okay? I heard Rudy left the show."

"I'm fine. Absolutely A-OK. Never better."

"That sounds Absolute-ish."

Absolute silence followed. She knew that trick. Cops and Horace and Hall Hamden all knew silence made people blurt out the truth.

"Can you talk?" she finally asked.

"Not really."

"If I come see you, will they let you see me?"

"Maybe."

"Okay, that's what I'll do then. You're in Tulsa?"

"Oklahoma City starting tomorrow."

"Give me the name of a hotel."

"How would I do that?"

"Nathan, for God's sake, look in a phone book or something."

"Nee, don't take the name of the Lord in vain," his tone was robotic.

"Never mind. Let's make this easy for you. There's got to be a Hilton, there's always a Hilton."

"How do you know that?" And for the first time, she sensed his old curiosity poking at his Moral Absolute persona.

"'Cause I've stayed in a lot of them? Just leave a message at the desk for me. I'll call you."

After a pause, he asked, "How's Mummy?"

"Okay I guess. But don't call her just now, will you?"

"Why?" he sounded petulant.

"Just don't, okay? Trust me. I'll tell you why tomorrow, okay?"

"Okay."

After she hung up, she called American Airlines and booked a ticket to Oklahoma City. Though most of her trips had been pre-arranged and carefully chaperoned, she had taken note of everything. Now, to her proud pleasure, she knew how things were done. She had even called American Express and found out her credit limit was $3,000 and would need to be paid in full at the end of each month. Since the bill went to Nevin's apartment, that gave her a month to travel incognito.

Still, she knew Nevin would be worried sick, so she called her. Much to her relief, she wasn't there. As she was leaving a message on their new answering machine, she heard her mother pick up. "Cornelia? Is that you? Please just talk to me. We can fix this."

Cornelia hung up.

On the taxi ride out to the airport the next day, she pulled out her wallet and perused her checkbook. After Nevin paid all the bills out of Cornelia's earnings, each month she had allotted her an allowance. The balance had accrued to $8,353, which seemed a staggeringly large sum of money to her.

She settled back against the plastic seat of the taxi, swallowing the surge of metallic saliva. Dr. Ruth Bergman had explained that she must eat first thing in the morning and continue to eat all day long; that would help stave off the nausea. Her messenger bag was stuffed full of snacks. She opened a honey nut granola bar and wolfed it down.

The plane landed in Oklahoma City at 4:23 p.m., all without event. She taxied to the Hilton, shoving her Amex card across the check-in desk as if she had been travelling alone for decades. And no one raised an eyebrow. Just by doing things with confidence, her confidence was building. When she reached her room on the fourth floor, she opened the note left for her at the desk. Nathan answered on the first ring.

Outside the window, a flat featureless city of low-lying buildings stretched out to a yellow-gray horizon. A scorched sun hung low over the smoggy sky.

"Are you here?" he sounded rushed.

"Yup, what's the matter?"

"Be there in twenty."

Just twenty minutes later, an exhausted Nathan knocked on the door. Before he came inside, his eyes darted sideways down the hall. He panted. His thin white shirt clung wetly to his mid-section.

"I ran the whole way here. I don't think anyone followed me," he panted.

"Does Hall Hamden know you're here?"

He twitched but didn't answer.

"Nathan?"

He drew himself up, pulled out his soaked shirt, shaking it out away from his ribs, then poked it back down into his pants, tucking it in too tight. "Nothing's the matter. All is well." He smiled a dazzling Absolute smile and a shiver went up her spine. "What could possibly be the matter? The Lord takes care of those who follow his commands."

"Nathan, this is me, remember? Don't give me that bullshit."

He flinched, then closed his eyes as if hurt.

"Sorry," she muttered, "Guess I've been on too many photo shoots."

His eyes fluttered opened and, to her delight, his lopsided smile looked more like the brother she once knew. But then he twitched all over, ever so slightly, as if settling back into a second skin, and began to preach. "We must *always* be on our guard. We must *resist* his temptations. We must say, 'Satan, stand *behind* me, *tempt* me not!'" His eyes narrowed. His freckles, like miniature stop signs, stood out in stark contrast to his too-pale face.

"Nathan?" She whispered, "Are you in there? Did you tell them you were meeting me?"

As she looked into his eyes, deep down, a frightened little boy looked back, but then as the dazzling smile snapped back into place, a stranger spoke. "Why are you really here, Cornelia? You can tell me? Do father and his foreign cohorts truly hope to lure us to their nefarious headquarters? That's what *they* said last night when I told them you had called."

Her heart lurched, "I told you not to tell anyone I was coming."

"Cornelia, we have no other choice. God mandates that we *must* be *absolutely* honest after all. Nothing else will suit." He chuckled. The hairs on the back of her neck prickled. But then suddenly the lost child returned. "But I came here alone; I didn't tell them I was coming. Was that being dishonest?" His expression was bereft. "Nee? Tell me. Was I bad?"

She went to him and held him close. His body was wooden, and she was reminded of their father. And then she wept for all of them, lowering her head to his chest and soaking his shirtfront with tears.

"Nee?" He patted her on the back, "Are you okay? What's the matter with *you*?" He sat down on the end of the bed and patted the mattress next to him, "Tell me," he repeated.

And so, she did. He hung his head and listened, not looking at her, but nodding along as she told him of the recent months, her dehydration, her almost starvation state, and now her pregnancy, and then of her running away from Geraldine and Nevin, and of how they had badgered her for an abortion.

"Oh no," he swung his head toward her, "That would be murder." He grabbed her hands. "You would never do that. Would you? Hall Hamden said that you were not to be trusted. That you would do just about anything, including lying, to get what you wanted."

She shook her head; the injustice struck her speechless. A crushing guilt descended. She should never have let Nevin persuade her to drop the charges against Hall Hamden. It left her alone and without defense. A profound sense of despair cloaked her.

He nudged her shoulder, trying to yank her out of her stupor. "We'll figure this out together, I promise."

His words pierced her ennui.

For one long wonderful moment her brother was back, and she welcomed that feeling of being a team of two against the world.

The phone rang just as there was a knock on the door. The desk clerk told her two men were on their way up.

A fist pounded on the door. "Nathan. Cornelia. We know you're in there, open up!"

Fear hammered her heart. Nathan jumped off the bed, ran at the window, banging against it, then veered back toward the bed, his hands fluttering in front of his chest, his eyes wide and panicked. His head twitched back and forth.

Cornelia gasped to see him in such panic.

"Miss, are you okay? Should I send security?" the front desk clerk asked.

"No," she said, "Not okay. Do that." She laid down the phone but did not hang it up.

Nathan wrung his hands.

Just like Nevin, thought Cornelia.

"What can I do?" He shook his head from side to side, and then, as if a cloak of disguise was being thrown over his shoulders, he stood tall, squared his shoulders, and looked back down at her with that awful smile and said, "I must do the right thing. The loving thing. Not to worry, Nee, he'll take care of you. He knows best after all, remember? He has that direct line to God, don't you know?" He raised one finger and shook it at her as if she were a naughty child and went to open the door.

Hall Hamden swaggered in. He cocked his head at his sidekick and pointed at the door. The minion wheeled around to guard the door, crossing his arms and facing inward. To her infinite gratitude, they didn't close the door, thinking, she guessed, of blocking her exit rather than the possibility of someone else coming in. Hall threw his arm around Nathan and slapped his other shoulder as if he were a prize bull. Nathan lurched forward, then recovered with an embarrassed smile.

"Cornelia," Hall Hamden bared his teeth, "To what do we owe this unexpected pleasure? And I understand you asked Nathan to keep it a secret? Up to your old tricks, I see." He chuckled. "You know we don't keep secrets in Absolute territory. Or had you forgotten?" And this time he winked. Her stomach twisted. The wink struck her as obscenely familiar, as if by not going forward with the rape charges, she was complicit. The wink also told her if they were ever alone again, he would hurt her. "Don't you recall we are only as sick as the secrets we keep?" And again, he winked.

Her gut knotted; her hands flew to her belly. With a beseeching gaze up at Nathan, she silently begged him not to tell Hall Hamden about the baby.

Nathan's brow furrowed. "Nee, he's right, you know. We are not meant to be alone. We must always take counsel from those who have a direct connection."

"No." A long shuddering moan came out of her.

"Listen to your brother," said Hall Hamden, "He has come to see the wisdom of our group guidance. You know how your self-will has always blinded you to the truth. Your brother knows we only have your best interest at heart."

"Let them take care of you," pleaded Nathan. "I was wrong. *We* can't do this alone. *You* can't do this alone."

Just as a part of her felt so besieged that she longed, in an old familiar way, for the comfort of others' righteousness, heavy footsteps thundered down the hallway. It jolted her courage back.

Nathan spoke woodenly, "It's for your own good, Cornelia, I cannot tell a lie for you."

Two massive security guards pushed their way past the minion and charged into the room. "Miss, are you okay?" one asked.

She nodded at Hall and his crony, "I will be if this man and that man leave now." She nodded at Nathan, "He can stay if he wants to. He's my brother."

"Why am I not surprised?" Hamden's face knotted. "You always did have a way of twisting the facts to suit yourself." He turned, as if it were his idea to leave in the first place, "Come!" he said to Nathan and snapped his fingers.

From the door, Hall Hamden barked back over his shoulder, "Nathan! Don't make me wait for you."

Nathan looked from Hall to Cornelia and a shiver passed across his face, wrinkling its surface. "I have to go," he said. "I don't have a choice."

"Yes, you do," she pressed him, "You always have a choice."

"No, I don't, God has a plan for me, and I must follow." At the door, he turned and, briefly, Nathan replaced the robot. "Nee, just do the right thing, okay?" Without another word, he followed Hall Hamden down the hall to the elevator. One security guard escorted them while another stayed behind.

"Will you be okay?" he asked.

"Stay with me while I pack up. And if you could call down and order me a cab while I get my stuff together."

He nodded.

Her hand shook as she found a twenty and handed it to him. He called down to the front desk while she quickly gathered her few toiletries and jammed everything into her tiny leather satchel. She waited another five minutes until the front desk called up to say that the men who'd been bothering her had just left in a car.

She bounded down the corridor, restlessly waited for an elevator, then bolted across the lobby floor, signed the bill, then loped out to the waiting taxi. The whole time her heart was pounding.

It wasn't until she was on a red-eye back to New York that her heart finally slowed down enough to let her close her eyes. She dragged out her pashmina, wrapped it around herself and her baby, curled up sideways and fell sound asleep, waking only when the wheels touched down at JFK.

| 5 |

In New York, she went straight to the Swissair terminal and booked a flight to Geneva. She spent the day holed up at the gate, thinking. Her options had been narrowing down and yet, finally, as she stayed still, her quiet inner voice finally returned. She welcomed it back, allowing herself a tiny quiver of delight, anxious not to spook it. But it spoke clearly. "You are right to reach out to your father. He will listen." She hoped that might be true.

Though she had not talked to her father, the receptionist at the Absolute headquarters in Vaux sur Valais, Switzerland, perched in the hills above a mountain lake, assured her they would send a car to pick her up in Geneva.

After the long overnight flight to Geneva, she was greeted, after leaving customs, by a young man who cheerfully said her father was expected back that very day from a trip to the Laplanders, high up in the artic wilderness of Norway. But not to worry, he had sent a telegram telling them to make her welcome in every way possible. She liked the fact that this young man named Alfred had a bright blue flower tucked into his vest pocket. When she told him she liked his flower, he smiled and, much to her relief, his smile reached his eyes.

"You'll find we have flowers everywhere in Switzerland at this time of year," he said, as he took her leather satchel, "No other bags?" He cocked his head to one side.

She shook her head, "I travel light."

"That's a good thing," he laughed. "I do that myself. Better not to be a beast of burden. I've always admired St. Frances and his vow of poverty. I used to be such a slave to possessions."

She reminded herself to be cautious. She remembered well how one of the tactics used by the Absolutes was to disarm you by sharing their own sins then asking, not quite naively, for you to share your own. And so, she clammed up and didn't respond to his various attempts to make conversation as he drove them along the north shore of Lake Geneva, then, after an hour, to the left up a long pass into a narrow mountain valley surrounded by peaks.

He threaded his way through a medieval town with dozens of clock towers out of a fairy-tale book, and up onto a narrow road that switch-backed three thousand feet straight up to the Absolute headquarters.

Back at the turn of the last century, Alfred told her, the structure had been a grand hotel for people seeking fresh mountain air and a respite from polluted cities. During the winters, this valley was so widely renowned for its fresh mountain air that celebrities suffering from consumption would often stay in residence for many months. In 1963, the Absolutes had purchased the by-then dilapidated building as a perfect place to have conferences. "The money came from many sources. Generous people like your father." Alfred smiled as he swung the car around an alarming switchback curve.

Off to the side, the drop was a dizzying thousand feet. The other side was a steep granite face studded with a brilliant array of wildflowers. "Many of the full-timers fixed the place up with their own hands. Even the chancellor of Germany came to spend a work weekend."

They pulled up in front of a gigantic building topped with turrets and built of fine old woods, with hundreds of windows along the façade facing the view. Several thousand feet below, the lakeside medieval town looked a toy, but the sound of its church bells floated up to this edifice they called Utopia.

"I know it's a bit corny," laughed Alfred. "Everyone is expected to carry his or her own weight here. There are no kings or princes here.

Neither are there paupers. All is one, and one is all." His tone was light, almost frivolous. "I'll leave you then; Marie will take over from here."

A tall young Swiss woman wearing a dirndl welcomed her. "Hope you don't mind my English, I'm practicing, yes, but still it's not so good as I would wish," she blushed. "Come," she said, "You must be exhausted. You'll meet everyone else in good time. Is that the way to say it?" And she shook her curly brown hair, making fun of herself. "But for now, I think, yes, you must rest. Yes?"

She nodded. "Yes please."

She followed her through a grand entrance hall decorated with ornately carved wooden chandeliers, elaborate paneling, and filled with comfy armchairs scattered all around the room, some overlooking the view, some arranged in front of a huge stone fireplace in which a cheery fire blazed. They trotted up a broad spiraling staircase, around and around until she was almost dizzy. As they went higher, the staircase narrowed and finally, at the very top, a short hallway opened to the right with just a few doors along one side. "You are so fortunate, or should I say lucky? Is that the correct idiom?" she asked. Her words had a formal schoolgirl rhythm.

Cornelia nodded. "Very correct."

Marie blushed, then with a lovely curtsey and flourish opened the door. "These rooms have the best vistas of the whole of Utopia."

Inside was a tiny but totally charming room. Tucked into a bay window, a slipcovered armchair looked out to a vast view of blue sky and dazzling snow-covered peaks. The four-poster bed was covered with a fluffy down comforter. A bouquet of wildflowers perched on the wooden mantel above a porcelain stove whose glass door showed off a chortling fire. "We, how do you say, sleeping here with the windows open? We very much like the fresh air. Therefore, the fire is to take the chill off how do you call it, the wind? The breeze? Which is more correct?"

She shrugged.

"You will like it. You will get the roses in your cheeks." She giggled and left.

Moments later, after washing her face and hands, Cornelia sank down into the armchair. Cowbells clanged as a large herd of cows picked their way up the steep pasture below her window. In a lovely contrast to the thick yellow sunshine flooding her sill, a cool breeze blew in, chilled by its passage across the glaciers.

Far below, a sapphire blue lake swirled with paisley patterns, etched by the wind. She sighed with pleasure and turned back to contemplate the tray of food on the table next to the porcelain stove.

Next to a pink teapot with a curving spout, slices of mountain cheese, a dolt of butter, a pot of homemade strawberry jam, and a pile of hot croissants tempted her. She buttered one croissant, covered it with jam and shoved it into her mouth. It melted into buttery flakes. She washed it down with a huge mug of green tea laced with honey, then picked up a slice of cheese and took nibble bites as she sighed again, leaned back in her chair and put her feet up on the windowsill.

From below, a train tooted as it trundled up the hill, stopped briefly at a tiny station, then continued its upward passage through a pasture stuffed full of indigo gentians and bright red poppies.

Her brain and body, for the moment, were at peace.

She stumbled to the bed, pulled up the duvet to keep cozy, loving the way the fierce mountain air fired her cheeks, and fell soundly asleep.

Hours later, she awoke refreshed. She lay in bed listening to a cacophony of cowbells and church bells, a sound that was mildly chaotic but peaceful. It gave her hope that there was some way to settle the jumble of her own thinking. As she stayed under the covers, stretching her legs and wiggling her feet, she cupped her hands over her belly and prayed for that quiet inner voice. At first there was nothing but a clamoring: strident Geraldine, needy Nevin, brutal Hall Hamden, and parrot-like Nathan, all vying to be heard. Gradually, the uproar fell away, and that quiet inner voice reverberated as clearly as if only one cowbell winged its way across the snow-covered peaks through the sunshine all the way to her window. *Go find your father*, came the zing. She hadn't seen him in a long time. They had only in rare moments ever been close. But there it was, ringing as quietly and insistently as a bell.

And so she got up, pulled on her jeans and hoodie, brushed her teeth, washed her face, finger-combed her hair, laced up her high-top sneakers and went to see if her father had arrived.

She trotted down the tower stairs and into the lobby. A crowd of chattering young people smiled and nodded at her as she passed. Several older people pored over newspapers by the fire in the grand lobby. People bustled by carrying trays of food or bundles of magazines, waving and laughing as they passed others. She went to the reception counter and identified herself to the young woman wearing a formal kimono. The young woman bowed.

"Oh, so *you* are Mr. Woodstock's daughter. We are so honored and delighted to have you with us. We've all been so very curious. Indeed, your father *has* arrived while you were resting. No one wanted to disturb you. After all, most of us are all too familiar with jet lag."

"Thank you," Cornelia said. "Do you know where he is now?"

"Indeed, I do." She bowed again. "When he's here, he spends most afternoons outside. You must go out the front door," she nodded at the entrance. "Follow the path up the hill. You'll see him after a while." She tittered. "But here, you must take some chocolate." She pushed a chocolate bar across the counter. "It helps with the altitude."

"Thank you. So I just walk up the hill?" She felt like she had landed in Never-Never Land. It brought back unpleasant memories of her time at other Absolute conferences, when everyone on the inside seemed to have the key while she was still knocking on the door.

The young woman shook her head, bemused by the question. "Just go ahead, you'll see."

And just as she had said, Cornelia did see.

Outside the sweeping entrance there was a signpost with an arm pointing up a hillside path. At first, the pathway was paved and ran between two stonewalls. It soon turned to dirt but was well-marked and led steeply up hill. Within minutes her heart was beating fast, and she was inhaling huge draughts of pure mountain air.

After passing through a shadowy area with pines bowing down from either side, she broke through to a sloping meadow that was filled with green grasses splashed with bright yellow and orange wildflowers, glowing like jewels in the thick sunshine. A lovely perfume filled the air. Drowsy bumblebees nodded down into flowers, their hind legs kicking as they pushed in to drunkenly suckle the nectar.

Down below at the far end of the steep meadow, a herd of cows trundled along, their large bells clinking, their heads held down to graze. Above and beyond, fluffy cumulus clouds danced in circles around snow-covered peaks; the sky was a deep, glorious indigo blue.

Halfway down the meadow, a man sat perched on a campstool with an open sketchbook in his lap. His head bobbed up and down, first looking up at the view, then down at his work, his hand flickering out to the paper to leave a few marks on the page.

Her heart pounded as she realized it was her father, Cornelius Woodstock (C.W.). Leaving the path, she walked across the meadow toward him, parting the grasses and flowers as she went.

He must have heard the rustle of grasses because he startled and turned. For one long moment, C.W. stared at her as if she were a stranger. Cornelia almost turned to flee. But, just at that moment, he sprang to his feet, dropped his pencils and sketchbook onto the stool then strode toward her, a welcoming smile stretched across his face.

Cornelia's heart hammered. She had never seen him look so relaxed. His walk was confident, his skin was tanned, he wore an open-necked white shirt rolled up to the elbows, with a grey woolen vest buttoned across his chest and thick wale corduroy pants of a dark forest green. She immediately wanted his outfit, and indeed the following day took the tiny hillside train down to the town below to purchase just such clothes for herself. But, at that moment, her heart still hammered. She didn't know exactly what she was feeling. It felt half like fear, half like longing.

"Cornelia, I am so glad. I have prayed for you to come. And here you are. Finally." And he stood in front of her, awkward once more, as she remembered him, nodding in pleasure, but still stiff and formal in his stance, not touching her at all.

"Come," he said and turned. "I have something for you." And, without waiting to see if she were following, he stalked back to his campstool.

"Here," he said, handing her a brand-new sketchbook and a tin of colored drawing pencils, "These are for you." He sat back down and picked up his own sketch again. "I just want to finish this. The light is so wonderful right now. And the clouds so fleeting. Look," he ordered, but kindly, "look around until you see something that pulls at you. And then that is what you must draw."

Without another word he went back to that quick bobbing of his head and the flickering movement of his hand that she had spotted from across the meadow.

Silence fell between them as it always had, but this time it didn't seem odd or nervous, just companionable. She wandered off about thirty feet then plunked down into the grass. She peeled the tin foil off the chocolate bar, then let square by square melt deliciously in her mouth.

Flowers swayed in a slight breeze, chill in its temperature but offset by the brilliance of the sunshine. Bees buzzed from flower to flower. Clouds cast violet shadows across the lake far below. Steep canyons carved parabolas across the silver snowfields on the towering peaks above. The kaleidoscope of light and color filled her senses and stilled her thoughts.

Finally, she opened the tin of pencils and reached for lavender and put pencil nub to paper and let her hand have its will as it perfectly captured the shadow of a clock tower far down the hill. And then her hand reached for Naples yellow to match the slant of late afternoon sunshine striking the other side of the tower. It sprang to life on the paper. And her hand flew back and forth from page to tin and back again, her head bobbing up to see, then back down again to draw. And all else fell away as time stopped.

Yards away from each other, father and daughter drew.

The rest of the day passed in a lovely blur. They stayed in the meadow for several hours. Cornelia did three drawings. They looked unfinished and weak to her, but she had truly been absorbed in doing them. She loved the way the world fell away and all that mattered was the moment. There was no one making demands or reminding her of the pressing nature of her calendar. Perhaps, she thought, the bliss of enjoying the present moment might be the most precious thing of all.

She had briefly experienced that pleasure with Alexander. But she was also reminded of how, as a younger child, she had run across the beaches of the Bahamas with Nathan, drinking in the play of light and color across azure seas. Finally, sighing deeply, she lay back in the grasses and let the sun and breezes caress her face. She dozed off but woke when a shadow fell across her. Her father was looking down at her sketches.

"They're not finished," she said.

"No, no, they're not. But I can see your intention. Here." He pointed at the clock tower, "You were seeing the light and that the shadow was on the opposite spectrum of color. And here," he pointed at a mountain peak in another, "You naturally made the snow fields paler than the foreground, that's atmospheric perspective. Most people don't often get that." He beamed. "You have the makings of an artist. You must keep drawing, every day, exercise that muscle until it feels easy rather than difficult."

She blushed. She couldn't remember the last time she had been so pleased by a compliment.

"Come," he said, "we must go back for tea, and then you must have a good dinner and go to bed."

They walked for a while in silence, then, without breaking stride, he said, "Your mother called earlier today. She guessed you might come here. She was wild to know that you were okay."

A flood of metallic saliva gushed into her mouth. She splayed her fingers out over her belly.

The unspoken hung heavily between them. He was quiet for another hundred yards or so, then in time to his step, he chanted, "The

Lord is my Shepherd; I shall not want. He maketh me to lie down in green pastures; he leadeth me beside the still waters. He restoreth my soul." And then he stopped for a moment, turned to her and his face was earnest. "Cornelia, it is time for you to restore your soul. There is rest here for the weary."

A painful knot jammed her throat. Unshed tears stung the corners of her eyes. She stumbled along, unsure of what to say. He launched back into his long-legged march, "Not to worry. It is not time to talk yet. That will come." And so she fell back into step beside him, grateful, for once, for his ability to be silent.

They sat by the roaring fire in the great hall, and he brought them a tray of hot tea and cheese and crackers. Then he showed her the library, which was a large room with ceiling-high bookcases and cushioned window seats built into the windows overlooking the lake and mountains. He pulled out several books for her to study, one on Sisley, the other Cezanne. "Study the way Cezanne paints a pear, the way he grounds it. Look at the way Sisley captures the passage of wind on water. Learn from them. Here, I'll leave you for a while and come find you for dinner."

That night they ate dinner in the large communal dining room with several young people: two girls from Sweden, two young men from Cambridge, and an older man from London who sat beside her father and who she remembered slightly from the days of Tall Pine Island. Though the conversation was lively, ranging from self-deprecating anecdotes about learning how to wait tables – this from the young British men – to a serious discussion of a recent détente between Russia and Germany, there was no mention of fashion or makeup or gossip about movie stars. She was beginning to realize she had been living in a very narrow version of the universe.

"Have you thought about where you might want to attend University?" asked one of the young women.

"University?" She stammered, looking up from the golden-crusted chicken and vegetable pie she was devouring, "I hadn't really thought…"

"Oh really?" she looked surprised. "C.W. told us he hoped you would go."

"Oh," she said, looking quickly up at her father, who was deeply engaged in conversation with the man next to him. And then the general conversation veered off onto the subject of an upcoming conference entitled "Breaking Down the Barriers of Borders," about which they were all very excited.

"I still think it should have been called 'Healing the Wounds of War,'" said one of the Swedish girls.

And the others laughed and said, "You may be right." And so it went.

She rolled into bed that night, pulled the down comforter up over her ears and slept for almost twelve hours. The following day, they went down the mountain on the tiny trolley train to the lakeside town where she bought some much-needed clothes, since she had fled the hospital with only one pair of jeans and two T-shirts. She bought green corduroy trekking pants, a lamb's wool vest and a light wool shirt, which she rolled up to her elbows. No mention was made of her buying everything in a man's size small. "I like my clothes baggy," she volunteered, but her father said nothing.

She giggled.

"What?" A lift of his eyebrows crinkled his high forehead.

"Nevin would think these clothes were just *so unattractive*." She drawled these last in a perfect imitation of Nevin.

His lips tightened into a rueful smile. "It hasn't been easy for you with your mother, has it?"

She shook her head.

"She means well."

"Does she? I'm not so sure about that. It always seems like a competition with her."

He darted a quick glance of interest at her but said nothing more.

The weather stayed fine though a squall settled blackly into the high valleys across the lake. In the afternoon they sketched, and he proffered advice and her hand became just a little surer in its choice of color and line and she was almost pleased with the result. And nothing serious was talked about. And the next days passed in a glorious blur of sunshine and flowers and walks and sketches and meal after wonderful meal.

Four days later, a gloomy day arrived. Clouds rolled in to fog the ramparts of Utopia and the view below was totally invisible. Wreaths of mist streamed past the windows, and she curled up in an armchair next to a fire and slowly studied the art book on her lap. She was awestruck by the purity of Northern light that made the cheek on a girl in a Vermeer painting glow with an opalescence that matched the pearl in her ear. A throat clearing made her look up.

"Sorry to bother your study, but they asked me to deliver this to you. It came by special delivery." Marie handed her a brown manila envelope, lumpy with contents. The handwriting was Nevin's and the return address was their apartment on the Upper East Side of Manhattan.

She sat for a long moment, breathing deeply, waiting until her pulse calmed and then she slowly opened it. Two posted envelopes addressed to her tumbled out. But though she shook the manila envelope nothing else fell out. There was no note from Nevin. Typical, she thought, her non-communication was pregnant with displeasure. Tightlipped at her own inadvertent pun, she knew her mother's silence was to signal how hurt she was, and also meant to punish her for running away. At least, she thought with gratitude, her mother had not opened the other mail.

She studied the envelopes. Though both showed a Los Angeles postmark, neither had a return address on them. But on one her name and address were typed. On the second envelope her name and address were handwritten in Alexander's printed scrawl. Heavy anxiety raced up her legs and arms, as painful as if liquid metal had been poured into her veins. Her heart thudded painfully in her chest. She tore open the handwritten first, noting it held an earlier postmark.

Dear Mighty Monkey,

I miss your sweet self and all your ways. Where are you? Do you miss me as much as I miss you? Peter wants you. Just thinking about you makes him hard.

Thought I'd tell you I'm about to leave on that long-planned trip to find the perfect wave. Bali here I come!

But before I go, I need to hear from you. I need your support. It's going to cost me. Big bucks.

How's your father? Have you talked to him? Does he still imagine you to be absolutely pure? Does he know what his Mighty Monkey does when he's not around? I would hate to think of him finding out. I know how important it is to you to have his approval. Given that he's so religious and all. He would hate to see certain things, wouldn't he?

Looking forward to hearing from you.

No matter what, I love you.

Peter

She crumpled his letter up and was about to throw it in the fire when that small quiet voice commanded, "Stop!" She slumped down in the chair; anger and shame sparked her face. Before she even opened the second envelope, she knew what was coming. And indeed, the typewritten words were bold and spare and each one of them speared her heart.

Disappointed not to hear from you sooner. Wire $25,000 to Western Union, 23468 Hollywood Blvd, West Hollywood, California, 90046 within three days or certain pictures will be sent to your father.

| 6 |

Quickly scooping up the two letters, she poked them back into the manila envelope as if their very touch could sear her. She jammed the envelope into her messenger bag and lifted it up over her head, placing it across her body and over her chest. As if those letters were glowing coals, the leather felt burning hot even through her thick lamb's wool vest. With tunnel vision, she ran across the library, out the hallway and down the corridor to the great room, where she picked up speed. She bolted out the door. She was vaguely aware that several people turned and stared as she passed, but she was afraid if she halted, she would start sobbing, and she wasn't sure she would be able to stop.

She charged up the hill, her heart pounding, her brain awhirl with awful thoughts of naked pictures and of a shocked and horrified Woodstock. She felt an acute sense of shame. And yet, in the midst of all the madness, that clear small voice reminded her that the lovemaking had been joyful and freely given on her part. She shook her head in astonishment at this possible acceptance of herself. The shame drained away to a trickle, replaced by a sense of self that seemed clear and strong. She would own her sexuality, she thought. No one could take that away from her. And then she thought back to the Degas and Renoir art books her father had given her to study just the day before.

There had been many paintings of naked women: some bathing, others combing their hair, and some even lounging on divans in what were obviously post-coital poses. With that memory pre-eminent in her thoughts, her headlong bolt up the mountain slowed and she came to a halt.

The valleys below roiled with clouds, but snowy peaks soared above, free of mist and glowing golden with the tail end of the setting sun. *Out of confusion comes clarity*, said that inner voice. And peace settled inside her just as she also realized the wind blowing up the side of the mountain was damp and chill.

She turned to go back.

Her mission was clear.

She must face her father, tell him the truth, and accept the consequences whatever they might be. If he reviled her, she would have to endure that. But perhaps, she thought, he might understand. No matter what, she would not be ashamed. Besides, she thought, and cupped her belly, making love had brought another life into being. That the embryo inside her continued to grow, despite any confusion she might be feeling, was an astonishing imperative. She wondered whether it had a heart yet. She hoped not. She couldn't bear the thought of killing something that had a heart. If it was still just an undifferentiated multiplying mass of cells, she might be able to abort that.

On the way back down the hill, the clouds moved in and dumped stinging rain. She was soon soaked and trembling. Half an hour later, as bedraggled as a mouse caught in a drainpipe, she knocked on her father's door. "Come in," he called.

"We must talk," she said.

He was sitting by a fire. His little black book lay open on a table next to him. His silver fountain pen still had its nub exposed. He had clearly just been getting "guidance."

It was a small room, monastic in its tidiness. A twin bed was tucked under the window. Rain lashed at the glass panes outside, the sky a deep sapphire blue, almost black. The ceiling flickered with light from the fire. A bible lay on the bedside table. There were two chairs in front of the small fireplace, and he nodded toward the empty one.

"Come, sit down by the fire," he nodded. There was no welcoming smile, but his hazel eyes were kind, and his large brow was clear, not furrowed with worry. "Draw your chair close; you look cold. And wet."

"I am." She pulled her chair so close to the fire that her wool sweater and pants soon steamed. She was quiet for a moment, holding her hands out to the flames. Then, with a shuddering breath, she launched right into it, "I'm pregnant."

He was silent, looking down into the fire. But his face had not flinched. "I know," he said. "Your mother informed me."

"You're disappointed in me."

His head bowed low. "I wouldn't exactly say that. Of *course*, I'm disappointed that you chose to have love without the sanctity of marriage. I would be lying if I didn't say that. But disappointed in *you*? No."

Relief flooded through her. His words were measured but held no censure.

"You see, Cornelia," he raised his head. His sheltering brows cast a shadow across his eyes, but they were clear in their direct gaze. It was the first time she could remember him holding eye contact for so long. In the past, his eyes had always jerked away within microseconds. "I've had clear guidance that *all is well.* I have faith that you have an intense relationship with your own divine power. And that you must consult that inner voice yourself. And then you will know what to do."

"You're not going to tell me what to do?" she asked, not quite believing what she was hearing.

"No, I am not," he shook his head for emphasis.

"How did this happen?" she asked, "What has caused such a change in you? You always seemed so ready to criticize me and Nathan."

"Aha," he said and chuckled, "I have much to be sorry for. You see, Cornelia, the death of Horace made us all think a lot about how the movement had gone all wrong. How it was possible for someone like Hall Hamden to gain such power. We had looked to Horace for the answers, even though all along he kept telling us the answers were inside of us. But we were like children, wanting to be told what was right and wrong. It was easy for me to think that our way was the only right way. I owe you an apology for being so critical of you. I'm sorry for that."

"It's okay," she muttered, "I guess you were only doing what you thought best."

"Aha! That's it exactly. And Hall Hamden, may he be forgiven, fell right into that same trap of thinking only he knew right from wrong. He was happy to tell everyone how to behave. And a lot of people followed him. You know there's a tremendous peace that comes when you give over your will to another. Then you're not responsible for your own choices."

"Nathan," she whispered, thinking of how he blindly followed Hall Hamden, perhaps in order to avoid the pain of his own decisions.

"Yes," he said, "He may be a bit of a lost sheep at the moment, but he'll find his way."

"You think?" she asked, suddenly pierced with worry for Nathan's wellbeing.

"He's in God's hands." His words were simple, but it was clear that he believed them whole-heartedly. And she took faith from his faith.

She sighed, "There's more."

"Tell me," he said.

And so she did. She told him about Alexander, of how they had met, how free she had felt. And finally, she told him about the blackmail letters. He asked to see them.

When he read the first letter, the handwritten one, he recoiled several times, and she knew it was because of the crude language. The second typewritten one with the actual threat brought anger to his face.

It was her turn to flinch since she thought his anger was directed at her. The old fear of him stampeded back, but instead of shutting down, she dared to ask, "Are you angry with me?"

He looked surprised, and she wondered how different their relationship might have been if she had dared to ask questions all along. "Not at all, but *this* has to *stop*," he waved his hand at the letters, "You need protection. We must go to the FBI with this. This man must be stopped from hurting you and possibly others." His tone was stern.

"The FBI?" she faltered. It had never occurred to her that he might want to take action. "Is that necessary?"

"When we find evil, we must cast it out."

"It wasn't all bad, you know."

He looked taken aback. "You gave your heart to him?" He cocked his head to one side, obviously curious and wanting to know.

"If not my soul, my body's heart." She lowered her head, abashed that she had loved a man who could so choose to hurt her. "And I want you to know," she blurted out, "the pictures aren't crude; they were loving. I know they were."

"Cornelia, look at me."

She raised her eyes to his. Again, his look was tender and in no way critical. "Next time you will be wiser in your choice."

"Yes," she said and felt a surge of hope as she allowed herself to believe that might be true.

"Does he know about the baby?"

"No," she shook her head. "You're not going to tell him, are you?" Horror filled her at the thought that her father might insist that was the Absolutely Honest thing to do.

"No, I think not." He slowly shook his large head. His large features and ungainly frame made her think of Abraham Lincoln. "Given his actions," he continued, "I don't think it would be wise on our part to tell him. You know the old saying, 'Be as wise as a serpent but as harmless as doves.' Let us be wise here." He paused for a moment to think. "We must *always* be honest, unless to do so would be to hurt others. Sometimes *love* must precede honesty. I think this is one of those times. I don't think it would be a loving thing to do to you or the baby to have him know."

"I agree." She had come to the same conclusion herself, but to hear him clarify and express her somewhat-muddled thoughts comforted her tremendously.

"I want to add something here," he cleared his throat. "I've thought long and hard about this. I've wrestled with my soul. But just for the record, Cornelia, I will support you no matter what your decision is. Only you and your divine power can make this decision. If you decide," he harrumphed as if the words were difficult to get out, "*not* to have the baby, I will understand. If you decide to keep the baby, I will help you, financially, and in any other way I can."

"Really?" It was hard for her to believe that he was telling her he would accept her no matter what she did. She thought again of Alexander saying, "No matter what, I love you." In his own warped way, perhaps Alexander had loved and accepted her, too. A sudden clear insight told her that a sick part of him was making him act this way. That the highest and best part of him would know it was wrong to hurt someone you loved. Instead, he was indulging a baser part of himself that felt he was owed something by life and those around him, that he was entitled to behave however he wanted because he needed the money. How odd, she thought, that love could dwell right alongside evil. They might even sometimes go hand in hand.

She looked deep into the flames and allowed her thoughts to expand. By giving in to his demands, would she somehow be affirming his need to feel potent in a world that often squashed those with no power? Though she would never know if her take on his actions was correct or not, it felt right, as if a puzzle piece had fallen into place. She thought she understood how he felt. It was a twisted way to feel powerful.

She hoped he would understand her need to stand up for herself. By accepting her right to make her own decisions, her father was empowering her. She did not have to bow down to anyone else's demands: not Alexander, not Nevin, not Nathan, not Hall Hamden, not Geraldine. She was in control of her own destiny. And, it turned out, the destiny of an unborn child.

Her thoughts turned to the baby. She still didn't know what the best thing was to do. Keeping the baby even though she might not be old enough to even take care of herself? Get rid of the child and give herself a chance to grow up? Or go through with the pregnancy and give the baby up for adoption? These three choices whirled around and around in her head. According to Dr. Ruth Bergman's timetable, she had less than two weeks before she should make a final decision about whether she would abort the other life inside her. After that, it wouldn't be safe to end the pregnancy.

"Really?" She repeated the question to C.W., just to make sure that she had heard him correctly, "You would understand no matter what I decide?"

"Really," he nodded. "Whichever way you choose, you are the one who has to live with the consequences of your actions."

"I can't believe it. You're the only person who hasn't told me what to do."

He chuckled, "Sometimes blind old dogs can learn new tricks. If they bang their head against the wall too many times, they learn to walk another way." He looked bemused.

And she threw back her head and laughed at the thought of him being an old dog learning new ways. But most of all she laughed at the relief of being told that only she and her own inner voice knew where the right path lay for her.

"You don't have clarity on this yet, do you?" he nodded at her belly.

"No, I don't."

"You will. Just live with the chaos a bit longer and the answer will come to you. You will know the right thing to do, I can promise you that."

"I will?" her voice trembled.

"Yes, I promise."

For a moment, they were both silent and looked back into the dancing flames of the fire. "Now I must ask you," he said, "are you clear about how you want to handle these letters? Perhaps I jumped the gun by saying we must go to the authorities?"

"Yes, I want to do something about it. I'm clear about that. I want Alexander to know he's done something wrong. That it hurt me. And I certainly don't want him doing it to anyone else." She thought about how she had allowed her mother to persuade her not to take action against Hall Hamden. She sighed. It felt wonderful to have her father do the opposite.

"Good, that's settled then." He stood up and moved toward the phone that was on a table next to the door.

"Have some tea," he nodded at the pot on a table next to his chair. "It should still be hot. And there's a toasted cheese sandwich. I asked them to bring two, just in case you showed up. I'm just going to make a call or two."

He picked up the phone and she heard him ask for the receptionist to connect him with the American consulate in Geneva. Within half an hour he had spoken to several people. It turned out, he shared with her after he got off the phone, that the FBI didn't handle this. Instead, the United States had something called postal inspectors who handled mail fraud and extortion attempts. Since no money had passed hands, an extortion attempt was what the letters she received were called. He had set up an appointment for the next day with a postal inspector stationed in Geneva.

"Will you come with me?" she asked.

"I don't think it's something you should have to do alone." He reached out and awkwardly patted her hand.

She bowed her head and felt she had been blessed.

*   *   *

With a ten-foot-high steel fence around its perimeter and small bulletproof windows spotting its façade, the American consulate looked more a jail than a gracious diplomatic residence. Alfred, the young man who had originally picked her up at the airport, had driven them down from Utopia. They had left before dawn, but the kitchen had sent them off with a picnic basket filled with a hot thermos of tea, several croissants, and a chunk of Emmental cheese.

It was a gray day and the mountain peaks were shrouded with clouds and the water on the lake was an unpleasant steely texture. When they pulled up at the gate to the consulate and a gun-bearing soldier asked for their passports, she felt a frisson of fear. She almost balked but didn't.

Instead, she closed her eyes and thought back to her best moments with Alexander. She saw them walking down a street, arms wrapped around each other, thigh to thigh, in sync, laughing and sharing stories. She saw him riding on the crest of the wave next to her, arms outstretched, mouth open with a cry of joy. She saw him hovering above her, lust and love comingled in his eyes. She saw their bodies joining together. And she remembered the explosion of colors as she came. And of how he had cradled her afterward and praised her for being such a good loving girl to his Peter. The fact that their pet names for body parts would now come under the scrutiny of some nameless official made her cringe. And yet, she thought, with a flash of anger, none of this would have happened unless he'd chosen to send her those letters. This gave her the courage to open her eyes and face the forbidding façade of the American consulate.

The main floor lobby was all hushed tones and marble. After their passports were checked for a second time, they were ushered to a steel cage of an elevator and taken up to the sixth floor, where they walked out into an entryway that faced what looked like a bank vault door. This opened to an office where once more they showed their passports, were patted down, and then told to wait.

C.W. sat down across from her on a small plastic couch, leaning forward, circling the brim of his felt fedora in his hands, looking up from below his furrowed brow at people as they passed. He must have picked up on her anxiety because he nodded without even looking at her and said, "Not to worry. All is well."

She took a deep breath and felt herself settle down.

After fifteen minutes of waiting, they were ushered into a small office where a large desk was placed under a bank of tiny windows. Behind the desk, a portly man wearing a blue serge suit yanked one finger inside the neck of his shirt. A bulge of red flesh rolled up over the back of his white collar. He waved at the two seats facing the desk. His other hand held a phone to his ear. He raised his eyebrows to show them he'd be off in a minute then after a few abrupt yesses and of courses he slammed the phone down, tightened his lips, stood up to shake C.W.'s hand and nodded abruptly at her.

He rocked backward into his wheeled desk chair. She had the feeling he wanted to put his feet up onto the desk but stopped himself just in time. There was nothing on his desk to identify him in any way. "And just why exactly are you here?" His tone was brusque.

"My daughter, Cornelia Woodstock, received these letters in the mail. Show him, Cornelia."

She took out the manila envelope and shoved it across the desk to him. Without comment, he read the two letters then looked her up and down with a scornful appraisal. "How the hell did a classy girl like you get involved with such a creep?" He made classy sound as if it were a joke.

She blushed and was infinitely grateful when C.W. broke in. "Is that important? It's difficult enough that she should have to go through this."

"Yeah, I guess." He nodded his head, "Okay then, what can I do for you? You haven't sent him any money, right? God, I hope not."

"No, I haven't," she said. Shame flickered along her face. Her fingers tingled.

"Well, let's be grateful for small favors. On the other hand, that makes it harder to go after him. Because you see, technically, a crime hasn't taken place until money changes hands. So what we have here is an extortion *attempt.* Crude attempt, but obviously a real one. Stupid of him to think that typewriting the actual threat and then not signing his real name in the first letter would somehow protect him. I'm assuming, am I not, that Peter is not his real name?" He looked up at her from under his patchy eyebrows and again his look was scathing.

"No, it's not," she said.

"I assume you *do* know his real name." His tone was sarcastic. He shoved Alexander's letters back across the table, pushing them with just the tips of his fingers as if their very touch might soil him.

"Of course she does," snapped C.W. She was pleasantly surprised at how he was coming to her defense. Nothing he had ever done before made her think he would have been capable of such assertion.

She gave the postal inspector Alexander's name and address and, sighing heavily, he wrote them down.

"Okay," he said, pushing his chair back as if he were about to wash his hands of them, "Here's what we're going to do. I'm going to call my compatriots out in Los Angeles. And we're going to pay a visit to this little piece of crap, and we'll scare the hell out of him, shake him up a little bit. Tell him we know what he's doing and that we'll be watching him and that he'd better not ever in this lifetime get in touch with you again. Hear what I'm saying? And we'll get the negatives from him – you bet we will – and we'll send them on to you. And you can either rip them up or keep them as a memento of this creep, that's up to you. But that is what we're going to do!" He slammed his hand down onto the desk, then stood up to usher them out. He slapped C.W.'s shoulder and said, "Hard having daughters, ain't it?"

Trembling, C.W. raised himself up to his full 6'4" height and glowered down at him. "You should be ashamed of yourself. Trying to humiliate. How you could want to add to her shame and misery at this moment is beyond me. Haven't you ever in your whole lifetime made a mistake you were ashamed of? Haven't you?"

The man looked stunned, the color drained away from his face, he looked down at his feet, and then, gaze still averted, quickly went back to sit behind his desk, shuffling the papers in front of him. "We'll take care of it. We'll do that."

"See that you do so." And with that last rejoinder, C.W. cupped her elbow and ushered her out.

They said nothing to each other until they were back in the car. He was tight-lipped. They were both silent until the consulate gates swept closed behind them.

"Thank you for defending me," she said.

"Well," he said, "that wasn't fun. But it's over. And if they do what they say they're going to do, that should end the matter. Now we never need to speak of this again." And with that he looked out the window.

But, for some strange reason, now that it was over, she felt giddy. And she dared to make a joke, "How did ever I meet such a creep? Because *I'm* a creep, you know what I'm talking about?" All said in her best imitation of an Italian mobster.

Alfred looked over his shoulder, looking puzzled. "What is a creep? A slow skulk? Yes, that is right?"

Startled, C.W. looked up at Alfred and then at her, and she saw a flicker in his eyes; his head bobbed down up and down; then a burst of chuckles exploded out of him like helium out of a balloon. The high-pitched sound of his snicker made her giggle too, and it went back and forth between them like laughing gas, each of them darting pleased little looks at each other, and then, just as they were about to settle down, one or the other would giggle again and off they would go, rocking back and forth, and finally crying out, "Stop! Stop! Don't make me laugh again!" because their stomachs hurt so much.

Alfred solemnly asked, "Please share about what is so amusing. Is it something I said?"

"I'm sorry," she said, "It's nothing you said, Alfred. Oh my, it's just too hard to explain. I'm sorry."

And with that, they were back on another round. In fact, the laughter lasted almost all the way back to Utopia, though it would occasionally lapse as they tried to recover, only to be overtaken by another whole round of giggles, and all the while they acknowledged their satisfaction with each other with small, pleased nods and smiles.

Three days later, she received an official-looking Special Delivery packet from the consulate, inside of which were the copies of the letters to her, another manila envelope holding a bunch of parchment-paper sheathed photo negatives, and a letter from the consulate. They recounted that postal inspectors in Los Angeles had indeed made a visit to the attempted extortionist at the given address, where they informed him they knew of his actions and would be watching him from now on. In answer, he freely admitted sending the letters, gladly turned over the negatives to the postal inspectors, then tried to explain it away by saying that it was all just meant as a joke. The inspectors told him they knew it was no joke, and he then promised never to attempt to contact the complainant, Cornelia Woodstock, ever again.

She took a quick glimpse of the negatives before she threw them in the fire. As the images twirled to their death in the flames, she saw the curl of a sleepy smile on one of them and knew that she would always remember that Alexander was the first one to capture her smile, and the first one she believed when he told her she was beautiful.

But he would never know he had left her with something even better. His crude attempt at extortion had given her the gift of daring to trust her father. Alexander had assumed she would be ruled by her fear of C.W.'s cobwebby disapproval, while instead the exact opposite had happened. Instead of being snared by it, his malice had resulted in her breaking free of old binds to a new laughing, joyous place. Once more she was struck by the irony of love surfacing from evil.

She kept only one of the many photos sent. It was a shot of her taken from across a bathroom. Standing in front of an old-fashioned porcelain pedestal sink, she was reaching down to wash between her legs. Shyly looking sideways over a rounded shoulder, her uplifted thigh was perfectly curved, her hip swelled, and her face was smudged soft with pleasure. Not a fierce little monkey after all. But an incandescent young woman.

| 7 |

Three days later, she and her father boarded an overnight flight out of Geneva to India; a trip, C.W. explained, that had long been in the works.

In the years since she had seen Hadji, he and his Moral Absolute followers had been busy. After several cross-country marches, he had accrued thousands of followers. With donations of money from all around the world, they had almost completed a conference center in an old hill station tea town, high up in the mountains of Maharashtra, where the cool of the heights had once offered escape to the old British Raj from the fevers of Mumbai during the monsoon season. He had asked C.W. to come visit the new conference center. Of course, the invitation had gladly been extended to Cornelia.

To see Hadji once more, after such a long time, was intimidating and exciting. Would she even recognize him? Would he her? Would he still make her heart beat faster? Would he be judgmental of her years as a model? Would they still feel like kindred spirits? Or would it be awkward and horrible and meaningless? Would any of it help her to make a decision about the life inside of her? She had no answers yet. But by now she had learned to trust that more would be revealed.

After takeoff, as the plane broke free of a thick cloud cover, the range of the Alps appeared below like a row of golden temples, their ramparts and minarets reaching high up into the blue-black sky. Just above, a planet swung by the scimitar blade of a rising crescent moon. As the plane swung east, dark pounced on them. She slept and awoke when the engines roared on their descent into a land where gas flares marched across empty stretches of a night-blackened desert.

As the plane refueled, a score of Indian families carrying infants and huge bundles of cloth filed in. She could smell sweat and spices and thick perfumes and heard the jingle of many glass bangles.

Again she slept but awoke to an early blue dawn and to the un-mistakable stench of human feces wafting into the plane as the vents opened and they circled over Mumbai before landing.

Their hosts in Mumbai, an English Moral Absolute family, picked them up at the airport and drove them into Malabar, a beach area of Mumbai where black from mildew high-rises towered over surrounding slums. They were to stay in Mumbai for three days, waiting for the once-weekly flight to Poona where Hadji would send a car to fetch them at the small regional airport for the six-hour drive to the new conference center high up in the Maharashtra Mountain range.

With her hair tightly permed and anxious pleats on her upper lip, their pasty-faced hostess showed Cornelia to a closet of a bedroom. Mary quickly told Cornelia that it hadn't been *her* choice to come to India, but that her husband had received "guidance" that overruled her objections. Her hands twitched at the tightly cinched belt of her mid-thigh polyester dress. "The heat is unbearable," she complained, "but we must keep up good appearances. I'll have the driver take us downtown tomorrow to buy you some suitable clothing. Jeans just won't do here at all. It'll just make you the target of a lot of unpleasant attention."

She could have told Mary that her own thick stretchy stockings and synthetic fabrics weren't helping her deal with the humidity. But she suspected that suffering was part of Mary's modus operandi. And so, like always when she was in the company of strong-willed women, she kept her mouth shut. After giving her a litany of dos and don'ts, Mary strongly suggested Cornelia must need a rest and firmly shut the door of her small room as she left. She went to the barred window and looked out.

Crows perched in rows along a tiny ledge running from one window to the next, occasionally swooping down to peck through three-story-high piles of garbage that lined the small parking area far below. Several small children picked through the debris. When one crow fluttered back up with a tiny bit of glitter in its beak, the other crows complained bitterly then flounced off to find their own scrap.

Far down in a canyon below, trains swept past, their roofs smothered with thousands of men, clinging on for dear life, their black hair streaming behind them like flags. On either side of the tracks, in the mud-blackened slums, the brilliant pink and orange saris of the women glowed like jewels.

She pulled out her sketchbook and pencils and quickly drew the scene. The world fell away as she worked.

Above her head, a fan whirled as fast as a plane propeller. When she pulled the string to make the fan stop, the caws of crows floated in, along with the distant cry of children. From inside, she heard the prim voice of her hostess reminding the cook that she was in charge of measuring out his hand-ground spices.

After an hour, the skies blackened, and a torrential rain fell. She ran to the window and let the rain splash her face. The street below quickly turned into a raging river, and black umbrellas sprouted like instantaneous mushrooms all along the sidewalks. She drew it.

The call for dinner came as a surprise. She had to pull herself away from the work.

After breakfast the next day, a turban-wearing Sikh driver drove their hostess, Cornelia, and C.W. downtown to an emporium that sold clothes. She was told once more that jeans were just not to be worn in India by women at any time.

It gave Cornelia a frisson of pleasure to remove Mary's hand from her elbow and walk right past a row of dummies wearing conservative shirtwaists. Even as she did so, she realized, with some chagrin, that she had not yet learned a good way to deal directly with bossy women. She was still wed, it seemed, to behaving in a way that she knew could irritate. She sighed. She had some growing up to do. She needed practice in asking for what she wanted. Once more she wondered if she would be capable of taking care of a child. Probably not, she thought, and felt a deep sadness pierce her.

On the other side of the store, a lovely older woman wearing a bright crimson sari beckoned to her.

Mary raised one eyebrow. "Well, if you insist on going native then I guess there's nothing I can do." She raised her hands in defeat. "I'll go out to join C.W. and wait for you in the car."

As she studied the stacks of colorful silks, a pang of pleasure shot through her as the saleswoman waggled her head just as Hadji did. "Would you be needing silk for a sari?" she asked.

Cornelia shook her head. "I don't think I'd be any good at all the folds and pleats. How about those tunics?" She nodded her head toward a mannequin.

"Ah yes," said the woman, "perhaps the salwar kameez would indeed be more appropriate for a Westerner." These were, explained the saleslady, the traditional outfits worn by women in Northern India consisting of tunics with contrasting leggings and matching scarves.

Within minutes, Cornelia had chosen two. A gauzy celadon cotton tunic filigreed with gold, leggings of citron green, and a silk scarf that combined all three colors. The other, a silky mauve with silver threads in a paisley pattern, and leggings of eggplant. She also chose a pair of gold leather sandals and two stacks of glass bangles that she layered on both arms. Then she added another simple white tunic and leggings. The woman waggled her head at this last choice. "White is usually worn only by men or by women when they are mourning." Cornelia bought it anyway, because it reminded her of Hadji.

Cornelia wore the new green outfit, shoes, and bangles out of the store. She left her jeans behind, delighting the saleslady. She said her son would be most delighted to be the proud owner of real Levi's from the United States.

Cornelia didn't share that the waistband of her jeans had been starting to chafe at her thickening waist.

She was grateful for the looseness of the new garments and their tie-string waists, allowing the breeze to blow right through the delicate fabrics onto her skin. And she liked the way she could take a scarf and fling it over her head to hide her blond hair from the piercing gaze of Indian men.

Back in the car, she tried to be nice to Mary. "You should try wearing them too," she smiled. "You'd be much cooler."

"Oh no, I couldn't do that," Mary sighed. "Though I must say they quite suit you, don't you think so, C.W.?"

"If you say so," he said. "As for me, I quite liked her in men's woolens."

Cornelia laughed.

Taking a cue from the long hair on Indian women, she swept her long wavy hair to one side and braided it until it hung like a thick cord of bronze down over her tunic and breasts, which were suddenly much larger and more tender than they'd ever been before. She cast her eyes down and smiled. She felt like a goddess of fertility.

The pleasurable thought soon faded as the reality of the streets outside sunk in. For minutes, while they were stuck motionless behind a spewing-black-smoke bus, she watched a woman squatting on a sidewalk bathe her tiny baby in the brown water slushing past her in the drainage ditch. A man, presumably her husband, wearing nothing but a loincloth, towered over her, grabbing at a large silver bangle on her wrist. She shook her head and cowered away from him. He tried to yank it off her wrist. She looked up at him with sadness, then calmly took off the bangle and handed it to him. She watched him stalk off, turned back to her baby, lifting his shining wet body up into the air where he squealed in delight. The fact that she could so lovingly care for her child even though they were living on the street made Cornelia feel guilty for even wondering whether she could care for a baby. It occurred to her that all the choices that her modern culture gave her were perhaps not such a good thing after all. Seeing this young woman so happy despite her desperate circumstances made her feel ashamed of her own selfishness. For the first time, she felt sure she should keep the baby.

Finally, the bus in front of them moved off in a belching cloud of black smoke and their car swept on, honking as it pushed through throngs of cheerful people.

The car drove past a crescent beach where thousands of people walked out across the low-tide flats. Gamboling gymnasts twirled across the sand. Bands of young men raced each other. Ancient sadhus sat cross-legged as the incoming tide tickled their feet. The cries from vendors of balloons, ices, and spicy fried parathas sang through the crowded air. The ubiquitous crows circled above everyone's heads. A lone vulture circled over a tower where the Parsees laid out their dead. By the time they got back to the apartment, her brain was whirling. And she was truly excited to be in India.

That afternoon, an excursion to a local cricket club was planned. Much to her relief, it was to be without their hovering hostess. She and C.W. were dropped off at an old wooden house with encircling verandahs, ushered through a series of salons with highly polished floors and old varnished portraits of jewel encrusted Maharajahs, out to a covered porch with brown wicker furniture, overlooking bright green lawns on which white dressed cricketers bowled and danced to their own mysterious rules.

She couldn't help but think of Hadji and Nathan and wonder how they both were. They were ushered to a table where they ordered iced teas and chicken tandoori. And finally, she and C.W. had a chance to catch up without the oppressive presence of their hostess.

At first, he was quiet, but then he began to talk. "I am sure you have heard Nevin's version of my life, but I am pretty sure I've never given you my own."

"No, you haven't," she said, dipping a piece of spicy chicken into a cool yogurt sauce.

"I would like you to understand something about myself and of how the Absolute movement happened to become so important to me."

"I would like that," she said.

Halting at first, then more and more polished as he went on, the story poured out of him. She ate her curry and drank her tea. And still he talked. After an hour or so they brought another pot of hot tea and spicy nuts and sweet flaky pastries rolled in honey. And so she nibbled and drank and nodded some more to let him know that she was listening. And sometimes she asked a question.

As he told his story, a murder of cawing crows circled above the mango trees. Below, their clothes a startling white against the vivid green of the lawn, the cricketers danced their mysterious dance, advancing and retreating, their arms spinning. There was a sharp crack of a bat as the ball was struck. And a high-pitched voice cried out the score.

"And your parents?" she asked. "Didn't you ever spend time with them?"

"Yes, well, from time to time, I was asked to have dinner with the two of them, Father and Mother. My father would ask me things like, 'So C.W., where *are* you in school these days?' And I would pipe up in the manliest voice I could muster, 'These days I'm attending Groton.' And so it went."

He looked out over the garden as if the view extended far past the mango trees and cricket lawns to a distant time. "There were only two things that saved me from an early suicide. Painting and your mother. But painting came first." He leaned down to stir his tea even though he had already stirred it twice.

"My mother had taken a house to rent up in Old Lyme on the Connecticut River, and an American impressionist was hired to take me out painting. The man told my mother he thought I had some talent."

"'His *fath*er will *never* let him paint,' she said, 'but if you really think he has even a smidgen of talent I suppose another day or two won't hurt.'"

C.W. came to a grinding halt in his story and dozens of facial muscles danced as if a series of tiny lightning bolts were striking him at random. "Won't hurt?" he shouted, making her jump. "What did she think?" His whole body shuddered. Finally, he sighed, "Horace used to tell me that the resentment toward her was just hurting me. And that in order to move forward I had to let it go. And forgive her." Again, he shook his head. "It took me a long time to get to forgiveness. How do you forgive somebody for *not* only *not* loving you, but for hardly even taking note of your existence? No wonder they nicknamed me Living Statue. I was stiff for sure. All hollow inside."

"I'm so sorry," she said and meant it. Her heart broke at how much he'd been neglected. It went a long way toward explaining why he had been so remote with Nathan and her. No one had ever taught him how to love. "And so?" she prodded him. "He was allowed to take you out painting again?"

"Yes, that day and the day after and the day after that as well. Until I was dispatched back to Groton in the fall. I'll never forget that summer. It was as if I had been blind, and he taught me how to see. The full whirl of color and light made me drunk with happiness." His face filled with wonder at the memory.

"And then you went back to Groton in the fall?" she prompted.

"But everything was different, don't you see? I began to show evidence of a bit of stubbornness. I insisted on spending time in the art studio rather than playing football. And somehow the headmaster let it slide," he snorted. "He knew I was an oddball, guess he was glad I had found something I was passionate about. God knows I wasn't much use on the football field. Anyway, all went well until my next-to-last year when it came time to apply to colleges. My father was insisting on Harvard, of course. And the very thought filled me with horror. I wasn't a club sort of person and that was what was expected of me. To join all the right clubs and do the right thing. So, I bargained with him. I said I'd be cooperative if only he'd let me go to Paris to study art. I begged him for just one year abroad. And much to my surprise he finally relented, and I was allowed to go with the firm understanding that the following year I was to go to Harvard, with no ifs, ands, or buts about it."

"And then?" she asked. "What happened then?" She was so glad to be finally hearing his story. She felt as if puzzle pieces were falling into place.

The breeze waned; shadows crept toward them, and a thick humid heat rolled in off the cricket lawns, arching now with long glittering sprays of water from clicking sprinkler heads. A white turbaned man stood behind them, yanking a braided rope-pull that slowly flapped a giant palmetto fan back and forth above their heads. A group of young men still bowled on a far-off lawn.

"I went to Paris," his head sank low, "and I was a failure."

"No." She could hear by the flat tone of his voice that just remembering brought back the despair. "Why?"

"Because no matter how hard I tried, I just wasn't good enough. There was always someone better. Or someone with more flair than I had. I had an eye, but it wasn't enough. And so I came home with my tail between my legs and dutifully went to Harvard. But I didn't get tapped for any of the clubs. Despite being a heritage. And depression nipped at my heels like a persistent terrier working at an old pair of black leather shoes. At first there's just a little hole, and then it starts to rip and tear and fall into shreds until your life is all full of tattered thoughts and fractured feelings, and all is dark."

The murder of crows startled up again, whirling up like thick black ashes from a distant fire, then settling down upon the top fronds of several palm trees, where they set up an awful raucous chattering, their mouths wide open as they complained about their day. A gardener moved slowly past, snipping at the dead heads of roses. C.W. stirred his tea and the leaves whirled in a dervish dance up from the bottom of his porcelain cup. The group of young men, dressed all in white, left the cricket field and walked toward them, arms thrown around each other's shoulders, their voices high and strident. In the late afternoon sun, their black hair gleamed in the same way as Hadji's did, and Cornelia felt a throb in her loins at the very thought of him. Ashamed, she immediately pushed the thought away.

"And Nevin?" she asked. "How did you meet Mummy?"

He looked up at her, sadness cloaking his eyes. This was clearly not an easy tale to tell. "Well, turned out one of my mother's old friends happened to be related to Nevin's great aunt. And Nevin had just had her heart broken by a beau from Yale and all the ladies were desperate to keep her entertained. And so, it was arranged that I would take your mother to a Harvard/Yale boat race dance."

"How did that go?"

He looked up at her from under his hooded brows. "It went as well as to be expected, I suppose. She was a famous belle of the ball, you know."

"Yes, I know. I've heard about *that* ad nauseum."

"Have you now?" And his look turned curious, as if he were a crow turning over a piece of glitter in its claw.

"Go on," she said.

"Well, you see, she just made it all very easy. She was so good at talking. And I was good at listening. She misunderstood my reserve for lack of attraction and that piqued her interest just enough to secure me a second date. Because I was a lost cause from the first. I fell for her hook, line, and sinker. She just seemed so alive, so ebullient; I felt her blithe spirit as an almost unbearable light shining down upon me. I grasped at her as if I were drowning. Which indeed I was." He took his knife and raked at the crumbs that flecked the white linen tablecloth.

"And her? What about her?"

As if the memories had indeed once more plunged him into a black pool of sadness, he swam back up to her through long moments of silence. "Well, I guess her family thought the Woodstock connection would offer security. Her family didn't have much money, you know. And her debutante days were numbered. In those days, beauties had a short shelf life. She had wasted, as she saw it, four years on a beau who had, in the final analysis, dumped her. Her options were fast closing down. And here I was offering her a good name, a family fortune, a house in Pennsylvania, and I was presentable on her arm, if a bit shy."

He shuddered at the memory. "It all just went along. After graduation, I came into a good bit of money, and it seemed the thing to do, to get married. And of course, I was besotted with her, if you will. I let her do whatever she wanted. She wanted horses, so we bought horses. She wanted servants, so we had servants. She wanted dinner parties, so

I learned to mix drinks. And all the while my soul was festering, and I was lost, and it took me a long time to see it."

"And Nathan and me?" she said quietly.

"Well, you just came along like everything else did. I didn't question whether it was right to have children. It was just what you did. Procreation was expected of you, after all. But I must say, though I had little to do with you and I'm sorry for that, when I did pay attention you delighted me, both of you. But I just didn't have the skills to dandle babies or change diapers, and to be honest with you, it wasn't expected of men at that time. It was only later that I realized I missed out on all of it."

"But what happened? How did it all work out? Why did it end in divorce?"

"Well, Nevin began to tire of our way of life. She had everything she said she had ever wanted: the big house, the two beautiful children, horses, men paying attention to her, but there was something restless inside of her. I could see her drinking more at our cocktail parties. And her flirting became more overt and less casual. I guess in hindsight there were probably more than a few flings during that time. Then two things happened almost at the same time."

"Ray and the Moral Absolutes," she whispered.

"That's right," he looked up at her in surprise. "How did you know?"

"Well," she said, "I'm not exactly a dummy, you know. And I can count backward."

His lips tightened into a thin straight line. "We bought this little caravan. Nevin thought it would be fun to spend the winter months camping along the Florida Keys. I could get back to my painting and it would be good for the kids – you were still toddlers – to run naked along deserted beaches. She had such fun decorating the little trailer, and I liked the thought of sketching again. I was rusty. And I suppose I leapt at the thought of an excuse to get out of my pretend job shuffling papers in a brokerage firm."

Out on the now-empty cricket fields, the shadows had lengthened and turned purple. Above the trees, cumulus clouds boiled up into golden thunderheads, and a curtain of rain slanted down from one of them, gradually moving in their direction.

"Isn't it beautiful?" he said. "I've always loved clouds."

"Me too. Do you mind if I sketch while you talk?"

"Not at all. It makes me happy to have you sketching." His eyebrows lifted in pleasure, then he sighed and continued.

"For a few months, the new distractions worked for both of us. But it was close quarters in the trailer, and Nevin missed having hired help and missed her horses. She began to pace up and down the beaches. Finally, one day, she drove into a marina where she hoped to hire a boat to get us out to the Gulf Stream where we could troll for tuna. And who should be running the marina but Ray? And so, they started up. And soon he had her convinced that the only thing they could do was both dump their respective spouses and run off to the islands where they could have a simple, meaningful, hardworking life together."

"And the sex was great," she quipped. "Don't forget that."

"She told you that?"

"Yup."

"Well, not that I can blame her for looking elsewhere. I wasn't giving her much in that department."

Hearing that made her uncomfortable and so she switched the subject back to him. "And the Moral Absolutes?"

"Well, I think Horace once told you that he had met me when I was a teenager. My father had been persuaded to have him for dinner. He kept in touch with me over the years. And I followed his moves around the world. And it just so happened, just when Nevin was falling for Ray, I began to hear a call to my spirit."

"Your spirit?" She thought of her own inner voice that spoke up so clearly in times of conflict. She wondered if that was what he meant by a call to his spirit.

"Yes, you could say that for many years I had been blind, deaf, and dumb to the call of anything spiritual in my life. I had rejected the old Episcopalian ways as hypocritical and a bunch of ritual that held no meaning for me. And I was so absorbed in my own angst that God's clear, quiet voice was drowned out by my own selfish desires. That the world was in bad shape, and perhaps needed warriors such as myself hadn't occurred to me at all."

His face shone, as if a candle had been lit in a darkened room. "You see, there was nothing in my life that I hadn't failed at. Art. Being a husband. A father. A job. And here was Horace offering me a chance to make a difference in the world. That what I did *could* matter. That my money was a gift that could be used to further the cause of good in the world. That God actually *needed* me in the fight against evil. I was inspired. And I guess," he chuckled, "I still am. I gave myself to the cause wholeheartedly and I have never looked back. It has made my life worth living." His voice had fervor, and she believed that indeed Horace and the Moral Absolutes had saved his life. And that he was the good and stalwart man he was today because of them. "And now I'm starting to draw again. And my daughter is with me. And suddenly life is quite, quite wonderful."

"Thank you for sharing all that with me." Her eyes welled with tears; she blinked them back because she didn't want him to think she was sad. They were, in fact, tears of joy that she was finally feeling close to her father.

Above the trees, now a lurid green, a grey veil quickly moved toward them, and the first drops of rain splattered the old wooden steps leading down to the lawns, then clattered across the tin roof above them, drowning out the possibility of any further conversation. They stood up and moved through the old club out to where their driver was waiting for them in the car.

| 8 |

Two days later, thick monsoon clouds clogged the sky. Their prop plane pitched up and down. The engines screamed. A grey-green soup streamed past the windows. The engines snarled and the plane bucked to one side, then swerved back up and around and abruptly down.

As the plane lurched, so did Cornelia's stomach. Her hands clasped her belly. Finally, just as she thought she might start screaming, the plane broke free of the clouds. A runway appeared several hundred feet below the plane. Nose up, tail down, the plane dropped fast, jolting down, bouncing back up, swerving as it slewed through a puddle, straightening up, then roaring down the runway and braking hard. Rain swiveled across the window.

Beyond the tiny airport, charcoal grey clouds capped steep green hills.

Two men wheeled a staircase up to the plane, the door opened and out they went, bolting down the stairs and across the runway splashing through the downpour as fast as they could. Despite their dash, they were drenched by the time they reached the one-room terminal. Cornelia yanked at her clothing, trying to unstick it from her skin.

From across the room, a young man greeted them with a waggle of his head. He loped over with a broad smile. He was extremely thin and dressed all in white cotton. His head looked alarmingly large for his slender frame.

In a sing-song voice, he said, "Indeed, you must be the famous Cornelius Woodstock and his daughter Cornelia. You are most welcome!

Namaste!" His hands met at the apex of his forehead, and he bobbed down into a little bow. Cornelia followed suit. Her father nodded.

"My name is Mohammed," said the young man. "I am originally from the Punjab. But now my family, as you can see by my presence here," accompanied by another head waggle, "has come to take our proper place near Hadji and follow the Moral Absolutes. We are *changed*, you see. We have taken it upon ourselves to serve something larger than our own needs. We met Hadji when he walked into our village and asked us to simply come with him. My mother packed up her cooking pots and saris and here we are, living in the green hills of Maharashtra."

He stretched and inhaled deeply before launching into another torrent of words. "Hadji chastised me for fretting about coming to meet you. He assured me that I would indeed recognize you. And so I have!" He beamed. "I am indeed very pleased with myself for having accomplished this task." He nodded and smiled.

C.W. bowed and nodded back. "You are a good man."

Mohammed flushed with pleasure. "Your bags will be here directly. And then we will most promptly be on our way. You see, it is a very long way to Cherrapunji most likely six hours of driving, or perhaps even more. We must set out as fast as we can in order to get you there for dinner time. There is an extremely singular evening planned for you. A very special meal, I believe. It promises to be most delicious, followed by singing and dancing all around. Everyone is most delighted at the prospect of your coming to visit us for the first time ever, is it not?" And he cheerfully smiled and waggled his head again and Cornelia could not help but smile back. A wave of anxious pleasure surged through her.

Within minutes, their bags were trundled in on an old loading cart pushed by several soaked-to-the-skin porters. As she stooped down to pick up her suitcase, Mohammed insisted on trying to grab it away. When he laid his hand across his heart she relented, letting him carry the scruffy old leather satchel.

His VW van had seen better days. It was all battered on one side. "Sideswiped by a bus I'm afraid," he shook his head sadly. "I'm afraid the bus drivers here in Maharashtra state are not often intimidated by other vehicles. They think of themselves as the lords of the roads, like tigers running through the jungles. All others must bow down and get out of their way."

She laughed, truly delighted at his rhetoric.

"Oh no, Miss Cornelia, it is a most serious matter I am afraid. Not a laughing matter at all."

"Oh, I see," she said, putting on a serious face. She looked over at C.W. and saw what was now becoming a familiar twinkle in his eye. She quickly looked away, afraid that they would have another fit of giggles in the car and hurt this young man's feelings.

With some effort, he slid open the banged-up side of the van, sliding it to one side and ushering her into the far back seat as if it were a throne. The upholstery on the seat was faded almost silver and had several holes in its padding, but someone had starched and ironed a white lace runner that hung over the back of the seat, making sure that if her head rested backward, it would touch the fresh linen and not the old seat. She smiled, and Mohammed noticed her smile. "It is my mother who is responsible for this splendor. She has insisted that all must be freshly washed and starched and ironed for your distinctive delivery."

"Thank her for me," she said, and resisted making eye contact with her father.

"You will have a chance to thank her yourself. She will indeed be a part of the greeting party; you can count on that!" He opened the front passenger door with a flourish and nodded for C.W. to take the seat.

In the back, Cornelia looked for a seat belt. But there was none to be found.

Ever alert, he swiveled his head around from the front seat. His face furrowed with a tragic expression. "I am so sorry that I have to tell you that I am most afraid the restraints are long gone. But we have them in the front seat, you will see." He proudly buckled her father in next to him then did the same for himself.

They set off down the busy roads at a fast clip. Mohammed played his horn as if it were a trumpet, scattering street urchins and even a sacred cow or two. "You see," he said, dashing a smile back over his shoulder, "It is only the Hindus who worship cows – we Muslims like to eat meat. But still, Hadji tells me that I must show respect and beep my horn in warning rather than run them down if they insist on getting in my way. You see, Hadji is, as you may or may not know," he waggled his head, "a Hindu, and therefore to him the cows are sacred. And since we respect that all their gods are our gods and our one god is the same as all their gods then we must take care not to run down their sacred cows, you see?"

"I do see," she laughed. She couldn't help herself. She hoped her laugh did not offend him. She had forgotten about Hadji's wonderful appreciation of the ridiculousness of life. She looked forward to his ability to make her laugh. Few people did. She so valued that quality in him.

C.W. shook his head in a serious manner, "that shows a very profound understanding, Mohammed."

From the back, she could see Mohammed's neck turning red with pleasure and she was happy.

The thought of seeing Hadji once again filled her with an almost unbearable combination of anxiety and pleasure. They had once veered very close to a special closeness. And they had always liked each other and been friends. She wondered what lay ahead. *More will be revealed,* whispered her inner voice. And she giggled.

The van soon splashed out of the town of Poona and climbed into the surrounding hills. Below them, terraced rice fields flashed silver in a shaft of sunshine that briefly vaulted down from between two storm clouds. Several water buffalo wallowed in a muddy roadside pond. Along the green borders of the road where grass grew in the ditches, two little boys with switches kept goats from scampering up into their path. Knee-deep in water, a row of women, their bright saris tucked up to their waists, leaned over to thrust their hands deep down into the watery rice fields.

Down in the valley, a toy train dashed across the emerald landscape, dozens of pilgrims, dressed all in orange, leaned out the windows of the entire length of the train, as decorative as garlands of marigolds. She committed the scene to memory, vowing to draw it as soon as she could. She leaned back against the seat, supremely happy to be here in Hadji's India, with a dazzling landscape to contemplate, an amusing driver, and a father with whom she was cautiously growing ever closer.

Hours passed as they rushed forever higher. The air grew cooler, and she was glad for the long mauve pashmina she had purchased in Mumbai. Not wanting to close off the rush of fresh air from the window, she wrapped the shawl around her head and shoulders and soon felt warm and cozy.

Bright turquoise birds swooped up into the big-leaved trees now lining the roads. Off in the distance, much higher up, the herringboned ridges of tea fields began to appear. The van ascended ever higher, switch-backing to climb up a ridge, then swooping down the other side, only to find another steep hillside waiting on the other side of a narrow valley.

The road grew worse. The van slammed down into deep potholes. A ligament at the base of her pelvis began to ache and she hoped it wasn't much longer. But when she asked, Mohammed informed them they still had several hours to go.

They came into a small town with teashops all in a row along a concrete embankment. Mohammed stopped, and they got out to have a pot of hot tea and a slice of garlic naan. Cornelia used the restrooms, which were basic with a black hole in the floor over which she crouched to pee. But there was toilet paper and a bucket of hot water with which to wash.

She splashed water on her face and smoothed the tangled hair off her forehead, flinging her thick bronze braid back over one shoulder. She studied herself in the tinny mirror above the rust-stained porcelain sink, wondering what Hadji would think of her now. All the eating of the past few weeks had fleshed out her face. Instead of sharp angles her cheekbones were now a bit rounded, and her arms had a soft subcutaneous layer of fat that gave her curves where before had all been bones. Her cheeks had a flush of pink. Her lips were rounded, her skin as smooth and tight as a nectarine. It seemed pregnancy suited her. She smiled at herself, chuckling at the thought of how horrified Geraldine would be by her new softness.

Back in the van, she turned sideways, curling her knees up toward her belly and once more swaddling herself in the pashmina. C.W. turned his large head back toward her and nodded. "All is well," he said.

"Yes," she nodded back, "All is well."

His presence comforted her. During these last weeks with him she had felt less alone than she had in years. With her endless need for approval, Nevin's frenetic demands had exhausted and alienated her. The false surfaces of the modeling world were no better. The glorification of façade and the dissembling pretense of instant friendship seemed designed to make trust impossible. Flattery was the language of that world, and it was a language she despised. And though she had briefly allowed Alexander to penetrate her loneliness, it had sadly ended in hurt and betrayal. Like a hermit crab, she had retreated back into her shell. But being with her father, who was the opposite of pushy and the antithesis of smarmy, a good man who awkwardly meant everything he said, made her realize that there must be people like her out there; she just had to find them. She could not help but wonder what kind of person was growing in her belly.

She fell into a trance-like daze as the damp landscape swept past the open windows, making minor adjustments to her body when the van landed in an axle-pounding pothole, or when they were thrown sideways in the swoop of a hairpin turn.

Outside, the air began to turn blue. She last remembered looking far down into a distant valley where the setting sun flashed gold along hundreds of water-covered rice paddies. She fell into a profound sleep.

Loud yells startled her awake. "Ala Allah!" Mohammed bellowed.

She lurched to an upright position. It was dark, and the valley to their right was a yawning black hole. The headlights shone up a long steep hill. The wet road was slick with reflections. Directly ahead, catapulting downhill, a huge bus had pulled out to pass a van stuffed full of people.

Ahead of the van was an oxen cart piled high with rice on which several children perched. The sides of their heads shone golden in the headlights, their wide-open mouths purple with shadows, the whites of their eyes glittering like stars.

With its horn and headlights blaring, the giant bus barreled straight down toward them, fully over on their side of the road. There was nowhere to turn. Time slowed and swirled all around her.

To her right, she saw only a yard of dirt between them and a sheer drop-off. To the left, the children on the oxen cart stared at her, their eyes shining in the headlights. She had time to study the rain. Each raindrop became distinct. Spiraling down toward them. Casting rainbows into her eyes.

There was one final scream of "Ala Allah!" from Mohammed, a grunt of shock from C.W., and then the bus slammed headlong into them.

For a millisecond, the Mercedes logo of the bus filled the entire windshield. Then there was a profound sound of smashing. Shards of glass whirled all around C.W.'s head.

The world spun into a million bits of glittering brilliance.

And then she was catapulted out into the dark.

* * *

Sunshine flickered gold on her eyelids. She opened her eyes to a glare that made her head pound. Outside the window, vermilion blossoms flared in a vividly green poinciana tree. She lay there for a while, letting her senses get accustomed to the bright light filtering through wide-open glass jalousies into the room. Where was she? Had she slept through their arrival at Cherrapunji?

She moved her toes and fingers beneath the rough linen sheet on her bed. She ached all over as if she had been pummeled by giant waves.

But she seemed intact. She wondered why she thought about being intact. She looked around the room.

There was a shiny concrete floor beneath her simple cot-like bed, a door opening to a corridor, and to her right this bank of windows opening up to trees filled with flittering butterflies. A dark-skinned woman dressed in what looked a Mother Teresa outfit of simple blue and white cotton with a headdress of the same color tiptoed into the room. When she saw that Cornelia was awake, she nodded. "Good for you! Now that you are awake, I will go to call the doctor."

And as she said the word doctor, all went black and she was flying through the night sky and smashing into the ground with a thud of stars, then tumbling down a steep hill to land in a painful and awkward tangle of limbs. She shuddered and came back to the room but now her heart flickered.

There had been an accident. Her hands went to her belly. Her father? Mohammed? Where were they?

An older man with dark hair grizzled with silver came into the room, wearing all white with a stethoscope hanging around his neck. Without a word, he came and touched her forehead, which caused a painful pressure. Her hand flew to her head, but he caught it in a strong grip, patted her kindly, then clamped a blood pressure cuff around her upper arm, pumping it as he said, "Shush now. Not to worry. Do not fret. It will not help in the least little bit."

She shook her head in confusion and tears spurted unbidden from the corners of her eyes. "Where am I?" she gasped,

He put his fingers to his lips as he listened for her heartbeat, then asked her to take several deep breaths. "Yes," he said, then, "yes," again and then "yes," again for a third time. He took a deep breath. "You are fine. Fit as a fiddle as far as I can make out. A bit banged up? Indeed, you are. Bruised and hurting all over? I have no doubt of that. And indeed, there is in fact a bump on your head the size of a goose egg. But all in all, other than that, as fit as a fiddle."

"But what happened?" she whispered, "And the baby?"

"Yes, you told us last night when they brought you in that you were concerned about the baby. As far as I can tell all is fine in that department as well."

"As far as you can tell? What does that mean?"

"It means that you are in the clinic at Cherrapunji. But this is just a simple shelter for the sick. We are quite far away from any modern hospitals out here in the hills. But in my humble professional opinion – and I am a doctor, you may rest assured of that, I used to be a surgeon before coming here to Cherrapunji to offer my services – it appears that you will be quite all right. You were brought in last night. You were a bit, in fact quite, confused and very sleepy. We kept you awake as long as we could, walking you up and down, but eventually sleep took over and, using my best judgment that all would be fine, we let you sleep. Do you remember nothing?"

As he had mentioned the walking up and down, a vague memory surfaced of being dragged between two women along a long corridor lit by a string of overhead lights glaring down from above. Her heart agitated as she suddenly remembered crawling up a steep embankment, slippery with mud, and finally clawing her way back up to the road that was writhing with a bewildering mass of people and animals. Spinning wheels and shining headlights and a smashed in bus, impaled by a van turned into an accordion. She pushed through a circle of people and staggered toward the van.

Her father was sandwiched between two plates of metal, his face contorted into an awful expression of wonder, but his body was way too thin and, most awful, his head was flattened.

Beyond him, Mohammed was obliterated as a human, just a pulpy mash of red flesh. She heard someone screaming as the horror of remembering flashed through her and the screaming went on and on and on and now it's her who's screaming in the clinic room, and she's up and out of the bed, howling as she paces up and down, cupping her head in her hands and trying to wail the image of their dead bodies out of her mind and spirit.

"Yes, yes, yes, you must let the pain out. That is a good thing, but then you must calm yourself." She felt firm hands trying to hold her still. "You are understandably most agitated," said the doctor, "But also please understand that this extreme agitation is not good for you or the baby. So, after a few moments of release, you must then work on trying to calm yourself."

And as he said that she folded in over herself, grabbing her belly and moaning as she rocked back and forth, walking up and down, screaming and sobbing until finally she could scream no more and she fell sideways to the floor, curling up into an exhausted ball.

Then, just as she was diving into oblivion, her father's flattened head floated by, and she screamed again. Her hands went over her face and bile rocketed up from her stomach and filled her mouth with bitterness.

She vomited, and then there was a slimy yellow scum all around her on the shining concrete floor and she moaned, "Nonononono, it cannot be. Nooooooo!" Her head rocked from side to side on the floor. "His mother starched my runner. My daddy told me all was well." She howled, "All is *not* well."

And then she felt hands lifting her back up onto the bed. Someone wiped her face clean with a lemon-scented washcloth.

"No," she moaned again, "Mohammed, my father ... please tell me it's not true." Her rocking slowed to a tiny twittering movement. She hugged her own shoulders, jiggling herself ever so slightly.

Beside her, she could hear the doctor's voice, soft in its pitter-patter singsong. "I cannot do that. Indeed, I cannot in full honesty tell you that all is well. I am very afraid you are right, my child. They both are gone. I am so very sorry. I understand from Hadji that your father was a great man. Let me be the first to offer my sincere condolences to you and your family. Hadji will be in later to talk with you about getting in touch with your family about the arrangements," he paused. "Indeed for all the appropriate handling of the remains."

A sob clenched her gut. Again, the image of his squashed face and body flashed through her brain. She covered her eyes in a vain attempt to not see it. But that only made the image more vivid, so she opened her eyes and focused instead on the light filtering through the trees outside her window. She continued to rock back and forth ever so slightly. Pain pierced into every appendage and poison sang through all her veins, but her breathing settled down and the sobs stayed swallowed.

Again, the doctor patted her. "That's better now. Sister Beth will come to sit with you. I would like you to rest for a while longer, please. You have been through a grievous shock, and you must be careful to stay as calm as possible so as not to risk damaging either yourself or the child, do you understand?"

She nodded and whispered a thank you. She turned her head back to the window and did what she had done so many times before in her life: let the light and shadows and colors oscillate her eyes and brain and allow her to shutter the monkey chatter of fear in her brain. Within minutes she fell back into a light sleep, half aware of the dark-skinned lady sitting in a corner, her hands folded in her lap, her quiet stillness calming.

She awoke at dusk. Her first moment of awareness was blessedly free of pain before all the memory and sight of their squashed bodies came slamming back and she moaned. The quiet lady from the corner came, stood next to her, and patted her hand. "There now," she said, "there now, settle down, you must live you know, your time to go has not yet come. Acceptance of your life will help you now. Look out the window again. Look up. What do you see, my child?"

As if she were indeed a child, she followed the nod of her head and looked up out of the window and up into the now purple-black silhouetted branches of the trees.

In the lovely violet spaces between the branches where the evening lay gentle upon the skies, flocks of large flying animals floated through the skies above, hundreds of them, then thousands, all slowly flapping past, moving across the evening sky like gathering denizens of a dark-skinned ilk, their tiny, furrowed faces wizened mummies, all peacefully following the lure of some unseen destination.

A sense of strangeness, of wonder, and finally an overwhelming awe flooded through her with a painful awareness that life had an inexorable pull, that her destiny still lay ahead of her beyond strange and uncharted horizons.

"What are they?" She finally whispered to the lady who kindly patted her hand. "Are they angels?"

"Let me answer that one," said a familiar voice, and she turned to see Hadji entering the room, his dear, thin, beloved face creased with a smile, his shock of black hair still swooping down low over one side of his forehead only to be swung back as he let her see the deep sharing sadness shining out of his dark brown eyes.

| 9 |

From the moment Hadji entered her room at the clinic, peace walked in with him. Despite the leaden sadness squatting on her chest, Hadji's mere presence helped her believe that her grief would not kill her. And that loneliness was banished.

Later, she was to find out that many people had this experience on first meeting Hadji. After just a few minutes of conversation, grandmothers left their kitchens and followed him halfway across a continent. Men abandoned their Ph.D. studies to work, hammering nails in the still-being-built conference center. Famous politicians officially announced their conversion to his way of thinking. Gamblers donated money. Rich women worked side by side with people they once would not even have touched. In fact, the Harijan, once called the Untouchables, not only dared to leave their protected enclaves behind, but under Hadji's careful tutelage went on to give speeches to thousands.

When asked why they had given up so much so quickly, a response from a wealthy Parsi woman from Mumbai was typical of many: "It was quite easy, you know. Hadji made it seem that nothing in the world was as important as what he was doing. And that all I had to do to be a part of something bigger than my own petty concerns was to follow him. I'm just grateful," she threw back her lovely silver-haired head and trilled with laughter, "that my husband felt the same way as I did."

Cornelia was certainly not immune to his charms. She had been feeling their siren call for many years. When he stood next to her bed, beaming down at her but also radiating sadness and knowledge of such, the full force of her attraction to him slammed into her with such a rush of blood to her head that the world spun wildly on its axis. She felt bathed in his radiance. His non-judgmental, cheerful warmth and innate generosity of spirit made her feel special, and that somehow, they belonged to each other. It was as if she had finally come home.

At first, all she could do was look up at him and smile back. Not a broad grin because her sadness was too deep to allow that, but pleasure creased her face with such strength that the grateful tears streaming down could do nothing to erase her smile. Behind his large tortoise-shell glasses, his warm brown eyes crinkled, and delight wreathed his face. His shock of black hair fell again across his forehead, and he swooped it back up, raking his fingers through the shining hank. She wanted to reach out and do it for him.

Only later did it occur to her that he never actually physically touched her. During that first encounter, she was just so incredibly happy to see him once again, so warmly embraced by his loving look that his physical detachment would only haunt her in the weeks to come. Then she would look back over each moment they had together and fondle them, pondering over their value as if those moments of intensity and intimacy were as precious as rare jewels.

But he did stand close and look down at her as if she were the prodigal returned. "I am so very happy to see you," he said, "I know you have been through a most terrible shock. Indeed, this truly dreadful accident has sent a shockwave through all our hearts. I have prayed for so long a time that one day you and your father would come to India. I told you always that I wanted you to come to India, do you recall that?"

She nodded. "Of course, I do."

He continued, his words had a thrilling cadence, each phrase following upon the next as if it were chanted poetry. "I remember telling you that one day you must have a chance to experience the true wonder and colors of India. I always knew you and your father would love it here. At the risk of repeating myself, let me say again that it is with true happiness that I welcome you now, knowing full well that for all of us, but most of all for you, it is bittersweet for your arrival to be accompanied by such an appalling loss."

She nodded but remained speechless. She felt if she talked, she might start howling again.

He continued but more softly, "Other than Horace and my grandfather, I believe your father to be one of the very best men I have ever met. He gave me, and many others, faith that all westerners were not greedy and grasping and petty dictators. He gave me hope that it would one day be possible to cure ourselves of the awful wound inflicted on us during the years of the British Raj. That there was indeed a way to mend the hurt that runs deep into our very souls. But I ramble on," he chuckled. "I must remember that Horace used to tell me that less is more. A practice I believe your father would approve of, no?" And he waggled his head in that way that had once, and still did, delight her. Then he cocked his head to one side. "Aren't you going to ask me?"

"What?" she stammered.

He nodded toward the sky and put up one finger as if he were about to make a solemn and sacred pronouncement. But his wink showed that he was also allowing the moment to be comical as well. One of Hadji's most endearing characteristics, she remembered, was his innate ability to make fun of himself. She followed the line of his pointing finger.

Outside the window, still visible in black silhouette against the setting sun, those mysterious flocks of winged creatures flapped slowly by, thousands of them, soundlessly passing overhead. Several times she thought she saw bright little eyes staring curiously down into her room. She blushed that she had forgotten all about them.

"Oh yes, of course, how could I forget? What are they?"

Hadji looked up at the passing cavalcade, his face filled with childish wonder. "Aren't they wonderful? Every night, just at the time of sunset they leave their trees and fly further out into the jungles, looking for figs and mangos and all sorts of blooming flowers. And in the process, they pollinate and disseminate seeds. Can you see how large they are? Their wingspan is almost five feet. They are fruit bats, largest bat in the world, I believe."

"They're bats?" she whispered.

"Yes. Can you hear them?" Again, he cocked his head.

She shook her head. "I hear nothing."

"Listen carefully, they communicate with each other in high-pitched squeaks. It is one of the very many special things about Cherrapunji. They pass over every evening and morning. When we sit in the mornings, listening for our divine guidance from our gods, the bats float past over our heads. And since many of us here are Hindus, we truly believe that the divine exists in every creature. So we are particularly blessed by their passage. You still don't hear them?" He cocked his head again.

She heard the call of a mother to her child from far away. She heard a clink in the corridor. Again, she shook her head.

"Listen again," he chided. "Very carefully. Attune your senses to the highest possible note you can imagine, beyond even that of a piccolo." He laughed. "I tell people that hearing the voice of the fruit bat is like listening for your inner voice from God. It takes practice to separate out the true sound from the clatter. And you must learn to fine-tune your frequencies until that divine voice comes in loud and clear." And he fell silent listening with full attention.

She was embarrassed by the silence at first, but it was clear he was intent on her hearing them, so finally she silenced that critical chatter in her brain, which often clogged her thoughts, and listened. In the beginning she heard only the slap of sandals out in the concrete hallway, the rustle of a slight evening breeze in the lacy leaves of the poinciana trees outside and the sharp cry of a child calling back to his mother, until finally, all at once, at a very high pitch, drifting above all the other evening sounds, she picked up a gentle chitter, a back and forth, not as loud as a twittering bird and oddly metallic, like a metal triangle rung by a kindergartner.

Like sounds coming back after making love, the chittering soon filled the air, and she couldn't believe she had not heard it from the start. She closed her eyes and listened to the chorus of what sounded now like tiny little harps tuning up for a concert, yet was in no way discordant, but resonating and singing through the skies and air all around them until it seemed that music was everywhere.

"Yes," she nodded. "I hear it now. It's like divine music."

"Exactly."

And she opened her eyes to see his smile of approval.

"Now," he clapped his hands. "We have much to discuss. Come!" He waved his hand at her. "The doctor tells me that you are good to go. A few bruises here and there but no broken bones to hold you back. The resilience of youth coupled with a strong life force, I suspect." Then he suddenly blushed and averted his eyes as she started to throw back the covers and swing her feet over the edge. "I'll wait for you just outside." He nodded toward the door and quickly left.

She gingerly stood next to the bed for a minute. The goose egg on her forehead was down in size but still tender to the touch. Her back and neck were stiff. There was a broad band of dark purple bruises across the center of her thighs, but her ankles were limber, and her feet felt okay. Later, in trying to recreate the accident, she came to the conclusion that she had popped out of the collapsing van like a cork out of a bottle and that, in in the process of being catapulted out, her thighs had been squarely struck by a band of metal. The bruises would linger for many weeks.

On the chair in the corner was her scruffy old leather satchel, filled with the clothes she purchased in Mumbai. She took off the cotton shift from the clinic, pulled on some leggings and a tunic, wrapped her pashmina around her shoulders, finger-combed her hair as best she could, splashed some cold water from a bowl onto her face, slipped on leather sandals, heaved her satchel over her shoulder and headed for the door.

Outside in the corridor, Hadji was deep in discussion with the doctor. "Good chap," she heard him say as he patted the doctor on the shoulder. The older man beamed up at Hadji as if he were a student pleased by the praise of a revered teacher.

As if he could feel her coming, Hadji turned to greet her. She saw his eyes flicker over her long unruly waves of hair, and down across her Punjabi clothes. His voice was harsh. "The clothes suit you."

An awkward silence fell as they both looked down at their feet. One of his feet, shod in old but polished leather, scraped back and forth across the shiny concrete floor. It touched her that his feet were large and awkward and that, though Nathan would have called them clodhoppers, her father would have understood the value of fine old leather shoes with solid soles. One of the earliest memories she had of her father was his daily polishing of his shoes with brushes and soft chamois cloths. The thought brought a sudden sting of tears.

The doctor broke the silence by patting her hand and telling her she was fine and could always come back if she felt poorly and how, at all costs, she must keep up her intake of fluids and foods and vitamins, the latter pronounced with such a short-clipped tone that she was reminded that India was indeed a foreign country.

Hadji seemed reinvigorated by the doctor's litany and, with a casual wave of the hand, suggested they continue their walk down the hall. They fell into step next to each other. His long legs and extra six inches on her reminded her of Nathan, but his jet-black hair and sing-song voice were all his own. Still, she liked that his stride was as long as hers.

As they walked down toward the waiting courtyard and out into a world of blue dusk, he slipped something familiar out of the pocket of his cream linen jacket and handed it to her. "I thought you should have this. They found it in the wreck. He would have wanted you to have it."

She took hold of the worn leather notebook her father had always carried with him. Its shiny sides fit in her palm and matched her fingers, and she could almost feel his hand above hers, holding it close.

"It's his guidance book," she said. Tears spurted from her eyes and rolled down in a stream to soak the silk of her tunic with large mushroom patches of damp.

"Yes, it is that." Hadji's tone was uncharacteristically sober. "It will be full of all his guidance from God. And I hope you don't mind, but I took the liberty of cleaning the blood off its cover."

"Oh my," was all she could manage, overcome with a mute grief.

"There will be time for all of that. For now, there are many people waiting to greet you. And we must discuss what is to be done with your father."

"My father? What is there to be done?"

"Exactly. That is what I need to know. Before we can make arrangements for his passage to the other side, we must endeavor to understand his wishes."

"Oh yes, of course," she said. "I see." But she did not see at all.

As they walked out from under the lacy poinciana trees surrounding the clinic, the sky above shone with a soft violet hue, stars studding its depths, silver spangles on a dark ocean.

In front of them, windows glowed along the side of a brand-new three-story building perched alongside a canyon. The canyon itself was empty of light and yawned like the black maw of a giant monster. She shuddered as flashes of a wild spin through air followed quickly by the slamming jolt of the earth sprang through her brain and into all her muscles. She shivered as the horn of the van and the headlights of the bus, and a cacophony of screams whirled above her in the night air. She covered her ears.

Hadji quickly turned to face her. "Are you okay?"

She swallowed hard. A lump of unshed tears throbbed in her throat. She hung her head for a moment, then shook herself, willing the flashback away. She nodded, "I will be."

"Look at me," commanded Hadji, but not unkindly. She looked up into his warm brown eyes, which were solemn, lacking their usual spark of levity. "It will hurt for a long time. You will see things in your mind that you would wish to never see in seven lifetimes. But I can promise you this. The pain indeed is tremendous, that you know already, but in time it will fade and there will come a day when your father will live inside you and talk to you as if he had never gone away. But for now, you must move forward. You must drink and eat to keep up your strength, even if you feel like doing the exact opposite of all of that."

Again, she nodded, afraid the tears would come and never stop if she spoke instead of nodding.

He began to walk again, but more slowly, and she fell into step next to him though her feet felt leaden, and it was an effort to lift them off the ground and move forward.

"Perhaps you are wondering how I know these things. In India it so happens that we have to deal with an inordinate amount of loss. Death touches every family more than in your part of the world. You will meet girls here who are the sole surviving child of a family of eleven. You will meet others who have lost both their parents to cholera in the space of twenty-four hours. I too have not been spared the experience of seeing death extremely up close."

"Tell me," she said.

His brow furrowed, and his eyes lost their focus. "My little brother drowned in the river that rose up every year during the monsoon season almost to the doors of our very house. It was me who found his little body in the rushes and carried him home to my mother, who held him close in her arms for many hours before she could accept that he would never smile again. But then she drew me close and said that I would now have to smile twice as much to make up the difference." He laughed. "I guess that is why I make so many bad jokes and laugh so much."

"But I ... we love that about you," she faltered.

"Yes indeed," his head waggled, "and why not?" But his eyes stayed glassed over and his expression was inscrutable. She shivered.

She wanted to reach out and hold his hand, which she might have done when she was ten, but knew that it would be inappropriate now that she was a young woman. If she had been in her recent world of modeling after a sharing like that there would have been many hugs and kisses, but perhaps no real feelings. Here on this hill in a far-off foreign land, the customs were different, and she wanted to tread carefully despite her desire to draw closer to him. "Go on," she said.

He took off his glasses and rubbed the bridge of his nose, then peered up at her from beneath his shock of black hair. He held her gaze for a long moment, and she felt the pulse throb in her throat. Blushing, she was the first to look away, but said, "But there *is* more, isn't there?"

"That is perceptive of you, but why should that surprise me? I always knew you had a knack for the truth. Horace saw it first. But I wasn't far behind him. And you are right, there is more." He waggled his head and sighed. "I haven't talked about this for a very long time, but I witnessed my father dying way too young due to a terrible mill accident. He was trying to save one of his workers from being dragged into the claws of a machine and he tripped and fell in himself instead, pushing the other man out of the way in the process."

Again, he stopped and looked deep into her eyes. This time she didn't look away though her heart beat fast.

"I tell you all this," he said, "not to belittle the experience you have just been through, but to let you know that you walk next to people who will love you and have compassion if you only let them. They have walked where you have walked and felt what you are feeling, and they still smile when they see the sunset and laugh when I make my most feeble attempts at humor." And then he chuckled, and the sound made a dent in her sadness.

"You are not alone. To be sure, in India, you will *never* be alone. There are just too many of us. Millions and millions of us in fact." He hooted with laughter.

This time a chuckle bubbled up in her, but it jammed into the sadness clogging her throat. She did manage a smile.

"That's my brave little Cornelia. It makes me happy to see you smile."

They reached the new main building and inside the lobby there was a throng of people to greet her. Some held their hands up to their foreheads and said, "Namaste." Others just smiled warmly. There were women of all ages dressed in saris, young men dressed in western clothes, and many older men in wool vests over long white tunics and leggings. Several young women in salwar kameez nodded their heads at her and scrunched up their faces in pleasure, then covered their mouths with their hands and turned away as if the sight of her pleased them so much that they fairly twirled with delight. Later, she would work side by side with them in the kitchen where they all labored to roll out puri and parathas for hundreds of conference attendees. But that night, their faces soon blurred away into the mass of many.

Only one face stayed etched in her brain from that night. A middle-aged woman with a very sad face stepped forward out of the crowd and walked toward her, holding out her hands in welcome. She clasped Cornelia's hands in hers and moved in very close, looking way up at her since she was a full foot shorter. Her Muslim head covering hid all her hair and the lower part of her face, but her eyes held all the wisdom of the ages.

Hadji explained that this was Mohammed's mother. She spoke no English. "She speaks only the dialect from her village in the Punjab. They buried Mohammed earlier today. It was a simple ceremony. They put him in the ground, laying him on his right side facing Mecca, but she was not allowed to go. For Muslim women it is the tradition for only the men to accompany the body to the graveyard, so she is very grateful to be here with you instead."

Cornelia moaned and, without thinking, hugged the woman close. She was tiny, and the woman's bowed shoulders looked as delicate as the bones of a bird. The woman clutched tight to Cornelia's tunic as if it could hold her back from floating away. Cornelia felt a tiny shudder run through her. Then Cornelia touched her chin and looked down directly into her eyes.

"He talked of you in his last hours," she said, hearing someone translate her words as she spoke, "He loved you very much." She nodded as if she needed no translation. "He bragged of how you had ironed and starched the linens for our seats. He went quickly. It happened in a flash." She snapped her fingers. "He couldn't have suffered."

"That is kind of you to say. She will appreciate your words. Come," said Hadji. "There is more we need to do. Come along with me." And he walked down a long hallway, knowing that she would follow. But before she went, she leaned down and kissed Mohammed's mother on the forehead and she clasped her hands and shook them, nodding her head all the while. She hated to leave her. She wanted to tell her Mohammed had called out to Allah just before he died.

Hadji was waiting for her at a door. He held it open but stood in the doorway blocking her way. "Prepare yourself," is all he said and then stood aside.

It was a simple room with a few chairs and a long table, and on that table was a laid-out figure shrouded from head to toe in a white sheet. She stood quietly for a moment. Her heart lurched, then stumbled back to life. She felt a small hand slip into hers and she turned and was happy to see that Mohammed's mother had followed them. She nodded and smiled up at her. She led her over to a smaller table where a large porcelain-lined tin bowl sat next to soap and a pile of washcloths. She put one of the washcloths into the water and nodded at her to do to the same.

But Hadji spoke first, and she turned to look at him. "Before I leave, Cornelia, you must tell me what he would wish to have done with his remains. It is humid here in India and bacteria grows very fast. We have already delayed measures until you were back on your feet. But we can wait no longer. He must either go in the ground tomorrow in the nearby Muslim cemetery, or there is the possibility of a Hindu cremation, also nearby. But if you want an English burial, we must go to the Anglican church, which is all the way back in Poona. And, of course, if you insisted, there might be a way to fly his body back to the United States, but the cost would indeed be prohibitive."

"No. He wouldn't want that. Nor do I. We did once talk about it. He wasn't big on funerals. I think he would like the simplicity of fire. So I guess it should be cremation then." She blurted this out, finding it hard to believe she was making these decisions. She inhaled deeply to settle her thoughts. "If you are sure the Hindus would allow one of us to be cremated, then I think that is what he would want."

"That will certainly not be a problem." He nodded his head, "For what it is worth, I am pleased. I think you are making the right decision."

"Thank you," she said, "I am glad you are pleased."

This time it was his turn to blush and look away. "Righto, then, I will arrange that as expeditiously as possible. There is one more thing. It is customary for the son to do the rites at the actual cremation and for the dispersal of the ashes. Except when no son is available then we call it putrika, and then the daughter takes over the role. You should know I have tried reaching Nathan to no avail. I will continue to try but I fear, no matter what, he would not make it here in time. Are you ready for this task?"

She swallowed hard, "Do I have a choice?"

"Not if you are the person I believe you to be," and he smiled.

She grimaced, nodded and turned back to Mohammed's mother who again nodded her head, smiling approvingly at her.

"By the way, her name is Aisha," whispered Hadji. "And I will send in one of the Hindu ladies to help you as well."

As Hadji left the room, carefully pulling the door closed, Aisha turned to the table and gently pulled the shroud back from the corpse, exposing his legs, which looked almost normal, leaving his head for last.

His face was almost unrecognizable. His large forehead was flattened and luridly purple with hematomas. She was grateful that his face no longer held that expression of surprised agony she had last seen. But now, with his jaw gaping open, and his chest and shoulders so tortured in shape, it was clear beyond a doubt that all life was gone. She gasped and drew back.

Aisha reached out her hand and made her dip it into the warm water then rubbed the bar of soap across the cloth, wrung it out, then led her back to the body. Aisha bathed his face gently, then nodded at her to do the same. Without understanding why, a strange sense of detachment settled over Cornelia, smothering her feelings. She fell to the task as if nothing else mattered. She let the washcloth soak off the bits of dried blood that clogged his hair. When the bowl turned to red, Aisha left the room to fetch more warm water. By then another older woman had arrived, wearing a white sari and bowing and saying Namaste as she entered.

The three worked on cleaning the body bit by bit, washing each and every part of it. She was grateful that Aisha took on the task of washing what her mother would have called his "nether parts." She had to avert

her eyes from that. Cornelia concentrated on his feet, which were almost wholly unbroken.

Though they were alarmingly cool to the touch, his skin there was
soft and golden. The sight of his toes wounded her. She felt sad that this
man, her father, had been so alien for most of her life. That, in fact, she
had probably never seen his toenails before this very moment. It filled
her with wonder that they had the same crescent moon arch as did her
own, and that his toes splayed out in an almost simian way, also exactly
like her own.

After his entire body had been washed, a fourth woman brought
them a vial of fragrant warm oil. Aisha made her cup her hands then
poured the oil in and nodded toward his feet. She rubbed the oil into
his feet, massaging them as if they were her own, fingering the high
arch, covering each and every inch of skin with the sweet-smelling oil.
When she had anointed both feet she went to his head, dipped her
hands into the oil then raked it through his hair, grieving that she had
only touched her father in his death.

All the while as she was tending to his hair, which was thick and silver, soft to the touch and undamaged by the death, there was a teasing
banter going back and forth between the two motherly women tending to the rest of his body. Later she was to learn that it was not all
understood on either side, one speaking Hindi, the other a dialect from
Punjab, but their nods and smiles and shrugs and eyebrows supplied
enough communication for them both to be pleased with their inter-
actions. Male thighs and belly and private parts they knew, and they
bathed and anointed and fussed over her father's body as tenderly as if
he were their own.

They worked on his body for what seemed like hours. Just before
they carefully wrapped him back up in the long white shroud, turning
him over and over until he resembled a giant cocoon, Cornelia leaned
down and gave him one last kiss on his flattened forehead.

Once the wrapping was done, they soaked the shroud with more
fragrant oil. Then the Hindu woman produced some soft yellow gold
yarn and tied the body up, one loop at the ankles, a second around the

thighs and a third across his chest and folded arms, ending up in the hollow of his neck. Cornelia was glad that the shroud hid the broken body and yet displayed his fine long shape and noble skull.

Signaling with the *namaste* salute that they were finished, the women ushered her into an adjacent room where a single bed lay under the window, with two sleeping mats laid out on the floor below.

A low table held bowls of soup and rice. The women proffered the food to her, but she shook her head. But then, stubbornly, they refused to eat themselves. Despite not being hungry she finally drank the soup and realized in the process that she was ravenous. They all ate.

With gentle nudges, they laid her down on the bed, insisting that she be the one to sleep on the mattress despite her being the youngest. When she finally gave in to their demands, they curled up on the mats below her and soon fell asleep. It felt right to be sleeping in the room next to her father, but she was grateful she didn't have to do it alone. She fell asleep faster than she would have thought possible, comforted by the tiny movements and slight snores emanating from the two women below.

Several hours later, pulling her up out of a deep, dark sleep, someone shook her shoulder and led her down the corridor to where a black phone stood on a tiny table. Hadji was holding up the phone, and even from a distance of several yards she heard the shrill tones of her mother.

As she listened to Nevin, Hadji stood to one side, far enough away so that he couldn't hear every word, but close enough to give her comfort. Cornelia's head whirled as she listened to Nevin's wild hysterics.

"This has been a terrible blow for me. What with you running away, and now poor C.W. dying in this most horrible fashion, it's been awful. Everyone says I look like death warmed over," said Nevin.

If you only knew what death really looked like you wouldn't say that, Cornelia thought to herself. But, as she often did with Nevin, she said nothing to contradict her. She feared the tailspin that followed any hint of criticism. And so, she let her mother fly on.

"Everyone thinks you're just being terribly irresponsible. And it's left me totally in the lurch. I mean, I can hardly be expected to pay the rent on my measly income. Did you know I've had to take a job as a receptionist? Do you even care? And Geraldine is no longer returning my calls. Oh, I just know you're giving me one of your black looks right now. I should think you would care about how desperate I am. Do you know how awful all of this makes me feel? Oh, what do you know about anything? You're young. You know nothing of how it feels to be old and all alone and unwanted."

"Mummy, I can't handle this right now."

"Now I know you're angry with me," she wailed, "What *am* I going to do?"

Cornelia said nothing.

"Well, I'm just going to kill myself then. That should make you happy."

Cornelia hung up.

Hadji cocked one eyebrow and waggled his head. "I gather that didn't go so well."

Her throat closed. Her voice came out all croaky. "She didn't even say anything about Daddy."

"Some people," he said, "Cannot see past their own pain. It clouds their vision totally."

"She can't see that I'm hurting."

"Has she ever?"

She shook her head, "No, can't say that she has."

"Then there's nothing you can do. We can't change others, you know. Only our reactions to them."

"She said she was going to kill herself."

"Has she said this before?"

"Yes."

"But she hasn't?"

"No, it all blows over after a few days of her locking herself up in her room."

"Go back to sleep," his tone was kind, "You need to rest." And then for the first time since she had arrived, he touched her, cupping her shoulder with one large warm hand while the long slender fingers of his other hand briefly massaged the knot of tension alongside her neck.

She closed her eyes and mewed. His hands fell away. She opened her eyes to see him standing still, looking pained, his eyes downcast. His feet were bare, and his toes curled under as if they were ashamed.

"We must both go back to sleep now," he said.

"Yes," she whispered.

The women had left a candle burning next to her bed. Briefly she opened her father's black book, a pocket-sized ringed leather notebook soft and shiny with age. The three-holed pages in the front were crisp and new, but several yellowed pages beckoned her from the very back. She thumbed one open. The date was from many years before, written on the day she and Nathan had sailed off with Nevin to have, she promised, a wonderful new life in the Bahamas.

He wrote of fearing he would never see his children again. His guidance was to commend his two children to the spirit of God. And that every day he was separated from them, he should continue that entrustment.

He had. Every day of his guidance started with, "Lord, I commend them to thy spirit."

And then she had slept, holding the book close to her heart.

| 10 |

At dawn, Aisha roused her once more. She stumbled to the shared bathroom down the hall, washed her face and hands, finger-combed her unruly hair into some semblance of order, then went back to the room where Aisha handed her a plate of mango slices on top of yogurt with wild honey drizzled over both. She devoured all of it, and then went into the other room to find her father's body gone. Speechless and with a skittering heart, she raced back to the other room, raising her eyebrows and shoulders to the Hindu lady, whose name was Bharati and who spoke English fairly well.

"Calm yourself. Not to worry, the men came before first light to put him on the elephant that will carry him down the hill to the cremation site. We will go there now. Are you ready?"

"I am," she nodded. Her heart slowed, and she put on her leather sandals. Sadness weighed down on her, but she was glad to be moving. She didn't think she could have taken another day of spending time with his dead body. Regret flooded in. Death took all options away. Now they would never have a chance to be close. She shook her head to clear the negative thoughts. At least she'd had the past few weeks with him.

Below the conference center, a steep path snaked down into the jungle and disappeared. They set off down the hill, slipping in the mud as they went. A light drizzle seeped out of the sky. The damp air was all silver in the hills and valleys around them.

As they slithered down the muddy hill, a shaft of pale golden light broke through the banks of gray rain clouds, slanting down into the thick jungle below. Far off the winding silver of a river shimmered as it cut a swath through the trees. Directly above them, the clouds still spritzed. Moisture cobwebbed their eyelashes and hair. Cornelia's tunic clung to her skin. When they paused for a moment, Bharati pointed down toward the cremation site on the banks of the river, where, small as ants, several people milled around a pile of wood.

Suddenly, Cornelia lost her footing on a patch of slippery clay. She yelped and fell heavily to one side. Something popped inside, as if a large rubber band had been stretched beyond endurance. She panted, and both hands went to her lower right side.

"Are you alright?" said Bharati, her face creased with concern. Behind her head a flotilla of fruit bats flew by. Their velvety wings seemed like the flapping cloaks of mourners. Cornelia labored to her feet, determined not to be weak.

"I'm all right." She headed back off down the hill, but shortened her steps to tiny ones, so that she felt like a little old lady. An ache throbbed in her lower belly, close to the groin, and each step sent a shooting pain down her right leg.

Though her vigilant gaze stayed fixed on her feet, in her peripheral vision she became aware that many young women whose names she did not yet know were falling in behind them on the hill.

Quiet and solemn, they all carried garlands of marigolds.

After twenty more minutes of walking, they entered the gloom of the jungle where vine-encrusted fig trees formed an umbrella over their heads, keeping the drizzle off. Piles of curling leaves slithered beneath their footsteps. The fruit bats chittered high above, settling down for their long day's sleep. The air was thick with humidity. Despite the cool of the mountain air, sweat trickled between Cornelia's shoulder blades, sheened her forehead and pooled between her tender breasts.

Finally, they broke free of the dense jungle and out into a reedy area where the path led through clumps of grass toward the edge of a river coursing down from the jungle and into a rocky streambed.

A group of men stood next to a huge pile of sticks, Hadji among them. Her father's shrouded body lay next to the pile. Eyes downcast, a timid young woman blushed as she handed Cornelia a garland of marigolds then nodded toward her father. Without needing any further instruction, she somehow knew to drape it across his body.

Dressed all in white, Hadji genuflected a *namaste* in her direction and she returned the gesture. One by one, everyone stepped forward until a thick necklace of garlands were laid all around his head, forming a kind of orange and yellow halo. An older man spoke in Hindi as he anointed each part of the shrouded body with fragrant oil.

Afterward, he handed the vial to Cornelia, and she poured more oil over his head and shoulders. The men all leaned down and picked up the body, laying it gently down on top of the pile of sticks. Then they carefully laid more sticks on top of the body, leaving only his shrouded head uncovered.

"Wait!" she said, holding up her hand as the man lit a torch. "Can I say a few words?"

Hadji nodded. "Of course."

She held up her hands to the skies, "Oh Lord, into thy hands I entrust the soul of your servant, Cornelius Woodstock." She cried out, "I commend him to thy spirit!" She let her hands fall and felt peace enter every inch of her being.

The man touched the body with the lit torch and flames sprang to life, licking at the oil, covering the entire shroud with a thin layer of blue light, flickering up and around the corpse until it glowed. There was a sudden crackling as the entire pile exploded into flames. Scorched, Cornelia shrank back from the heat.

Mesmerized by the roar and searing heat, she gasped as she realized why the body had been tied down in several places. For, as the flames consumed the flesh, the corpse writhed with life, bucking against the restraints as it curled up and began its passage to cinders. The shrouding cloth burned off and for one moment she saw his face again and the exposed teeth smiled and then that too disappeared as the bones began to crack and burn. Thick black smoke curled up into the sky and spiraled into the hovering clouds above.

She bowed her head. *May your spirit wander the mountains and clouds you so loved*, she thought, *and hover always above me in spirit.* She closed her eyes for a long time, and when she opened them there was nothing but a charred pile of ashes with glowing embers scattered through it. Though the heat still scorched her, she leaned down to the smoldering ashes, dipped in one finger, and then dabbed some between her eyebrows.

Hadji moved toward her, gently draping a garland of marigolds over her head. He gestured toward a clump of trees. Beneath the trees a small elephant stood with its keeper.

In wonderful swirls of paisley, the animal was painted scarlet and gold and pink, with a tiny platform perched on its back, all swathed with brilliant silks. A set of stairs stood next to her. As Cornelia approached, the animal turned, and her trunk curled out and touched her forehead. Her eyes were rimmed with curly eyelashes and her mouth turned up with looked to be a smile. She couldn't help but smile back. Her mahout, grandly dressed in a turban, bowed toward her, and gestured toward the stairs. A smiling young woman with a long plait of shiny black hair hanging down one shoulder already sat above her on the perch.

"Come," said Bharati from behind her, "Ride back up the hill with Anasuya. She will be a most suitable friend for you. She has recently lost the last of her ten brothers and sisters, so she knows well what you are going through."

Cornelia scrambled up the steps, hauling herself up onto the platform where two little seats allowed Anasuya and her to perch side by side on top of the elephant.

The mahout sprang up to sit just behind the ears with his legs on either side of the animal's neck. The elephant turned and set off up the hill with a heaving gait that swung them from side to side. As the hillside steepened, Cornelia felt an answering lurch deep inside her body as if a gear had turned and something had broken. She yelped.

Anasuya said, "Whatever is the matter? Are you in pain?" She could only groan in response. Anasuya reached out and with firm hands pulled her in, cradling her against her shoulder. She smoothed the hair back off her sweaty forehead. Cornelia relinquished herself to the embrace. They stayed that way all the way up the hill. Cornelia curled in ever closer to herself until she was almost in a fetal position in Anasuya's lap.

They reached the conference center half an hour later. As Cornelia stood up to descend the steps, there was a gush of fluid from between her legs. Blood ribboned down. She leaned heavily on Anasuya, who led her directly to the clinic.

Back in the clinic room she had so recently vacated, the next fifteen hours were a blur of pain. Every few minutes, a flurry of sharp knife-like thrusts sent her lower abdomen into spasms. Chunks of bloody tissue spurted out of her vagina, leaving her panting and exhausted. As the throbbing subsided, pale and trembling, she would slump back and curl up under the thin covers, her teeth chattering from shock and pain, unconsciously preparing herself for the next onslaught of contractions. She remembered the way their goats in the Bahamas had been during birth, eyes glazed over, panting, their abdomens roiling with tremors every few minutes. She understood now why they called it labor. All night long, every few minutes the process would start all over again, and for a few minutes there was nothing but dazzling pain. Then, between, a numbed-out waiting.

Sometime during the day, the doctor examined her and confirmed she was having a miscarriage. He explained that it was better not to interfere at this point. "Let nature run its course," he said in his mellifluous tone. "I always hesitate to hasten along a process that has already started. The body knows exactly what to do."

"It feels like I'm breaking apart," she moaned.

He laughed at that, "Hardly, my dear. The more you hold back, the longer the pain will take. You must relinquish yourself to the pain."

"But maybe if I just rest, I'll be able to stop the bleeding and the baby will be okay."

He laughed, and his laugh was not altogether kind. Not mean, but rueful, exhausted perhaps. "If wishes were facts, then the world would be a very different place. The truth is, I do not think that anything could stop this process. Your will has nothing to do with the end result. But you shall see, you shall see."

"What did I do wrong?"

Like a ferret alerted to a sudden movement, he peered at her over his glasses, "You didn't do anything foolish, did you? You didn't take any drugs, did you now?"

"No, not at all. But I fell down when I was walking, and it hurt, and then I rode on an elephant, and it felt like something broke when the elephant lurched."

His lips tightened but he shook his head, "We'll never know for sure, of course, but I don't actually believe that had anything to do with it. Far more likely, the fetus was just not developing properly and so your body has rejected it."

"You mean there was something wrong with it?"

"Possibly, possibly. Later, after it is finished, I will have the lab in Poona take a look at the tissue and let you know." And with that he swept from the room.

For the next twelve hours, the nurse changed her pads every half an hour or so, carefully saving all the bloody tissue in a plastic bag, "The doctor has asked me to do so," she would say each time. Then, during the evening hours, Bharati and Anasuya sat with her, chatting quietly in Hindi. She was glad of their company.

The pain consumed her all night long; so did guilt. A part of her had so hoped to cherish this child, to give it safety and love in a way that had not been given to her. And now that chance was bleeding out of her. And yet – and this caused even more guilt – she was relieved the decision had been taken away from her. She was aware that she truly needed to grow up first before taking on the responsibility of another.

After Bharati and Anasuya left for dinner, she felt hopeless and very alone. She tossed and turned, and finally, so exhausted she could no longer clench her abdomen muscles, she gave herself up to the pain as the doctor had suggested, letting it take her over like a runaway horse.

An hour before dawn, when the light turned a deep sapphire blue and the pain finally eased off on its vise-like grip, she fell into a deep sleep.

When she awoke, the doctor was checking her blood pressure, "Low," he shook his head, "but that is to be expected; you've lost a lot of blood. But the nurse tells me the bleeding has slowed way down to a trickle. I think we are through the worst of it; indeed I think we are." His hands massaged her belly, "Good, good, your uterus feels relaxed. Finally. You must be relieved." He looked tidy and clean in his starched white coat with his thin hair combed well off his benign, rodent-like face.

Even though it was the truth, she wanted to yell at him that she was anything but relieved. She felt a monster. Her armpits and crotch reeked and there was a rank metallic stench of blood in the room. Every part of her ached, and she felt humiliated and scoured as if she'd been whipped and raped and discarded by the side of the road. "I'm such a mess." She wiped at her nose, which streamed with mucus.

"Nonsense. I know this may sound harsh, my dear, but has it occurred to you that this might be the very best thing that could have happened?"

"What do you mean? How could losing a baby be a best thing?"

He considered her, his brow furrowed, "You cannot be so naïve as to think that an eighteen-year-old girl all alone without family and without a husband would be successful at taking good care of a baby, much less herself? I find it highly unlikely that you hadn't at least considered abortion in such a set of circumstances."

A blush of shame shot across her cheeks. He was right. Of course she had.

From the tree outside, dancing shadows flickered across his face. A weakened part of her thought his eyes looked hooded and judgmental, though another healthier part of her knew he meant to be compassionate. Still she couldn't stop the anger that flared up from somewhere deep inside of her. "I would have done a good job of being a mother. I would have done my best."

He paused and nodded. "I don't doubt that you would have tried. And you may even be right about that. Stranger things have happened in my experience." He leaned down and took hold of her hand, patting it lightly, "You do have an astounding resiliency. But now you must listen to me. You will be as weak as a kitten for at least a few days, and your hormones will make you feel as if you want to die. You must fight that with all your heart. You must walk. And eat. And get strong again, so that one day you can live to have a baby in all the proper set of circumstances." And with that he turned and sighed, "I'll be back tomorrow. And in the meantime, I'll have the lab take a look at that tissue."

She fell asleep right after he left and slept through most of the day, waking up only to drink huge amounts of hot broth brought to her by Bharati.

Late that evening, she got up and went down the hall to a bathroom where a single showerhead sprayed down into the room, draining down into a hole in the center. After scouring every part of herself with a scratchy washcloth and a thick bar of yellow soap, she felt somewhat purified. After putting on a freshly laundered hospital gown, she felt almost human again.

When she came out, the nurse handed her a typewritten letter brought from a clinic in Poona, written by the doctor, stating that some of the tissue examined was indeed that of fetal extraction but much of it was undifferentiated tissue mass. This showed evidence, he elucidated, that the fetus appeared not to have been developing properly, just as he had suspected. He conjectured that something had gone askew in the preliminary division process. He wrote that he had informed the nurse that as soon as she felt strong enough, she could leave the clinic as long as she promised to rest and to not exert herself too strenuously for several weeks.

He ended the missive on a less scientific note, "Upon my return from Poona, I presume I will see you well and as happy as can be expected given these circumstances. And, so my dear, in conclusion, you may rest assured that it is a blessing that this child was not born to this body. Its external shell was definitely not evolving as it should have been. And now, the spirit, which is eternal, is free to go out and find another skin to inhabit, another perhaps more favorable set of conditions. And who knows, stranger things have happened, perhaps your father's soul will fly right along next to hers?"

She clasped the note to her chest, extremely comforted by this odd conglomeration of scientific fact combined with a belief in rebirth.

The next morning, Anasuya arrived holding the white tunic and leggings she had found in Cornelia's leather satchel. Her round face was wreathed in smiles. She tossed her long braid back over her shoulder, fidgeted with her sari, then launched into chatter.

"I am most delighted to tell you that you will be rooming with me and several other girls in a very lovely room, much the nicest room I've ever slept in. You will like it. And you will be most welcome. We range in age from 17 to 23 and we come from all parts of the country, but we manage to get along nonetheless." Cornelia wondered how she managed to be so happy even though she had lost ten brothers and sisters.

"How do you do it?" she asked as she was getting dressed.

"How do I do *what*, may I ask?" Anasuya cocked her head.

"Be so happy."

"Well you see," Anasuya's smile faded to a look of melancholy; "It would be most ungrateful of me to waste my time being wretched when I am the only one in my family to be spared. I look upon it as a charge to try to be aware of all the minute joys every day brings me. A lovely, crunchy puri, a magnificent sunset, the sounds of the birds singing in the trees, these all bring me joy, and now, best of all, life has brought me a new friend from overseas. How could I possibly be unhappy when so many wonderful things are happening every day?" She clapped her hands and once again her whole face glowed. She reached out to Cornelia and wrapped her arm around her waist. Cornelia flinched. She was not used to physical affection.

"Did I hurt you?" Anasuya looked puzzled.

"No." She looked down at the much smaller girl. How could she tell her she was only used to people touching her to yank at her hair or grab at her butt. But Anasuya's physical touch seemed as natural and thoughtless as a puppy scrambling up on top of a heap of other puppies for a quick catnap. So she decided that it was very much okay and made herself return the simple embrace.

Arms around each other's waists, she and Anasuya walked out of the clinic and across the yard to the long main building. Their room was on the bottom floor at the back, with a view of crotons and a yard where laundry was drying. The room was simple. Four cots lined up in a row, four benches for keeping neatly folded clothes up off the floor. The walls were bare of decoration, the windows had no curtains, and the floor was a washed and shiny concrete. If this was the loveliest room Anasuya had ever seen, Cornelia realized she must have grown up in real poverty.

Anasuya laughed as if she knew what Cornelia was thinking. "Indeed, my entire family of thirteen lived in one mud-and-wattle room. Only my grandmother had a rope bed. So this is very grand indeed."

Anasuya leaned down to unstrap her sandals and placed them next to two sets of shoes that were lined up next to the door, so Cornelia did the same. And then they walked barefoot across the room to meet the two other young women.

One was a thin Muslim girl from Delhi, sitting cross-legged on her cot. She was very dark skinned and intense with hairy arms and a low forehead. "My name is Zaina, which means beautiful, but, as you can see, I am not so lucky as all that." Her head waggled and, as always, the gesture made Cornelia laugh, though her laugh hurt and came out more like a snort than an expression of humor. She hoped it hadn't injured Zaina's feelings, but she seemed impervious. She smiled, and her smile was dazzling, her teeth as white and shiny and regular as kernels of late-harvest white corn. "You see, I make up for my lack of physical attributes by being a brilliant cook. Or at least my friends tell me that." And again, her head waggled, and Anasuya chimed in that indeed she was a most excellent cook.

Zaina continued, "I will ask for you to be on my kitchen shift, and I will teach you how to make wonderful curries. And tender tandoori chicken. And you will grind all the fresh spices and the wonderful smells will delight you, I am sure," she promised, and her smile was so warm and welcoming that a smile cracked open the strain in Cornelia's face.

"I am sure," she nodded.

The other girl was a rich Parsi girl from Mumbai. She was a plump girl who was, more often than not said the other girls, curled up on her cot asleep.

"Deeba comes from a very rich family," scolded Zaina. "She is most thoroughly spoiled."

"Zaina works her so hard that Deeba is always sleeping after her shift." Anasuya's beautiful round face beamed. She flicked her head, which swung her long, thick braid over her shoulder and into her hand. She leaned down over Deeba, using the very end of the braid to tickle Deeba's face. Her nose twitched, but her eyes stayed firmly closed.

"You see," Anasuya explained, "she comes from such a wealthy family that she is more used to eating honey pastries than she is rolling out the dough for them. It's the first time she's never had a servant to do everything for her. So we let her sleep a lot and pick up after her. At least most of the time," she chuckled. "Sometimes I am most severe with her." And again, she flicked the tail of her braid across Deeba's smooth-as-silk face.

As the doctor had warned, Cornelia's hormones wreaked havoc with her equilibrium in those first days of healing. One minute she was in tears, the next consumed with rage, followed almost instantly by a blank, empty feeling which was almost the worst. But no matter her mood, there was a calm acceptance of her by all the girls. Not once did she ever feel a moment of censure from any of them. She found herself relaxing into their company in a way she had never experienced before. As the days passed, she could almost physically feel the healing taking place inside, knitting and growing as fast as a plant does in the April sunshine after a long, cold winter.

She was encouraged to sleep as much as she could, eat whenever she was hungry, and take small walks along the pathway that wandered along the top of the cliff overlooking the deep valley.

When the girls were at work in the kitchen, she found a favorite place to perch. Beneath a lacy poinciana tree, a small wooden bench overlooked the valley. Far below, meandering through the green jungle, she could just glimpse the silver thread of the river where her father had been cremated.

She took her sketchbook with her and tried to capture the beauty she saw, thinking of all her father had taught her. And perhaps more importantly than whether she succeeded with that or not, her sadness and grief, and the confusion surrounding her future fell away, and she descended happily into a world of color and light as her hand danced across the paper.

And that is where Hadji found her upon his return from a speaking trip to Northeast India.

| 11 |

She jumped when he sat down next to her on the bench. "You startled me," she laughed. "I didn't see you coming."

"Indeed, you looked most preoccupied. I hated to interrupt."

"You are always welcome to interrupt me," she joked.

But his expression was serious, too solemn by far. Her heart raced. "Indeed, that is what I've come to talk to you about. You must not talk to me like that." He sat down on the bench but left a yard-wide distance between them. He sighed and leaned over, propping his elbows up onto his long slim thighs. He raked his fingers through his glossy hair, sighed deeply again, and then looked up over the view, his eyes definitely averted from her. "Cornelia," he said, "I have been thinking much about this while I was away. You must not form too deep an attachment to me. I cannot be available in that way."

"I don't understand. What makes you say that?" A flash of shame seared through her.

"Perhaps I am speaking out of turn, but there has always been something between us that now makes me uncomfortable, a yearning for a physical bond I know now can only lead to pain and suffering. I know we spoke of it once. Long ago, it seems. But things have changed since then. Life has changed me. Leadership has changed me."

She felt stung. "But why does it have to? I understand that you're telling me you don't want me anymore. I'm not a fool. I can see that." She blinked furiously, determined not to cry. She felt a fool for thinking that after all these years he would still care about her. Besides, her recent pregnancy no doubt disgusted and horrified him. But she was determined to fight for some connection. She whispered, "Can't we still at least be friends?"

He looked quickly at her, then away. "Can we be friends? I doubt it."

"Why not?" She felt like howling but it came out more a whimper.

"I have a mission. My life must be about helping others find their way to a better relationship with the divine. A way that endeavors to be purer, honest, loving, and unselfish with everyone."

"The Four Absolutes," she whispered.

"Absolutely. Yes indeed. You see, singling people out for special attention can only create division and conflict. That we have plenty of already." He chuckled and swung his head low as he looked down at his feet. Finally, with a deep inhalation, he drew himself up and looked back out over the view. "I seek to heal the divisions between people. Not to create them."

"But why does our being close have to cause trouble? We've known each other for so long." A small bubble of hysteria boiled up from deep inside. She quelled it. She would not be like her mother, she would not, she swore to herself.

Hadji shook his head as if to clear his thoughts. He cast another quick look at her. His gaze settled on the wild torrent of wavy hair that cascaded all around her shoulders. She had not plaited her hair that morning but instead washed it and come outside to let it air-dry in the rare sunshine that filtered down through the tree above and spun into golden spangles all around her. He shuddered slightly and quickly turned away from the sight of her. "You see, Cornelia," and as always when he said her name, each syllable was dragged out and it felt like a caress, "we come from different worlds. I can never truly fit in with your world. And you can never truly fit into mine."

"I see." She deliberately made herself sound calmer and more mature than she felt. Because it so hurt that he thought she could never fit in, just when she had been feeling so accepted by the others in the past few days.

Again, he let his gaze go out over the canyon and she followed it. Banks of clouds were building up over the far hills, smudging the horizon a dark charcoal gray. Shooting down from a hole in the cloud above, a shaft of sunshine stalked the valley, striking gold wherever it landed.

His foot tapped. His fingers interlaced almost as if he were praying. "I have learned from the Absolutes that the needs of the cause must come before my own. That is a struggle for me. You see, as a child, I was so indulged, so catered to, that, from all accounts I was a veritable tyrant of a boy. Quite horribly imperious from what my mother and Dida tell me."

"Dida?"

He turned to her, one eyebrow arched in amusement. His head waggled. "You see," he crowed as if his bishop had just taken her rook, "that just proves my point. You don't even know what we call our grandmothers here."

She blushed; hurt flickered in her.

"But then I was off to Oxford and jumping Jehoshaphat was I in for a rude awakening. There I was just another skinny East Indian boy. Up until that moment, I never knew that the color of my skin mattered much. Oh, my mother would brag about the lightness of my sister's skin and how that was going to help secure her just the right husband, but I never paid it much mind."

"Is that really true? I find it hard to believe."

"But my dear Cornelia, that is most naïve of you. Of course, you would know nothing of that prejudice, being so light skinned yourself. But at that time at Oxford, I was made very much aware that because of the color of my skin, I was *not* going to be allowed into the best clubs. Oh, I managed all right. I fast learned how to cultivate a facetious manner to hide the fact that I very much felt an outsider. Indeed, I acted as if I didn't care, when actually I cared about it all very much indeed." He laughed, shaking his head at how foolish he'd been. "It was all a ridiculous, pretentious folly. I drank far too much whiskey, simply because I was trying to fit in. I found out that the good old English boys quite liked me when I was making jokes and causing them to laugh, but would they ever ask me home to meet their sisters? Not likely." He paused for a moment.

She yearned to touch him below the rolled-up sleeves of his white oxford cloth shirt. His lower arms were a lovely chestnut color, the hairs a shining bronze. "Nathan and I never cared about the color of your skin."

"That's true, that's true. You two always accepted me, that you did. But believe me when I say that not everyone did or does." He stood up and began to pace back and forth in front of her.

"And so you see," he continued, "the end result was that I became quite resentful during those years. Just when it seemed that I was destined for a life of bitter immorality, I happened to stumble across Horace and found another whole way of being. I thank God that I found him and the Absolutes when I did. Otherwise I might just have been another dissolute arrogant Indian boy who flashed his money by buying fast cars and dating very blond women just to show he could. So you see, it just cannot be between us."

His curt tone sparked her hurt into anger. "That's all very well," the words snapped out of her. "And I *thank* you for sharing your story with me. But don't you understand anything? Don't you realize why Nathan and I were so drawn to you? We're outsiders, too. I've never fit in anywhere."

"You? I always thought you were the ultimate one who fit in." His eyes widened with astonishment. "Truly?"

"Truly. Are you kidding me? My father comes from this weird, crazy family. And my mother? After she divorced my father and that whole upper-class way of life, she ran off with a guy she met in a gas station. A man who never went past the third grade in school. Oh, he was okay by me. He was funny and smart and taught me how to work hard. But in the islands, we lived in a shack. And when we were with our father, we lived in a mansion. Or we were the only kids in a cast of a thousand Absolutes. Who was I? Where did I fit in? Who the hell knew? I didn't fit in anywhere."

"I didn't know that about you," his head cocked; he looked surprised.

She was afraid of how vulnerable she would feel if he saw how much she cared. On the other hand, since he had made it clear he couldn't be close to her, she had nothing to lose. She pressed on. "You were one of the first people I ever met who seemed to like me for just who I was. So maybe it's already too late for me, Hadji, have you thought about that?" her tone was sour. "Maybe *my* feelings are already attached. Maybe they have been for a long time now. I don't know why you should look so surprised. We talked about this once."

He shook his head. "That was a very long time ago. Much has happened between then and now."

"Don't you think I know that?" She stopped and swallowed hard, afraid she might yowl. The outrage hissed out of her; she felt deflated and sad. "The only other person I ever felt right with all the time was Nathan, and he's lost to me now."

"Look at me Cornelia."

She looked up at him and lost herself in the warmth of his brown eyes.

"Do you truly feel attached to me?" Though his hand was over his heart, he looked disturbed, which made her pulse skip with fear.

She didn't know what to say. Her unreciprocated feelings for him made her squirm. She could only nod.

"Does not the world of modeling still call out to you? Money and fame and I don't know ... I am sure you must have a plethora of young swains dancing at your attendance." He twirled his fingers and laughed. But it sounded hollow to her, not at all his usual spontaneous outburst of joy.

"Please," she snorted, "You must realize that whole world back there means nothing to me." She gestured sharply downward as if she were throwing it all into the canyon below.

"Honestly?"

And she could tell he was now staring intently at her but now she felt shy and couldn't make herself turn back toward him. "Of course. Didn't Horace always say I spoke the truth?"

"He did indeed," he chuckled. "He did indeed."

She looked up and saw Anasuya and Zaina, arm in arm, slowly walking toward them.

As the girls drew closer, Hadji beckoned, "Come. Be with your friend." And then in a lower voice to her, "You have given me much to think about, Cornelia. I promise you I will ponder all of this. I must have guidance about our talk. But whatever you may think of me, don't be too sure about having lost Nathan."

His words startled her. But now, as if they were opposing magnets, his eyes darted away from her. "What do you mean?" she faltered.

Finally, his gaze slid back to meet hers, and there was kindness in his eyes and a limpid sadness that matched her own. She reached out to touch him, but he leapt back a foot as if she were a too hot flame. "Nathan is arriving this very evening. I came to tell you that, but I allowed myself to be distracted by our conversation." He looked down at his watch. "If we hurry, we can be there to greet his arrival."

"What?" She sprang to her feet. "Nathan here? How is that possible?"

Hadji beamed his wonderful smile and his eyes crinkled with pleasure at having so delighted her. "Indeed, it is possible." He held up his arms and whirled around in a wild dance of happiness. "All things are possible if we just take the time to believe."

Anasuya giggled at the sight of Hadji spinning around in circles. Zaina's face bloomed with color. Hadji clapped his hands, "Come, come girls, we must go to greet Cornelia's wonderful brother, Nathan. I taught him how to play cricket only to have him promptly beat me at the game." He threw back his head and laughed. And they all laughed with him. "Come, come," he clapped his hands, "we must run to get there on time!"

Looking at the expressions of joy on the girls' faces Cornelia wondered just how many responded to Hadji with such intensity. Was she just the thousandth victim of his charms? Was this gathering all about a cult of personality?

They all turned and raced back toward the main building. Cornelia fell behind, her hand falling down to her side. She still felt slightly broken, as if she might rip further apart if she ran too fast. She could not help noticing Anasuya, ahead of her, stumbling on her long sari skirts. She almost fell, then blushed intensely when Hadji reached out to check her fall.

They got to the entrance of the conference center just as a battered taxicab pulled up.

Nathan tumbled out of the car, a tangle of rackets and duffel bags strapped all around him, all long limbs, jittery knees and freckled face. She catapulted herself at him, grabbing him around the middle and almost knocking him over.

"Whoa!" He half pushed her off him, but his smile was broad, and she was so happy and relieved to see him that nothing could have held her back. She rocked him back and forth, holding on for dear life. He laughed with delight. "Let me put my bags down," he pleaded. She extricated herself from him, allowing him to drop his bags and then went back in for another bear hug. Hadji pounded him on the shoulder. The girls stood off to the side, giggling and casting shy looks his way.

"Jolly good show, my man," Hadji shouted. "Welcome to Cherra-punji."

And then, as she looked up at him, she saw Nathan's jaw wobble. His shoulders slumped, and he oozed into her hug. "Oh, Nee," he moaned, "we never got to know him."

"Not much."

They held each other for a long time and the rest of the world faded away. After what seemed an eternity of shared sadness, they broke away from the hug, gathered his bags and found his room.

That night at dinner, Nathan told Hadji and her what had most recently happened with the Moral Absolutes in America. After Hall Hamden had learned of C.W.'s death, he had quickly contacted the estate attorney. It turned out most of the Woodstock wealth was gone and the little that was left had been placed in a trust that could only be used for his children's education.

The very next morning, Hall Hamden shared that his guidance from God was that Nathan had other paths to follow. Now that Rudy had been lured away by Broadway and Hollywood, it seemed that Nathan's talents as a back-up singer were no longer needed and furthermore, Hall smiled his crocodile smile, he was sure Nathan would be happier in another venue. Of course, the crocodile smile broadened, he should know, he was always welcome to come back if willing to use his educational funds to procure further opportunities. In other words, he hammered the point home: pay if you want to stay. Nathan had caught the next plane to New York and the following day had flown to Mumbai.

"And ready or not," he flung his hands wide, "here I am!"

Only she knew him well enough to know that beneath his bravado swam pain, lurking, waiting to snap at his thoughts and dreams. But she was glad to see that the robotic quality had vanished, leaving behind an uncertain young man.

"What a scoundrel that man is," snorted Hadji. "The only good thing I can say is that I'm glad I don't have to live, as he does, with his own conscience." He frowned, looked around the room, then back to Nathan. "You are most welcome here. We have plenty of need. And wherever there is need, there is no need to be stingy about the giving of your time." He waggled his head. "I know I must sound monstrously pompous, but believe me, I am being most sincere."

He stood up and his laugh rang out and its silvery threads turned most every head in the room. His voice grew louder, and his arms swept out to include everyone in the room. Their faces brightened, rows of flowers turning to the sun.

"You are *all* most welcome here. Hindus. Muslims. Jains. Harijan. Even Woodstocks! No one will be kicking you out!" He mimed a large boot kicking Nathan out. "Not while I have anything to say about it. Each of you must examine your conscience. You alone will know when it is time for you to leave. I can promise you that I will not be doing the kicking."

| 12 |

During the next days, the monsoon hit hard and heavy with a steady relentless downpour. Rain knocked on heads when running from building to building, drenching clothes and hair. Umbrellas popped inside out from gusts of wind. Leather sandals grew mildew overnight. Cornelia's hair never fully dried, and soon developed a musty odor that did not go away no matter how often she washed it.

And her hormones were still running amok. The loss of her baby and father had left her with a profound sense of emptiness. And yet she knew there was no point moaning about all she had lost. She was learning from being in India that everyone suffers; no one goes through life without painful loss. And it is not tragedy that defines us, she thought, but how we react to it that matters. She could be consumed with bitterness, or she could stumble along, trying to be of service to others. During the day, as she ducked her head when dashing through the rain, she felt gratitude for being here, now, where people understood, without having to wail about it, tremendous hurt. Just that morning, during a meeting, a man had shared that he had lost his entire family on a border crossing during partition. Nothing she had gone through could compare to that.

And yet, at night, she tossed and turned, wracked with an inchoate desire to be penetrated and filled. She yearned to run along the cliff tops and let the wind and rain tear at her hair and clothes. But the rain was so thick that it was hard to breathe even during her brief sprints to the main building from her dormitory. And so, she had thrown herself into her service work in the kitchen.

The kitchen was a huge room, designed to handle the feeding of hundreds. There were three eight-burner stainless steel stoves along one wall, a row of deep sinks along another, and in the middle of the room, several long, narrow wooden tables over which dozens of large aluminum pots and skillets hung on hooks. The wooden tables were where they chopped the vegetables and ground the spices for curries. She was not considered skilled enough to actually cook, so her job was to prep and learn what she could from watching.

Despite her young age and tiny frame, Zaina was a stern taskmaster in her area of the kitchen. Other cooks were in charge of the tandoor ovens lining the hallway where two older women cooked the meat curries. Zaina's station handled making dhal and a half dozen or so different vegetable curries.

When Cornelia was first given the job of peeling and chopping three dozen yellow onions, Zaina snapped at her to make the chunks smaller. "Otherwise the flavor will spring out in the mouth, dominating what should be a complex mix of tastes. The pieces of onion must be so fine that they will blend in with the spices when we roll them together for frying. It will be most marvelous if it is done just right."

Tearing profusely, Cornelia furiously chopped the onions into finer and finer pieces. When Zaina came to inspect, she blessed her with a brilliant smile, then shouted to the others, "Look at this. She has done them *just* right." And with a genial head waggle, she lectured the others, including Anasuya and Deeba, who were also under her charge. "You could learn a thing or two from her in terms of her level of energy. *This* is what Hadji was talking about at this morning's meeting. We must *always* prepare our food with passion and love." She paused to peer over her glasses at several people, most particularly their heavy-eyed roommate Deeba, who moved always in slow motion.

But something about Zaina's barbed comment prodded Deeba to speak. "Must you always speak of Hadji as if you are the only one who listens to him? Indeed, we *all* listen to him."

Cornelia could not help noting that Deeba bridled as she spoke of him. She suspected now that many of her companions had crushes on him just as she did.

Sighing, Zaina jammed her glasses back up to the bridge of her long nose and peered down at a detailed menu of the day. Her thick glasses were always slipping down her nose and fogging up in the steaming hot kitchen. Yet she never complained. *No complaining, no explaining*, she could hear Hadji speak inside her brain. It was a more gracious way to go through life, he said.

Most of them sported a constant sheen of sweat from the steam that continually swirled up from frying pans and boiling pots. Only Anasuya never seemed to sweat. Her golden complexion seemed naturally matte, and Cornelia envied the ease with which she seemed to inhabit her skin. Next to Zaina and Anasuya, Cornelia loomed as large as a giraffe among a herd of gazelles. To compound the feeling, when she leaned down over the too-low table to chop, she had to spread her legs wide, just as a giraffe does when stooping to drink. Among the hundreds of visitors and full-timers at the center, only a handful of people were as tall as she, and only Hadji and Nathan loomed higher.

Looking up from her list, Zaina frowned, then strode around the kitchen table to plant herself, arms akimbo, in front of Deeba. With her typically placid expression, Deeba looked up at Zaina and smiled. She had long eyelashes, a very large body and huge, liquid eyes. Her skin was as smooth as pale, yellow butter.

Zaina chided her. "Deeba, honestly now, are you *still* working on that one set of carrots? I *must* have them for the vegetable curry I'm making. You're as slow as a water buffalo to leave his mud wallow."

Deeba pursed her full lips. "You know I have never had to use my hands in this way before. I am trying my very best. Truly I am."

Zaina tsk-tsked and patted her on the back. "Most likely I am being a most impossible brute. My mother used to say I was bossing everyone around even when I was very little."

Anasuya tossed her braid. "Well, your bossing doesn't seem to be doing what it is supposed to do. Deeba may indeed be trying, it's just not taking her very far." She smashed a handful of cardamom seeds with the rounded end of a pestle. The pungent scent of the spice rose up into the air from the stone mortar.

When Anasuya saw Deeba's large eyes flood with tears, she dropped her pestle and leapt to her side.

"I am so *very* sorry," Anasuya said. "I did not actually mean to be unkind. I am very afraid it is a fault of mine to make fun of people. Indeed Deeba, I hope you know I am indeed *very* fond of you. Will you possibly forgive me now?"

Deeba's soulful smile was enough answer for all of them. They all went back to work and for a while there was little sound but the chop-chop of knives, the grind of stone on mortar and a whistling steam from kettles, always boiling, ever ready to be poured into the endless pots of black Assamese tea which they brewed and drank from dawn to night.

Their kitchen was a microcosm of India, Hadji said. If the Muslim Zaina, the Brahmin Anasuya, and the Parsi Deeba could get along, then so could India. And if you threw an American such as Cornelia into the mix, he said with a toss of his head, then so could the world.

Cornelia thought back to that morning's general meeting, over which Hadji always presided except for when he was off travelling, which he did frequently. At first, she had dreaded the morning meetings, afraid that they would evoke awful memories of Hall Hamden and the witch-hunt atmosphere she had last experienced in Absolute meetings. But these meetings in India were very different. They were casual. No one dominated. In fact, they were set up in such a way that everyone sat in a huge circle: rows deep, but a circle, nonetheless. Hadji often sat himself several rows in from the center so that there was no sense of him being in a superior position to anyone else. Ministers of states were treated with the same deference as the housekeeping staff. There appeared to be no hierarchy, simply a group of people dedicated to eliminating the prejudices of class and caste that they had all grown up with. There was no forcing of sharing, or even a hint of preaching. If people had a story to tell, or a bit of guidance to share, they were encouraged to do so simply by raising their hand and waiting their turn.

Yet Hadji seemed to have an innate sense of knowing which people were too shy or scared to raise their hand. That morning, Hadji had gently persuaded a man from Rajasthan to speak.

He stood up. He was a small man, dressed in a white tunic and leggings with a Nehru cap perched over a smooth, bald head. He told his story in a sing-song voice. "This story is about my family you see. We were forced to leave Pakistan during the partition. In order to understand, you must know we were Hindu, and the government, at that time, was Muslim. We had three days to put all our belongings into old cardboard suitcases, which were difficult to close and then would split all along the stitched linings. My mother would become hysterical and send me out to go buy more of them in the bazaar." He stood silent for a moment and his face darkened as if a cloud had cast a shadow across him.

"Go on," urged Hadji. "Your story is very important. It must be heard."

The man nodded, swallowed hard and continued. "You see, in the end it didn't matter at all what we brought. None of the packing and the choosing what to take and what to leave behind. It just didn't matter at all." He shook his head as if he might possibly get rid of images that clearly haunted him. His gaze went up over their heads, out the door and into the past. "Because you see, they stopped our train just before we reached the border, and we were all told to get off the train. And then they lined us up and shot us. I was the only one of my family to survive."

They had all gasped in horror.

So now, they were all working hard to make that man a very special vegetable curry. Zaina had started off their morning work shift by saying, "We must show him that not all Muslims hate Hindus. Here in this kitchen, Muslims work next to Hindus. We will show him love by making the most perfect pumpkin curry we ever can accomplish."

Just as Cornelia was finishing up her onions, Nathan ran into the kitchen, bringing a fresh blast of wet air that further clouded the already steamy room. His hands and legs twitched. His eyes darted from side to side. He sputtered with indignation, "I can't do anything right. I can't even hammer a nail in anymore. What's the matter with me?"

And then he bolted back out.

Anasuya's eyes widened. "He's as jumpy as a goat when a leopard is on the prowl."

"You think?" Cornelia said.

He was certainly no longer dazed or robotic, but this new manic phase was equally disturbing.

Their first days back together had been blissful. They had stayed up late in the dining room, filling each other in on everything that had happened since they'd last seen each other. He wanted to hear every detail of her time with their father in Switzerland. She could see by the twist on his face that he was jealous, but he only expressed a wistful, "Wish I could have been there, too."

"Me too," she had said.

He wanted to hear every detail of the car crash. "You must have popped up out of the car like a cork. Do you remember flying through the air?"

"Sort of. I remember entering the dark as if it were a tunnel."

"Do you remember the impact when you landed?" His eyes bored into her.

"Yes. It was almost like a cartoon, like the sounds shazam and kapow were exploding in bubbles all around me. I remember thinking how weird that was, that the cartoonists had it right after all."

"And then what happened?"

She tried to remember more details to slake his insatiable curiosity; despite the fact that it crushed her each time she told the story.

"Well, at first I didn't move. I thought maybe I was dead because I felt so slammed. Then I moved my toes, and they worked. But then I was afraid to move anymore, so I just lay there. I don't know how long I waited; it seemed to go on forever."

"I remember the time I got cut by the boat propeller. Everything slowed down."

"Exactly. Well, eventually normal sounds came back, and I could tell there were a lot of people on the road above me, yelling and screaming. And lights were flashing, and I felt like I had to go find Daddy, and so I slowly rolled onto my knees and crawled up the embankment. People were running around like ants after you uncover their nest, yanking at the front of the van, trying to extricate it from the bus, trying to get ..." And then the image of her father's flattened head shot into her brain and her hands flew up over her eyes as if she could erase the image by closing her eyes, but of course she couldn't. Instead her throat closed, and it was hard to breathe.

"Go on," demanded Nathan.

"I can't."

"Yes, you can. You just don't want to."

"Stop it. You weren't there..."

"Obviously not; I wish I had been. Maybe I could have done something to save him."

"No, you couldn't," she said, "he was dead."

"How do you know?"

"His head was ..." And she slammed her hands together with a loud clap. Then she bent over, holding onto her stomach. She retched. The spasms kept coming up empty but left her breathless and sweaty.

Nathan patted her on the back, reminding her of her father. "Sorry," he whispered, "sorry, Nee, I didn't mean to make you miserable, I just wanted to know." Then finally, she turned to him, grabbing his shoulders and they clung together. And for a while, it seemed, as C.W. would once have said, all was well.

But as the days passed and her own work shifts kept her more and more in the kitchen, she and Nathan spent less time together. Their work schedules didn't jibe.

One evening, having begged off clean-up duty, they arranged to meet after dinner in the rec room. She was yawning, almost too tired to talk but wanting to connect. She slumped down in a chair next to a table and put her head down across her elbows, but sideways so she could keep her eyes on him. It was late and there was no one else in the room. Nathan literally paced up and down the room, unable to sit down, hardly able to follow a conversation, his eyes darting from side to side.

"Did you go to the meeting this morning? I don't think I saw you there," she asked.

"Nah," he snorted, "I'm taking a break from meetings. I've had enough meetings to last me a lifetime."

"You're so fidgety. Like you used to get when Mummy had the blues. What's wrong?"

"Well, my father's dead. My girlfriend dumped me. And the American Absolutes made it clear they don't want me. Isn't that enough to make anyone fidgety?"

"Ray would say you were a cat on a hot tin roof."

To her relief, he laughed, but the frown soon returned. "The problem is, I can't seem to keep my thoughts in order. The only thing I do know, is what the hell am I doing here?"

"You're seeing me." She sat up straighter. "Our father just died."

He stared at her as if she had grown an extra nose on her forehead, "For Pete's sake, Nee, I can't be hanging onto your skirts. I've done enough of that already with Rudy and Mom." His hands slashed down as if he was literally cutting off knots.

"Have you talked to Hadji?"

"No, I have *not*. Don't you get it? I'm tired of always being told what to do. By Rudy, by Mummy, by Ray, by Hall ... you think now I want *Hadji* telling me what to do?"

"He wouldn't do that."

"Oh yeah, we'll I'm not so sure about that. And you? What the hell are you doing here? Mooning after Hadji like you're in heat." A deepening frown caused angry red-and-white folds to appear on his forehead.

"Nathan, that's cruel." The memory of Gertrude mooning after Hall Hamden surfaced and she felt ashamed.

"Well you should see yourself," he snorted, "It's obvious how you feel about him. You never have been able to hide your feelings, have you? Whatever you're feeling just shows right up on your face. How the hell you do that, I'd like to know." He stopped pacing for a moment then wheeled on her. She flinched away.

"You know that movie we were shooting when you bailed on me the last time? Well, not that you care, I was useless. On camera my face was dead."

"I'm really sorry," she said, "I didn't mean to bail on you then. It was just that … Hall Hamden … and I had to …" Once more, her failure to follow through with Hall Hamden struck guilt into her.

Nathan studied her. "Well, at least you're honest about what you're feeling. With Rudy, it was all about pretending. After a while, I didn't know what was real and what wasn't. I'm not sure *she* even knew."

Though he was finally sitting, his thighs couldn't stop jittering up and down. And his head swung from side to side. "What became increasingly clear," his shoulders twitched, "was that she was just stringing me along, making me feel like she cared, when all the time she was just waiting for her chance to bolt. Well, maybe it's *my* time to bolt now, have you ever thought about that? Have you?" He scowled at her.

"I don't want you to leave."

"I know you don't, Nee. That's clear. But what's less clear to me is what *I* want." And with that, he bolted out into the dark and the rain.

The next day, she cornered Hadji as he was leaving a meeting. He held up his hands to ward her off, "I really can't talk right now, Cornelia. I must go, I must really, *really* go." He turned away from her. She steeled herself. After all this wasn't about her but Nathan.

"Look, I know how you feel. You don't want me to count on you. But this is *not* about me. This is about Nathan. I'm worried."

"In that case," he turned back around, but kept his distance. He signaled to the man next to him that he'd be right with him. The man walked off and looked at a map of India hanging on the wall.

"I'm not going to bite you, you know," she joked, hoping to lighten the mood.

He waggled his head, "Please, Cornelia, don't be hurt by my apparent indifference."

She held up her hands, "I know how you feel. You've made it abundantly clear. I get it. But, as said, this is about Nathan." And she blurted out everything Nathan had said about bolting. "I need your counsel, Hadji. Please help me understand."

He closed his eyes, and she could almost sense him reaching for clarity. Finally, he sighed and looked down at her with so warm a gaze that she could only listen to what he was saying with all her heart.

"You must let him go. He needs to find his way just as you do. We are each on our own independent journeys. We each have our own precious relationship with the divine being that rests inside us all. If we happen to travel together for a while, we must consider ourselves lucky,"

"Let him go?" she whispered. "When I so want to pull him close?"

"Yes, let him go. With love. Let him know that it is all right. He must find his own way. If this restlessness in our Nathan means that he must go climbing mountain peaks or even wallowing in the marijuana dens of Goa, then so it must be."

He paused again to reflect, and she noticed the fine lines around the outside corners of his eyes, pulling the skin into pleats of anxiety. Dark shadows pooled beneath his eyes. She began to understand what a huge burden it must be to carry the responsibility of the Moral Absolute movement throughout the whole subcontinent of India.

She forced a smile. "Never mind, Hadji. I didn't mean to bother you. We'll figure it out."

"It is not a bother, Cornelia. You and your brother are never a bother to me. But you must learn not to take things so personally."

"How can I not?" Even to her, her tone sounded harsh.

"One of the things you must learn about our country might help you understand. There is a tradition in our country for men," he paused, then laughed, "and indeed, women of course, to repudiate everything at some point in this present existence to go out in search of the meaning of their lives. In fact, Buddha did this. He left off being a prince to go live in the jungle." And with that, he turned away and walked off to join the man waiting for him.

*　*　*

Puffy monsoon clouds raced in from the far-off Indian Ocean, stampeding up toward the high mountains. But today their bellies were only a light gray, not black with moisture, and for once the rains held off.

The trail leading down into the valley was thick with mud, too mucky for small humans, but the four elephants, each with their own mahout sitting just behind their ears, plodded single file slowly down the hill.

Nathan and Cornelia rode behind a mahout on one of the animals, Hadji and a Hindu priest on another, several men from the conference center on the third and fourth. These elephants were not gaily painted as they had been for the cremation ceremony. Instead, they were a sober gray, properly attired in just their own skin for the final part of the death ceremony for their father.

Nathan and Cornelia were carrying what remained of their father's ashes, safely housed in a porcelain jar, to a sacred spot in the jungle where the headwaters of the river sprang out of a cliff face. There, Hadji told them, they would scatter the ashes into the river to flow down to the sea.

Below her, the elephant lurched to one side. Her hand shot down to her lower belly. Every time she thought of the baby, pain pierced her. She blinked rapidly in an effort to return to this place, this time, this moment.

Again, the elephant pitched, but steadied itself by coming to a complete halt. Birds called out, a large butterfly flitted past, the wings all blue when wide open and flashing yellow when up. The canopy of jungle arched above them; the sky only visible in crescent-shaped slits.

"I've had it with this. Too slow. Here, take this," Nathan jammed the porcelain jar into her hands, turned gracefully and slid down off the elephant. He landed in a crouch, stood up, calling back over his shoulder, "I'll catch up with you all later."

He loped down the slippery path, leaping, arms spinning, almost out of control, disappearing around a turn of the path. Soon, they heard a whoop of delight from far below.

She looked over to the other elephant to see Hadji staring at her, his face bleak and full of pain. Why he was feeling such pain was a mystery, so she turned her gaze away.

The mahout called out to the elephant, chanting to it in a high singing voice. The animal shuddered, then carefully placed another foot on the slippery slope below and down they went toward the sacred headwaters.

A spring gushed out of a hole in a cliff, dashing into a swirling pool. The sun had skulked off behind a hill. The arching vault of the jungle washed the dim light green.

Nathan crouched down next to the spring, naked except for a loincloth. A Hindu priest stood behind him, shaving all the hair off his head. Tufts of blond hair littered the ground around Nathan's feet. His scalp shone lurid and white in the green gloom, as if the priest had shaved down to the actual bone of his skull.

Hadji called out to Cornelia from the other elephant, "It is customary in our country for the eldest son to shave his head when his father dies. Indeed, Nathan asked to have it done."

Nathan stared in her direction. He looked nothing like her brother. His gaze went through her. The muscles around his mouth were rigid, his cheeks yanked back in a silent snarl. His round skull looked as fragile as an egg.

She clambered down from the elephant and tried to hide how bereft she felt. But she knew from Hadji's quick, concerned look that grief must have been evident on her face.

She handed the jar of ashes to a priest then told herself not to cry, and to stay firmly in the background of the small crowd of men standing along the riverbank. This was Nathan's time to honor their father's passing.

The men dipped their fingers into the pot of ashes, then rubbed Nathan's head as they blessed him. With a smudged gray head, he scattered brilliant marigold petals into the stream, then poured the remainder of the ashes into the whorl of golden petals. The petals and grey bits swirled into a greasy paste on the surface. They roiled for a moment, then hit a vortex and were sucked downstream. One last petal floated in an eddy.

Not waiting for Nathan, Cornelia turned back to her elephant. The mahout pointed to a stump in the ground on which she was able to clamber up onto the elephant's back. The elephant plodded back up the hill. Sitting astraddle behind the ears, the mahout sang softly to his elephant. She wept without making a sound.

By that afternoon, Nathan had packed his bag. She deliberately tried to keep a light tone when she said goodbye but failed.

They stood next to the taxi waiting to take him down the hill to the train station in Poona. She jammed her sandals into the mud, splashing muddy water up around her ankles.

"Don't do this," he snapped. His baldness made him look both fierce and vulnerable.

"What?"

"Make my leaving a big, dramatic deal. Don't be like Mummy."

"I'm not. But you want me to be happy about your leaving? Well, I'm not. I know you have to go, but I guess it's my turn to feel you're leaving *me* in the lurch."

"Well, so now you know how it feels." One eyebrow was arched.

"But you had Rudy. And Hall Hamden."

"And now you have Hadji."

"But Hadji's no Hall Hamden. He's good."

"Maybe yes, maybe no. Time will show us, won't it now?"

"He's different. He's *better*. He's more like Horace was."

"Truth was you always liked that old blowhard more than I did."

She bowed her head and blinked furiously, still angry enough to hang onto her pride. She would *not* descend into drama like Nevin would.

"Listen, Nee," his tone softened, "I'm *not* leaving you. I'm just going away from here. I need to know who I am. I need to know what I feel and think about things. *Please* don't stop trusting yourself. I always loved that about you. That no one, not even Horace Baker or our father, could tell you how to feel. Don't let yourself be in sway to anyone else. You hear me?" He grabbed her shoulders and shook her.

She continued to scuff her feet in the mud, glad to be making a mess. She was happy that she had splattered the bottom three inches of his khakis with droplets of mud. "Where are you going? Do you even know?"

"Nope. Not entirely sure. That's the plan, to not be so entirely sure about anything for a while. I'm just bone tired of everyone else telling me what I should believe. Maybe for just a little bit I won't believe in anything. They say Goa's nice. Maybe I'll just surf. Maybe that's all I'm good for."

"Don't sell yourself so short."

"You know this Absolute stuff hasn't prepared us for much of anything. Or hadn't you noticed? Oh, we're good at being told what to do and where to do it. But when we have to decide what it is *we* want -- what *I* want," he quickly amended, "I find myself at square one." His tone was bitter as he continued. "We're not even prepared for college, have you ever thought of that? Gee willikers, admissions officer," he deliberately made his voice naïve and his eyes big and round, "I know how to milk a goat and chop down Kamalame trees with a machete, and I can write down thoughts from God, and I can sort of play the guitar. But can I write an essay or understand trigonometry? Gosh, I guess not."

"I get it. Go figure it out." She was thinking back to what Hadji had said about letting him go. To her delight, his face brightened.

He swung his backpack down into the cab, then leaned down to fold his long limbs inside the tiny black taxi.

"I love you," she called out. "Don't forget the moon shines down on both of us."

For one wonderful moment, her brother Nathan was back. As he stuck his head out the window, his smile was brilliant. His head was cocked back as if he could already feel the salty wind in his face. He waved jauntily as the taxi sped off down the long hill beneath the overarching jacaranda trees.

She stood quiet for a moment, her breath hurting as it passed over her tightened throat.

The monsoon rains returned in earnest that night, hammering so hard on the ground that the first three feet of every building in the complex was splattered with mud. The rains were so ferocious that the world closed down around them. The valleys below disappeared into the mist. Many left for other parts, including Hadji, who was off to speak at a university in Delhi.

Mudslides covered the road below the conference center, cutting them off from the rest of the world.

Only a skeleton staff was left to man the place. The girls squabbled among themselves, then fell into a lazy torpor.

Day after day, the rain sluiced down without a break. Seven days in, the rain retreated for a few minutes. A crescent slice of blue sky appeared briefly like the slash of a blade through the surrounding clouds. For the first time in weeks, they could see beyond a few feet.

On the other side of the valley, miles of cataracts spilled over the hillside and down into the jungle below. Rainbows danced all along the escarpment.

Then the clouds closed back in, the view crept back into fog, and the rain resumed, relentless and biblical. It seemed to Cornelia that eventually the valleys below would flood and fill up, and she would float away up into the sky on their own little mud island of Four Absolutes heaven. She felt stranded and isolated.

As the mud-covered roads still had not been cleared, conferences remained cancelled. Then the power failed. During the day, they bottled pickled cucumbers and curry sauces; at night, they read by candlelight. The cheerful mood of volunteerism frayed. All the girls were crabby. Several of them had their periods and there was a metallic stench of stale blood in their room that never seemed to dissipate in the humidity.

Every morning, they scraped fuzzy clumps of fungus off their sandals. Tears seemed redundant. The world was weeping for them. They slid around each other, polite but no longer making any effort to be merry. Even Anasuya was subdued. At night, they clipped and cleaned their toenails, checking for signs of fungus growing under the nails, combed out their damp hair, then blew out the candles early, only to toss and turn all night.

One morning as they were just rousing themselves, a great hallooing came through the rain.

"Hadji!" Anasuya cried out, her beautiful face lighting up. They all jumped out of bed, flung on their clothes, and ran outside, huddling under their umbrellas. As they ran toward him through the rain, Hadji beamed at them from the steps of the conference hall.

"Come! Come!" he cried out. "I have walked through the night to get to you. I heard from a little bird that moods have dampened a bit with the rain." He chortled as he always did at his own bad jokes, and his head waggled with good cheer and they all laughed and clapped, so happy to see him, feeding off his joy.

They followed him into the entrance hall. A bedraggled group of about thirty gathered. They stamped their feet, shook the wet out of their hair and clothes, and wiped the rain off their faces.

"Come, come quickly now," Hadji called out again, clapping his hands. "We must have a meeting, and you must meet my important new friend." He reached behind him to pull forward a scrawny looking Anglo with thick horn-rimmed glasses and a soaked through trench coat. "This is Jonathan Wright of the *New York Journal*, and he has come to write of our efforts here. Cornelia, where are you? Come forward please." She could feel Anasuya's pretty little hands pushing her forward.

"Our friend Jonathan here is most anxious to meet you. He wants to interview you, Cornelia. You didn't tell me," Hadji smiled indulgently at her as he let the axe fall. "Did you know?" He waved his hand to include the entire room, "Did Cornelia ever tell you that the press' nickname for her was 'fierce little monkey?' It seems there will be quite a story about her hiding out here in our hilltop haven. It will certainly help to get us the international attention we most desperately need."

As if the clouds had rushed inside and surrounded her, she felt black thunder boil up inside her. She shot a look at Hadji.

"Oho," he laughed, and held his chest and staggered as if struck by lightning. "That look must be what they are talking about. Fierce monkey indeed."

She hoped her gaze would scorch him. She suddenly hated his smug little face, the waggles of his head and his oh-so-charming ways.

She stalked out into the rain and instead of hiding from it she embraced it, setting off down the cliff-side path, not knowing where she was going, not even needing a destination, just knowing that the swinging of her legs would stem off the soul sickness she felt creeping into every part of her body. How *dare* he exploit her! How could he flaunt this pathetic little creep of a journalist who wanted to pick at the bones of her modeling story? Suddenly she remembered the sycophantic slant of Horace Baker's face as he turned to charm a movie star or a visiting tycoon. How he would laugh off accusations of always sucking up to the rich. *If you could always just eat chocolate cake,* he would say, *why would you settle for plain bread?*

That Hadji meant to use her to publicize the Absolute movement in India made her sick. Perhaps she had fallen into the same doomed trap into which her father had once stepped. Work hard, do good, follow the rules and you'll get a pat on the head for being such a good follower, such a good devotee of the Absolutes. She thought of how the girls' faces had lit up at the sound of Hadji's voice. How each of them no doubt harbored their own secret fantasies of him singling them out of the fold for special attention. How each felt buoyed by his praise and cast down when he noted their shortcomings. She snorted and felt filled with disgust for being such a fool.

She must have walked a mile or so through the rain along the cliff, splashing over streams, watching the endless waterfall rush out over the side, the water vaulting and bouncing and slithering in spirals all the way down to the valley floor.

And as she walked, she calmed.

The air embraced her. The touch of rain stilled her. Her thin cotton clothes clung as if they were a second skin. She paused and looked out over the canyon. The rain had eased, and the clouds once again parted, though far away they still boiled along the horizon. I must capture this, she thought. She pulled her sketchbook out of her messenger bag. Peace enveloped her as her fingers flew to catch the play of light and dark, the dance of color all around.

It was then that she heard Hadji calling her name.

| 13 |

She meant to castigate Hadji, but as he ran toward her, he was so drenched to the skin, his glasses so fogged up that she laughed instead. When he stopped in front of her and took off his glasses, she noted the small red dent left behind on either side of his high, arched nose. Because she wanted to reach out and touch those tiny indentations, she turned away.

She heard a groan and he stepped forward and pulled her into him until the length of her body was pressed against his, and her heart kicked so hard that black spots swam in her vision and she almost swooned.

"Why are you laughing? This is what you want, isn't it? Tell me it's what you want. I'm going crazy. I can't stop thinking about you." He was shouting as he shook her by the shoulders.

Her anger ignited. She pushed him away. "Stop it," she said. "You're hurting me.

He stood a foot away. He shook the wet hair off his forehead, raking his fingers through it. Raindrops flew everywhere. "*Listen* to me, Cornelia. I can't go on like this."

"Oh, so now *you* can't go on like this," her tone was sharp, "but what about me? What about *my* feelings? Did you even think how *I* might feel about having some reporter surface just when I've been feeling safe from the outside world? Did you?" Her last accusation was shouted.

He looked at her, startled by her statement. "No, I have to admit I didn't think of how you would feel. I'm sorry. I can see I've made a mistake. You don't care about me after all. I've been a fool."

This truly infuriated her. She almost screamed at him, "What are you talking about? Of *course,* I care, you dimwit. What's *wrong* with you?"

"You do?"

She shook her head and a smile tugged at the corners of her lips. She couldn't stay mad at him. It was impossible. "Why don't you go back to what you were saying?"

"What *was* I saying?" His usual unflappable aplomb seemed shattered. "My brain is all mixed up."

She threw him a cue. "Something like you can't stop thinking about me."

His eyes looked deep into hers and he shuddered. His voice was low and heartfelt. "I can't stay away from you any longer. I have tried. God only knows I have tried to resist you. But I cannot do it any longer." His face was forlorn.

She held up her hands and beckoned to him. With a groan, he took one step forward and his mouth went down to her neck, and he kissed her passionately where her pulse throbbed, and she found herself arching back, thrusting herself both away and toward him until their crotches were slammed together. Her head swam and there was a roaring in her ears so loud that she almost didn't hear his other groan. His hand reached around, and he thrust his fingers into her hair and drew her face in even closer. He cupped her chin and made her look up into his eyes. His tall frame was equal to hers, and their thighs and hips and stomachs were pressed together until it seemed they snapped together as perfectly as long-lost missing puzzle pieces.

"This *is* what you wanted, isn't it?" His voice was hoarse.

She nodded, unable to speak.

His breathing was ragged, and his voice fell notes deeper than she had ever heard him talk. The low tone resonated throughout his body and thrummed into her in time with her pulse. His wet shirt, just above his heart, fluttered. She couldn't talk, but her answer was to pull him tighter, straining against him. His thigh naturally moved between her legs, and she pressed even more toward him, wanting to merge into every part of him. His face drew closer until his lips were so close that she could feel his sweet breath.

His lips were soft and lush, and her lips opened to him, not pressing, but melting. Then suddenly, there was a sucking sound as their wet clothes parted. Again, he thrust her out at arm's length, but gently, so that she knew it was not a rejection but a pause.

"We must go tomorrow," he said roughly. "We must do this right."

"What are you talking about?" her voice came out all strangled.

"I thought of you all the while I was up in the hot Rajasthan desert." His fingers stroked the wet tresses of her hair off her forehead. Though he kept their bodies apart heat radiated between them, her pulse sent errantly wild electric charges jumping across the gap. "Here you've been stuck in the rain, working hard, while I've been gallivanting all over India. Yet not once have you ever complained. Even though you too, like many here, have suffered grievous losses. Despite your courage, I had the clear thought that you must have warmth and new sights to recover your strength, or your spirit will be damaged."

"But instead you brought back a journalist?" The injustice of him having returned with a journalist swept back with full force. "You exploited me. How could you do that?" She tried to push him away, but he held her tight.

"Is that how you truly see it?" he asked, cocking his head.

"It is," but then she hung her head and thought some more. Hadji had been nothing but kind and welcoming. He had given her a place to stay, friends to make, meaningful work with which to fill her days. Why should she begrudge him a chance to publicize his center? Wasn't that just the way of the world? "No, I guess. Not entirely. It's just that I came here to hide, and I felt exposed."

"Look at me, dear Cornelia. You can't hide forever. Your flame is too bright, your spirit too strong. I know that of you."

"And what do you mean, 'We must do this right?'" she protested. "What on earth are you talking about?"

She saw the blush turn his cheeks a mahogany red. She memorized the color. She saw the thin blade of his nose, the arch of his lips, the firm slant of his jawline. But most of all, his soulful eyes. And she loved him.

He faltered for a moment, then cupped her shoulders and stared deep into her eyes. His face flickered with held in emotion. His fierce eyebrows drew close to each other. "I can see that my thinking has jumped way ahead of yours. Let me explain. If we must love each other – and we must, I see that now. I was a fool not to see it before – then we *will* do it right. You will *meet* my mother. We will take this *one* step at a time. Like I once said many long months ago." He threw back his head and crowed. "We will have the most wonderfully grand Victorian courtship this world has ever seen."

He broke away from her then and almost skipped with delight; his feet virtually pranced around in a circle. "We will go to visit the sacred temples. A pilgrimage of sorts. And I will show you my India. And we will kiss. Yes, we will kiss. But we will take it slow. Because we *must* be pure. And we will be honest with each other. And care for each other. Unselfishly. Yes, we will do this right, Cornelia, we must!" And he looked fierce suddenly. "Not everyone will be pleased."

She thought of Anasuya and all the other girls and nodded her head in agreement. But she also felt dazed, in shock. She had gotten so used to thinking she could never have him that she felt confused. It was as if he had sprinted ahead of her, and she was lagging behind. "I feel dizzy. You really want this?"

He drew her close again but this time it was not so much sexual and passionate as tender. "I can see you hardly believe me. Certainly, it is because I have been so harsh with you. But you will see. Don't you know, you little fool," again, he shook her ever so slightly by her shoulders. "Don't you know, I've always loved you. From the moment I first met you when you were only a little girl. And you dashed yourself against me with your wounded arm. You were so pumped up with outrage, so full of vinegar and salt, that I could not help but adore you."

Her heart beat fast. "I thought it was my hair," she laughed.

"That, too." He reached out to stroke the wet tendrils off her cheeks. His touch sent electric shocks through her body. She trembled.

"And then how could I forget you popping up in front of me from underwater, your body all golden and slender, your spirit so free and unencumbered. You seemed like a magical sprite, come to life just to pleasure my soul and sight."

She hung her head. "I didn't know. I was just a child."

He threw back his head and roared with laughter. "You were, Cornelia. That was all you were. The best, most pure thing I'd ever seen."

"And then?" She was greedy; she wanted more.

He looked down at her and his gaze was troubled. "And then to see you so mistreated by Hall Hamden and the others. Not just once, but twice. I feared for your spirit. I truly did. But you were not mine to have then, Cornelia. You were still growing up, and I had to let you do that by yourself. But we have been on parallel journeys my dear, and you were never out of my thoughts, believe me."

"Nor you mine."

"Truly?"

She nodded.

He threw back his head and laughed. His broad shoulders relaxed. She could almost see the weight of the world falling off him. He looked young and free of worry, and she loved that his feelings for her could do that for him.

"To know that you missed me," he said, his eyes full of wonder. "I had hoped for that. I guess the Almighty has a sense of romance after all. I should have known it. You were so far away for so long that I had given up all hope. And threw myself into the cause."

He sighed and looked back at the conference center. Pleats of anxiety appeared at the corners of his eyes. A furrow creased his forehead. His full lips compressed, but then eased as he once more looked down at her. "But then, when you appeared again, and this time in my beloved

India as I had always dreamed, you were all grown up and strong and beautiful and full of pain from your losses. And I so longed to hold you in my arms and comfort you." Again, he laughed, so joyfully that the sound rang out over the humid air and into the far ramparts of the canyons below, echoing back to them in a dozen different reverberations.

"There," he said. "Now the world knows. I *love* this girl!" He shouted out into the canyon. He turned back to her and drew her close. "I plan to treasure you, my sweet Nee Nee. I promise to cherish you." He leaned down to touch his lips to hers, and they were soft and full of promise. She swooned into him, holding him tight for balance.

Again, he pushed her away, and again he shook her ever so slightly, "But listen to me. We must take it slow. We will take the time to get used to each other. To let others get used to the idea of us. We will not rush this. No, we will not make that mistake. So, let us turn back now, and talk together of foolish things," he laughed at this, and she joined him, and bliss coursed through her at the sound of their laughter. It rang out over the world and reverberated in every valley.

"Yes, let us walk back together now. But not holding hands – though you now know that I long to. For now, we must stay respectfully apart. We must let them get used to the sight of us walking and talking together. Let us start there."

"Yes, let's!" And she skipped along beside him to keep up with his pace. They smiled at each other, and it all seemed suddenly settled and right, and all was well with the world.

When he left her at the door to her dormitory and she watched him walk away, his long legs striding, she allowed a tiny, deep, crawl of happiness to curl up inside her heart.

Not yet ready to face other people, she turned back and went for another long walk, exulting in her delight.

An hour later, even from down the hall, Cornelia could hear a twittering coming from their dormitory room. She slipped in the door, wishing she could be alone to revel in the sweet confession of love from Hadji. But that was not to be.

Instead, as she entered the room, there was a flutter of excitement and a lifting up of skirts and legs and arms as if the girls were a pack of butterflies, briefly excited by the passage of damp air brought in from the hallway, but soon settling back down.

Their faces, bright with excitement, looked up at her from their cross-legged positions on the floor and, for a brief second, she thought they somehow knew what had just happened. The encounter between Hadji and her throbbed so raw and deep she thought it must be obvious to all.

But it turned out their chirping had nothing to do with her.

The three girls were in a tight little circle on the floor, their knees almost touching, their cheeks flushed with excitement as they helped Anasuya carefully fold up her saris and tuck them into a raggedy old duffle bag.

"What's happening?" Cornelia asked, feeling tall and awkward, and, for the first time, shut out from their female closeness.

Zaina's sharp little face pointed up, her beady eyes peering brightly over the tops of her thick glasses. Her face was serious as she delivered the pronouncement. "Anasuya is to go away with Hadji. It is what she has been waiting for, a sign that things are moving forward."

"What?" Cornelia's brain began to whirl, and black dots spun in the periphery of her vision. "What do you mean? I don't understand."

"Come, come," said Zaina, her tone both kind and patronizing, as if Cornelia were a child. "Go fetch a towel to dry off, then come back and join us." She patted the floor next to her, moving over a cushion to welcome her. "Then we will tell you everything. It is truly the most wonderful news."

Cornelia went over to her bed, grabbed a towel that she had hung next to the window. Its rank mildew stench filled her with revulsion. What did they mean by saying Anasuya was to go away with Hadji?

"No, no, no," chastised Zaina. "She cannot take that silk sari, it is too rich and bride-like. Better to take the simple cottons until it is all resolved." She firmly yanked the red and gold silk sari from Deeba's plump hands and added it to a stack next to Anasuya. Then she patted the smaller stack of cotton saris. "This is plenty. You know," she chided Deeba, "she was told only to take as much as she could carry."

Deeba looked abashed, but slowly protested. "But Zaina, she will want to look pretty as well." She deliberately extricated the red and silk folded sari and put it back on the other stack, then held her hand down over it so Zaina could not snatch it back.

Anasuya sat between them, her hands folded carefully in her lap, a pleased look curling her lips.

Afraid to ask but needing to know, Cornelia spoke again. "What is going on? Please will someone explain what is happening?"

Zaina cocked her head and looked at Anasuya.

"Zaina, you tell." Anasuya flicked her long, thick braid back over her shoulder. Her golden skin held a faint stain of pink. She bit her lower lip, which swelled as fresh blood surged in. Her lips gleamed, as succulent and colorful as the inner chamber of a fresh picked conch. Beside her, Cornelia felt damp and rotten and even old.

"You see," said Zaina, swaying back and forth a little with the importance of the story she was telling. "Back, many years ago, Anasuya and Hadji's families knew each other. This was not unusual, even though Hadji's family had wealth and Anasuya's father was an impoverished schoolteacher with eleven children. But you see, all the many Brahmin families in that part of Maharashtra knew each other and thus, each time a baby girl was born, the cards were read, and it seems that the astrologers and matchmakers agreed that the stars were properly aligned for Anasuya and Hadji to be a perfect match. And so the reading was sent to Hadji's family. They received a polite response, but the families never came to a formal agreement. Nevertheless, Anasuya's parents felt there was an implicit understanding that one day a betrothal might be a good thing."

"A betrothal?" Cornelia felt sick. She closed her eyes, trying to control her reaction to these words. That quiet inner voice she often neglected still steadfastly appeared when she called on it, and it spoke calmly to her. *Listen carefully. Listen to every word they speak. Just as you must with Hadji. Despite your fluttering pulse, listen carefully to what people around you have to say. Then you will know what to do.* She opened her eyes and asked, "Truly a betrothal?"

Zaina's head waggled, "Well, it is not exactly that. Not just yet. But certainly, this bodes well for that to happen. You know, without some expectation of that happening, Anasuya's family would never have allowed her to come here. They hoped her presence would move things along a bit. And now it seems to have worked. For Anasuya has been told to pack only enough of her things to carry and that she, along with a few others, will walk out of here very soon and make their way to Hadji's house to meet his mother. That is a most momentous occasion. Meeting his mother!" Zaina clapped her hands, truly happy, it seemed, for her dear friend Anasuya.

Even Deeba, who flushed every time Hadji passed within five feet of her, seemed consumed with excitement for her friend.

"Along with a few others?" Cornelia asked.

"Yes, yes," Zaina was impatient now that she had finished telling the story. And she went back to supervising Anasuya's duffle bag. Her hand hesitated over the gold and red sari, then patted it to show Deeba she approved and carefully placed it inside the bag along with the plainer ones. It felt as if her pat were both a blessing and a letting go, of an ugly girl humbly acknowledging the luck of the prettier girl beside her. "Here is the note that came," Zaina pushed a piece of paper toward Cornelia.

She unfolded it. It was not Hadji's elaborate cursive but a more cramped writing that was unfamiliar. It said that Anasuya and Cornelia were to pack up their belongings, but only enough to carry, and be ready to join Hadji and the journalist, just after lunch, to start a long downhill walk to where a car waited just below the washed-out road. From there they would go to stay with Hadji's mother for a few days.

"But the note says I also am to go." Her words sounded clogged. She swallowed, trying to keep up with the gouts of anxious saliva that kept flooding into her mouth.

"But of course, someone has to accompany Anasuya," Zaina's tone was impatient.

Anasuya's head was modestly lowered, but her lips still curled up at the corners.

"You see," Deeba said slowly, her large liquid eyes meeting Cornelia's, "it would not be proper for Anasuya to travel alone with Hadji. You are to accompany them so that all will be done as it should be. No one would ever want there to be improper insinuations. It would not be seemly for a woman to travel alone with two men." This last part hissed out of her, and she leaned back against a pile of pillows, deflated by her explanation.

"Tongues would indeed waggle if Anasuya were to walk off with Hadji alone," Zaina snapped.

Cornelia stared down at the note. A confusing array of emotions swirled through her. She wanted to burst out with the truth, that they had it *wrong*, that actually Anasuya probably had been chosen to be *her* chaperone.

But she couldn't just blurt that out.

Hadji and she had agreed to keep things quiet. Besides, she couldn't crush the hopes of all these girls. One of them, in their mind, had been chosen, and that was a thing to be reveled in. She felt as mean as a spider lurking in her den. A sour part of her was angry that their excitement had so tainted her own joy. It seemed that she was once more cast as the outsider, the one who saw through the layers of artifice and denial and fantasy to the truth beneath. Was she always to be the observer and holder of hurtful truths? Couldn't she just once be the one to simply share her own joy? But how could she hurt this lovely girl? How could she crush her dreams?

She could not. And so she kept the truth to herself and made herself smile. And whether it was the right decision or not, she did not know. For once a path is chosen, and once you have walked into deception, there is no going back through the tangled woods to find another way.

| 14 |

Just after lunch, a group gathered at the conference center to bid goodbye to the four people scheduled to walk five miles downhill where a car waited just below the washed-out section of the road.

While Hadji lingered, giving last-minute pats of encouragement to those who were being left behind, Cornelia gave Zaina and Deeba heartfelt hugs then shouldered her leather satchel and started off at a fast clip. Cornelia wasn't good at long goodbyes and knew that walking would help settle her troubled mind. She could no longer linger and watch Anasuya, whose eyes were so glued to Hadji's back that Cornelia knew she would not make a move to start walking until he did.

Cornelia swung into a long-stepped gait, enjoying the feeling of stretching her legs and taking deep inhalations of fresh mountain air. With a lurch of sadness, she let go of her grief and felt her strength returning.

Off to her right, columns of light stalked the lurid green of the far-off hills. Black clouds still boiled on the horizon, but occasional peeps of a startling cerulean sky gave her faith that the sun was still there somewhere. When she heard pounding footsteps behind her, her heart flickered, thinking it was Hadji running to catch up.

But the voice that called out was all nasally American, not sing-song baritone at all. "Hey, wait up. What's the hurry?"

She did not turn or say hello. In fact, she picked up the pace. She had no desire to chat with Jonathan Wright, the journalist whom Hadji had brought back with him. She tried to stay ahead of him, but he was persistent. His raggedy breathing stayed just behind her on the trail.

Leaving the plateau and cluster of conference buildings behind, they headed down a steep slope. The path right next to the road was muddy, but easier to walk on than the pot-holed road full of deep puddles. She lengthened her stride until she was loping downhill, trusting her feet to land on the right places, allowing gravity to catapult her forward, down and down, until her heart raced with adrenaline. As the feel-good endorphins flooded her, she was filled with a skipping joy. She bounded from hillock to hillock.

After a half-mile, head-long plunge down the hill, she pulled over to where a small knoll looked out over the vast landscape. Just below, the land dropped off then stretched out endlessly, spangled with rice paddies, all the way to the West where she knew the Indian Ocean must be. But on the far horizon there was no strip of metallic sea, only a blur of golden-struck clouds billowing with light. As she allowed the beauty of the world to flood into her, that clear, quiet voice inside reminded her not to worry about the muddle with Anasuya. *Just wait and see. More will be revealed.*

Jonathan struggled down toward her. His camera banged on his chest; his many-pocketed safari vest bulged with notebooks and pens. He was sweaty, and too plump for his narrow blue jeans. And yet when he caught her observing him, his red face creased with good humor. "Guess I'm not such a pretty sight, am I? Wait up for me, will you? What's the goddamn hurry?"

She grimaced. "I just like to walk fast."

Behind him, still far up the hill, she could see Anasuya picking her way carefully down the slope. Behind her, Hadji carried her duffle bag on his head. When he saw her looking back, he gave a cheerful halloo, which echoed back to them from several canyons far below. She waved and hallooed back.

Even at a distance, his teeth shone white against his chestnut-colored skin; his glossy hair that always swung down low over his forehead no matter how often he tossed it back, caught the light and shone like a beacon. As always, her heart skipped a beat at the sight and sound of him.

"I guess you love him, too?" asked Jonathan. She must have looked startled, because Jonathan's eyes gleamed behind his glasses as if he had just scored a point.

"What?" she protested. "What are you talking about?"

"Oh, nothing. It just that it's very apparent, at least to this poor gent, that Hadji engenders adoration in people. Not something I get, mind you. Never have inspired that in others. Not even my mom adored me. Maybe that's why I notice it when others get it without even asking for it. It's called charisma, you know."

"I know that. I'm not stupid, you know."

His glance grew sharper as he considered her. "Then you know most religious leaders have charisma in spades. Hadji's no exception."

"Oh he's an exception, all right. He's got it in hearts." It bothered her that Jonathan assumed Hadji could be equated with other religious leaders. She turned back to the trail and again set off at a brisk pace. But this time Jonathan kept up with her. He panted behind her, a tiny, irritating terrier.

"You've known him a long time, right?" he yipped.

"You got that right." Her words were clipped. "Almost my whole life."

"Oh, and that is *such* a long time, right? What are you? Not even in your third decade, am I right?" His preppy sarcasm grated on her.

"Something like that."

"And so you know *so* much about life." He reminded her of the entitled interns who had hung around the photographers in the downtown lofts in New York, hoping somehow that by ridiculing and belittling people that they could bring others down a notch and prove themselves superior. She wheeled around on him.

"Look, I don't know what the hell you want from me. But get *this*, I am *not* interested in talking with you, okay?"

"There she is. There's that fierce little monkey scowl the camera loves."

"Jesus." She turned back around and ran away as fast as she could, bounding from muddy hillock to muddy hillock, vaulting down, unchecked, but wanting to feel that endorphin rush again. Anything to get away from this niggling invasive fool, and away from her once-more disordered, chaotic thoughts.

And so, she let her body fly, her legs extending out, her arms held out wide for balance, sweeping downhill toward her unknown future.

Jonathan caught this downhill plunge in what was to become a famous shot. With her arms outstretched and silhouetted against the golden light of the valley, her leaping feet expressing an out-of-control momentum, he labeled it, "Monkey seeking glory in East-Indian Ashram?"

It made the covers of every gossip rag that then existed.

An hour later they were bundled into a car, Hadji in front next to the driver, but corkscrewed around to chat with Jonathan about the last of the now-famous cross-country marches he had led the year before. Anasuya was at one window, Jonathan the other, and much to Cornelia's chagrin, she was jammed into the middle of the back seat between them. She had asked for a window but Anasuya, suddenly manifesting a silent but steely resistance, had resolutely refused to sit next to a strange man. Finally, Hadji had shrugged his shoulders, making it clear he hoped Cornelia would be the flexible one.

And so here she was, in the middle and not at all happy about it. Her long legs folded up so far that her knees jammed up almost to her nose. She stared out the front windshield at the horizon, hoping she wouldn't succumb to carsickness as the car plunged down and around the steep hairpin turns. The constant swaying, as she slammed first into Jonathan and then back into Anasuya, finally lulled her into a hallucinatory half-waking dream.

Nevin galloped past her on a runaway horse, her frightened eyes pleading with Cornelia to save her. Flashes of sunshine popped as Nathan cut a line down a crashing wave. He blithely waved as he twirled over the backside of the breaker and disappeared. Then Hadji was speaking from a podium, his face intent, one finger held high as thousands clapped. Her father, carrying an easel under his arm, strode next to the car, peering in the window at her. She gasped and came fully awake, but of course he wasn't there.

Instead, there was an eggplant sunset and the lights of an approaching town bobbed up and down like a strand of boats riding out at sea, waiting for the dawn to carry them in over the reef. And then as the lights flickered closer, she began to pant, and her vision blurred. A sideways tornado whirled in front of the car, and she screamed as the car plummeted down into the vortex.

Later she found out that Hadji commanded the driver to stop, barked at Jonathan to get out, and then had carefully pulled her up out of the car and into his arms. The first thing she remembered was him holding her close.

She sobbed into his chest as the safety of his arms folded around her. She vaguely remembered his telling the others that this was where the car accident with the bus had happened. Later she would also find out that Jonathan grabbed the opportunity of taking another photograph. This one showed her looking up at Hadji with adoration, her face shining with tears, and his hand carefully stroking ragged tendrils of golden hair off her face. This pic also hit the gossip rags, with the headline: "Model says Indian cult leader has it in hearts."

When she was finally able to stop sobbing and get back into the car, Anasuya's eyes slipped away from hers. It was probably then, Cornelia suspected, that a hint of the truth began to haunt Anasuya. She shrank into something small and frail, not at all the glowing young beauty she had been earlier in the day.

They drove through the night, down and around and down until they reached a vast plain where the car rattled over an old rusting suspension bridge with wooden planks and turned to follow the river road as it wound around the base of the mountains to another inland province.

A few hours before dawn, they arrived at Hadji's mother's villa. It was still dark, and frogs piped in the surrounding trees. Wraiths of mist rose from the river below. Dazed with fatigue, she and Anasuya were led up a huge flight of stone steps onto a large verandah, then inside to a large hallway where many darkened portraits of bejeweled ancestors presided, then finally into a huge bedroom with closed wooden shutters and a mahogany four-poster bed draped with a mosquito net. Saying not a word, they crawled up into the bed from opposite sides, curled up away from each other, and fell asleep.

When Cornelia awoke, she thought she was in the Bahamas. A rooster crowed. Way off, a dog barked. Women called out to each other as they snapped out the morning laundry. Chickens clucked and scratched for grubs just outside the window. A goat bleated, and its baby answered. But then she opened her eyes, and nothing was familiar.

The sun was up, slivering the closed shutters with bands of caramel light. A vividly hued silk carpet lay next to the bed on a highly polished ebony floor. Beside her, Anasuya was on her back, her mouth hanging open and a slight snore rattling in her throat. Deep, dark circles below her eyes smudged the golden skin charcoal. Her tiny gold nose stud nestled into the fold behind her nostril as if it, too, were taking a nap.

Ever so carefully, Cornelia crept out from under the white linen sheet, tiptoed into the bathroom, splashed her face with water, pulled on a white tunic over tan leggings, loosely plaited her tangled hair into one long braid, poked her feet into her leather sandals, then snuck out of the bedroom, scampering down the hallway and down the steps into the garden before anyone could spy her.

Several acres of lawn swept all the way down to the river, flickering silver in the morning sun. The garden was lush. Bright yellow and red crotons filled one flowerbed. In another, blossoms in every shade of red, from pink to scarlet, blanketed the tops of mature rose bushes. Brilliant vermilion marigolds danced in circles around their feet. Thick vines of jasmine climbed out of pots to the verandah roof. The air was drenched with perfume, and she breathed it in until she felt half drunk.

She opened her arms and ran down toward the water. A turbaned man weeding a bed of zinnias started as she swept past. She chortled at him, which made the whites of his eyes pop. She came to a halt at the water's edge.

The river was broad, swirling with eddies and smothered with water hyacinths all along its edges. A boat woven out of reeds swept past, trailing nets from bamboo outriggers. Two fishermen hunkered down in the gunwales, pinching out crabs from piles of small silvery fish, then tossing them back, claws snapping, into the whirling waters. A third man was at the helm, keeping a firm hand on the tiller. Even so, they slewed to one side as they carried past. She saluted them, and they stared gravely back.

"Do you always run everywhere, like a child?" the voice was a soft melodic singsong, but when Cornelia wheeled to face her, her face was anything but soft. Cornelia towered over her by at least half a foot, but the middle-aged woman's upright posture and carved-in-stone-features showed not the least intimidation.

Her hair was black and yanked back into a bun with a steel-white stripe running down the middle of her scalp. The thought of a fierce badger crossed Cornelia's mind. Her features were sharp and perfect; kohl smudged her eyes so that they floated like large, dark pools in her narrow face. Her lower arms were covered with golden bangles. Gold chandelier earrings glittered at her ears. Her pale lavender sari was thickly encrusted with gold. One large ruby pendant hung from her neck and nestled into the slightly crinkled folds of her cleavage.

Cornelia felt foolishly large and awkward. She stammered an answer. "I do tend to run a lot." She chuckled to cover up her embarrassment. But she knew her cheeks must be flushed crimson.

The woman's gaze went down to her feet and Cornelia wished she had washed them before coming out. Her toenails were rimmed with earth from the hike the previous day. And she imagined the size of her feet must be alarming. This woman's, just peeping out from under her sari, were tiny, and her toenails perfectly polished an oxblood red. Then her gaze went up to Cornelia's tousled hair, and she knew her unkempt look was not going over well.

"You must be Hadji's mother." She tried to smile but her face felt like it was cracking.

"Of course I am. Who else would I be?"

If her comment was designed to make her feel stupid, it worked. She felt dim.

"Well," the woman sighed, after finishing an up-and-down scrutiny, "Hadji certainly told the truth about your hair. It's a glorious color. He always used to tell me it shone like gold."

And then she really did blush. The use of the word *always* told her he had been talking about her for years. She thought back to when Hadji had first told her about his family many years before, about how he would wander through his grandmother's fabric factory, and of how her hair reminded him of those silk threads, molten gold floating in tendrils through the morning sunshine.

"Do you still have the factory here?"

Her eyes narrowed and again Cornelia was reminded of a badger and of how fierce it must look when it was digging for a rabbit. "He told you about that, did he now?" She looked down at her feet. A spasm twitched her forehead. "That's long gone now. That ended some years after my husband died." She turned to walk down a mossy path between camellia bushes, as tall as trees, covered with pink flowers under a sheltering jacaranda canopy. Her hand waved. "Come, walk with me. Let us talk."

Anxious to please, Cornelia fell into step beside her.

A snort came out of her curling nostrils. "I want you to know that I do *not* approve of this liaison. Not at all." Her tone was that of a chastising principal.

"It's hardly a liaison."

"Well, what do you call it then? I gather from my son that he's in a rather unseemly haste to make a match. What else could it be but lust?"

Cornelia was both shocked and pleased by her frankness and so she answered in like manner. "I like to think there is more to us than that. We've been friends for many years."

"Have you now? But hardly seen each other, I think. Only in passing, so how is it possible to be friends? Explain to me how that is possible."

She struggled to answer, "It's hard to explain. But every time we see each other it's as if we just stopped talking moments before. We just pick up where we left off. There's no awkwardness." She blushed again, "Well, that's not quite true."

Her glance was sharp, "Now what do you mean by that exactly?"

"This last time, when I arrived after my father's accident..."

"Yes, yes, yes, we are all very sorry about that." But oddly she didn't sound sorry, and Cornelia wondered whether there was any softness in this brittle woman, or whether she was all unforgiving metal. "Go on, go on," she waved her hand.

Cornelia chose her words with care. "Well, this last time, it seemed clear that something between us had shifted. We were no longer so at ease with other." She stumbled to a halt.

His mother's lips tightened, "Lust, just as I thought."

She had no answer for the woman, and for a few minutes they ambled along in silence. Finally, Cornelia broke the silence. "Your garden is lovely."

She peered up at her. "Don't try to deflect me with flattery."

"I won't. I don't flatter anyone. Actually, I hate flattery."

She nodded as if pleased. "So, you like gardens?"

"Yes, I do. My mother loved roses. And so do I."

"You said loved? Is she gone?"

"You might say that."

"What does that mean?"

"We're not in sync at the moment. She didn't approve of my coming here."

"Why should she? A daughter's place is by her mother's side."

Cornelia sighed. "It's complicated." And then she thought of the pregnancy, and tears jammed the corners of her eyes. She blinked furiously. And of course, his mother noticed.

"There's more to this story." Her gaze was ferocious.

"Yes." Cornelia would say no more. She was not going to let her poke at the still-raw part of her soul that grieved the loss of her baby.

"Well, this is a dilemma you see."

"What is?" For a moment, Cornelia was confused. In her own mind she was still thinking of Nevin and the baby.

"You see, there is no way around the unenviable fact that you are, indeed, not one of us." She leaned over to deadhead a camellia bush and her pinch was brutal. Browned petals soon littered the damp floor of the orchard.

"I know," Cornelia hung her head. "I'm sorry about that."

"*Are* you?" She wheeled on her.

"I am. Truly."

"Worse than not being a Brahmin, you're not even a Hindu."

"I know."

"What *are* you exactly?"

"That's a good question. That's something I've been asking myself my whole life. Who exactly am I? Am I the girl who grew up in the islands chasing stingrays across the flats? Or am I the daughter of a once-rich man who gave all his money away to a cult? What am I?" she laughed and spread out her hands. "This is what I know. I read. A lot. I think. A lot. I look at everything and try to make sense of it. Nature soothes me, and I would love to capture its beauty for others. I try to listen to the best part of myself for guidance as how to live my best life. But what religion do I belong to? I don't have the answer to that. I guess maybe the only thing I know for sure about my background is that I'm a WASP."

There was a long silence. His mother looked puzzled. Finally. she looked up and asked, "What exactly is a wasp?"

At that Cornelia laughed out loud. "Did you think I might have a stinger? WASP. White Anglo-Saxon Protestant."

"Oh, I see," the woman said, but she seemed taken aback by Cornelia's laughter. The power between them shifted slightly. Cornelia stood taller out of her hunched-over posture and whipped her loose braid over her shoulder.

"You see," she said, "Hadji and I have talked about how neither of us have always fit in. He has shared with me that when he went to Oxford, he developed a false persona in order to get by. You might say, an overdeveloped facetiousness which made them laugh and think he was a jolly good fellow, don't you know?" And she mimicked a close-mouthed British drawl.

She frowned. "He never told me that."

Cornelia gathered speed as she gained in confidence. "So, for him, you see, getting to know Horace Baker, he felt, for the first time since leaving India, that he didn't have to be phony anymore. He didn't have to pretend."

"I see, I see," and she waggled her head just as Hadji did and Cornelia laughed out loud to see it. His mother looked startled, but a tiny smile turned up the edges of her mouth.

Taking advantage of the small sign of pleasure, Cornelia plunged ahead. "Don't you see? He could finally be his authentic self and that was enough. I have had that same struggle. Oh, I know I don't come from the same background as Hadji. I know I am not what you might want for him, and I know it looks like on the surface that we have nothing in common. But you must know that we understand each other, we truly do. In fact, I believe," she finished simply after taking one long raggedy inhalation, "that we belong to each other. You might even say we deserve each other."

His mother visibly shrank away from her. "My, that was quite a speech. You're certainly no fool, I'll give you that."

"Thank you."

She drew in close to Cornelia and reached up to cup her cheeks. She looked deep into her eyes. "You do, in fact, love him, don't you?"

Cornelia did not waver in returning the gaze, but her throat swelled so she could only nod.

"Yes, I can see that you do. I did not expect that. Or you. You are not at all what I thought you would be."

Holding up her hand in a gesture of farewell, his mother turned in a gentle arc and headed slowly back up along the mossy path between the towering camellia bushes. "This," she hissed to herself, but loud enough for Cornelia to hear, "will *not* be so easy to dismiss after all."

| 15 |

During the next few days, Cornelia hardly saw Hadji. Jonathan Wright left after twenty-four hours, no doubt anxious, as they both surmised later, to get his story and photographs in print. After he left, Hadji was often sequestered in meetings with a serious young Parsi man named Behnam who was up from Mumbai for a few days. They were deeply involved in the process of starting up a magazine based on the tenets of The Four Absolutes.

Behnam looked both harried and full of purpose after hours long meetings with Hadji. He would bustle out of the library, his pockets stuffed with notes, his tiny but round belly struggling against the tight cut of his woolen vest. With his air of self-importance and even a gold watch chain arching from vest pocket to pants, he reminded Cornelia of the White Rabbit in *Alice in Wonderland*.

When she shared this allusion, Anasuya looked blank, which reinforced Cornelia's increasing sense of alienation from her. Just because Anasuya spoke perfect English did not mean she shared the same points of reference. In fact, Cornelia was fast realizing, most of their viewpoints on the world differed a great deal. In contrast to her own need to be always moving, Anasuya spent most of her waking hours on a divan laid out on the front verandah, still for hours at a time, with no book or magazine, just lying there, with her eyes open, staring at the slow turn of the wooden ceiling fan above.

"What is the meaning of this White Rabbit? Can you elucidate me?" A frown creased the gap between Anasuya's perfectly arched eyebrows.

She often looked cross when Cornelia talked of something she didn't understand.

But when Cornelia jumped up and began to mimic the foolish rushing movements of the White Rabbit, trying to make her laugh, she looked even more disapproving. "Honestly, Cornelia, could you not just sit still for even one little minute? I'm exhausted just listening to your toes tapping all the time."

They both started as Hadji shouted out to them through the open door of the library. He spent most hours of the days in there, writing dozens of letters, answering phone calls, having meetings, calling for tea, moving from a wheeled wooden chair that rocked in front of a large mahogany desk to then sit cross-legged on the floor on a large, embroidered pillow. Above him towered bookshelves over which hung many pictures of his grandfathers, one a general and former Prime Minister, and the other the great Mahatma who had so inspired Horace Baker. Now he dashed out onto the porch and greeted them with a brilliant smile.

"Here they are. The lovely ladies of leisure."

Though she barely moved from her languid position, Anasuya took offense. "I beg to differ. I've asked your mother to please give me a job. But she only says nonsense. Why can I not have a job? It would make me feel much more purposeful. I feel useless just lying here like this."

"Nonsense is just what it is," Hadji shook his finger at her. "I was only joking. It would serve you well to begin to understand something about humor, my dear."

"I will try." Anasuya averted her head as if she had been struck.

Cornelia's eyebrows rose. Hadji smiled but held his finger to his lips. He leaned down to pat Anasuya's hand.

"Truly, I meant no offense, my dear. In fact, you *both* are the very opposite of ladies of leisure. You proved that by those long weeks of subservience in the kitchen up in Cherrapunji. But now, try to be of good cheer. It's a respite for my poor swollen head." And he grasped his forehead between two hands, waggling it back and forth to show them how his head was so stuffed full of worries. Cornelia laughed out loud, but Anasuya again looked puzzled and even more irritated than she had before he came.

"Let's go for a stroll, shall we?" Hadji smiled. Cornelia nodded, but Anasuya sulked. "I am certainly not anxious to hold you two back. The last time I walked with you two, your long legs left me quite unhappily eating your dust."

"Are you sure?" asked Cornelia.

"Just go." She turned away from them.

And so they did, trying to hide their glee at a chance to be alone.

Down the garden they dashed, anxious to be away from prying and questioning eyes. Hadji insisted they must walk deep into the far reaches of the garden before he would even so much as hold her hand.

As they strode along, Cornelia pleaded, "*Please* tell me Behnam reminds you just a wee bit of the White Rabbit?"

Hadji looked sideways, his eyebrows arching in surprise, then barked with laughter. "You may be exactly right about that. I hadn't thought of it previously. But his air of righteous pomposity is *exactly* that of the White Rabbit. Still, he's a good man. But oh, Cornelia, what would I do without you?" His eyes sparkled. "You remind me to have fun, to poke just a little bit at the parameters of proper behavior. Come let us hurry." And finally, he took her hand, and they ran down the mossy path into the jungle of camellias.

Once again, she was reminded of Alice, except this time it was the thought of her being whisked around the confusing country through the looking glass, never knowing where she was going to land next, or which puzzling person she would encounter. Of course, Hadji was no Red Queen, she thought, but then perhaps his mother was, and then just as she was pondering that, Hadji pulled her into a dark grotto of the garden where a ledge of rocks was resplendent with trailing orchids and brilliant butterflies flitted everywhere.

He pulled her close and all thoughts and sounds disappeared until the world rounded down to touch and heartbeats as the barriers melted between them. Each kiss left her breathless and panting. Her knees weakened, and she clung to him, afraid she would fall if she even let go for a nanosecond.

But then, as always, he gently pushed her away from him. "That is enough of that. Or else I will lose my mind." He patted a mossy concrete bench built into the ledge. "Here," he commanded "sit here." She might have taken umbrage, but his tone was as indulgent as a mother. And so she sat as he paced in front of her, talking of their future. He could only think clearly, he said, if he kept her at a slight physical distance.

"As you know, my mother is not at all approving of us."

"Yes, I *do* know. She calls it a liaison, which I tried to tell her it is *not*."

He chuckled, "I wish I could have seen you taking her on. That would have been a sight to witness. No one crosses my mother's will, not even me. I have learned over the years to avoid confrontations and just to present her with a fait accompli. I think she resents my not taking her counsel as I used to when I was a child. When she questions me now about my decisions, I just point upward and say there is a higher person I answer to now." One finger pointed up to the sky and his expression was so self-mocking and comical that she could not help but giggle.

"Now it's my turn to wish I could see that."

"Oh, you will, you will, I can promise you that. But seriously," he stopped pacing and wheeled to a stop three feet in front of her. His dear thin face looked troubled. "It's important for me, for us, to do this right. We do not have your father to help us navigate these tricky matters. Your mother, who despite what you may say about her, I would like to meet because truly, Cornelia, honestly, she must have done much that is right, because look at you." His palms outstretched themselves toward her and he looked at her with such tender adoration that she colored.

It pleased her to be so approved of, but she feared something so good could not last. Would anxiety, she wondered, always flicker at the edges of her happiness?

"I have been thinking." He took off his glasses and rubbed the red spots left at the edge of the high bridge of his nose. Without his glasses, his eyes looked bigger and softer, and his vulnerability melted away most of her worry.

"You see," he continued, "there is a very wise old priest, still alive at the venerable age of 92. My grandfather used to consult him when he was troubled. My mother respects him as well. I think if we could capture his approval for our betrothal, it would go a long way toward relieving my mother's anxiety."

"I thought you said you got your guidance from above," she teased him.

"I do, I do." His tone was a bit impatient. "But there is a difference between knowing what is right and disturbing the peace of others. I have no desire for my mother to be so troubled. I want her to be on board. Believe me, it will be much easier for us in the long run if we have her approval. Not only for us, but for our unborn children."

At that her heart skittered. "You do want children with me?"

He looked surprised. "Of course, I do. They will be the standard for a new world view, a mingling of cultures under one banner, under one God..." he broke off suddenly, looking worried, "Are you ready for this, dear Nee? You know that I will not abandon my leadership just because I have chosen to join my life with yours?"

"I know that," she said.

"There will be new responsibilities for you," he said.

She nodded but felt lost. She wanted him, but she could not help but wonder what she was getting herself into. "So how do we consult with this priest? Where is he?"

"He's in Madurai, in the ancient temple there. In fact, you must see it. You will understand much about the mysteries of our country and religion by visiting this temple and others. We must all go. Mother included."

"And Anasuya?"

"Of course, Anasuya. She must go as well."

"She's not doing well, you know."

"What do you mean?"

"Haven't you noticed?"

"I can't say that I have."

"Well, she's just picking at her food. Hardly taking in anything at all."

"I love the way you eat. You approach your food with such passion," Hadji chuckled. She loved the way his eyes crinkled when he laughed. In repose, he could look almost austere, so tall and stork-like. But when he laughed the stern lines dissolved, his eyes almost closed, and he abandoned himself to the moment. "You eat the way you live the whole of your life." His face filled with wonder.

"That's because I'm happy. When I'm not happy, I can hardly eat at all."

He nodded as he made the synaptic connection. "You suspect she is unhappy."

"I know she is. You see, she's in love with you," she said, "and she suspects that I am the object of your affection."

"You must be wrong," he protested. "I've never thought of her in that way at all. No, it cannot be. Not at all. Perhaps she's just misguided. Perhaps she needs to be more fearless in her searching inventory of herself. It's not me she's in love with, it's an illusion that her happiness lies outside herself."

"You may be right, but you *have* been in her thoughts for a long time. Even before she came to Cherrapunji."

"What do you mean? How do you know this?" His beloved face creased with concern. As always, she was reminded of how much he cared about everyone in his group.

"Well, it seems, her family hoped to secure a betrothal with you. When she was born, the astrologers said that the stars seemed to be aligned, or at least that's what I've heard.

"I see," he looked subdued. "This is serious then, after all."

"Why is it serious?"

"Any Brahmin father and mother looking out for the future welfare of their children would take a positive reading of the stars quite seriously."

Later she would regret having said anything. After that, she saw him considering Anasuya, studying her, puzzling over how best to handle a difficult situation. It was perhaps her first serious inkling of how treacherous it was going to be to share Hadji with so many. Because as much as he loved her – and she was beginning to believe he did – he loved and fretted over many. He took his leadership seriously, and once a person came under his regard, his gaze never faltered. She just wished she hadn't brought his attention to one so pretty.

Every afternoon, during the heat of the day, when even the drone of insects stilled, everyone retired to their rooms for a rest. Perched on a windowsill, Cornelia noted the gardener snoozing under a hibiscus bush. She quickly sketched the curl of his body, and the contrast of his white turban to the gleam of the dark green leaves. A knock on their door announced the major domo, a grand mustachioed gentleman with a towering turban. He told them that madam requested for them to "dress" for dinner. Hadji's mother had arranged for a special concert of Indian music to be held out on the veranda after dinner.

Anasuya spent hours getting ready. Pulling out a small bottle of coconut oil, first she oiled her skin, then her hair. After plaiting it, she coiled it into a bun. She smudged kohl around her eyes until they floated like deep dark pools of water in the golden planes of her face. She replaced the simple gold stud in her nose with a small glittering ruby, and then carefully unfolded her red and gold silk sari, the one Deeba had insisted she bring.

After closing the shutters from the now blasting heat, Cornelia lounged on the divan, reading a copy of *The Jungle Book* that she had found in Hadji's library. Glancing up every so often, she marveled at the patient care Anasuya took with her adornment, as if her body was a temple and she the priestess given the task to anoint it.

It seemed to Cornelia that she was the opposite: more goal-directed, always rushing to the next step, reading a book, drawing a picture, spending endless hours studying and analyzing other people. Unless she was walking, she was rarely just quiet with her own thoughts. "I envy you," she finally said.

"Indeed, how can that be?" Anasuya's finely arched eyebrows rose even higher, "it seems to me that you have everything."

"But you have a talent for just being. I lack that, I think."

Her brow furrowed as she thought about what Cornelia had said. "Perhaps it is because, from a very early age, I was taught to accept things. Our tradition is, as you know, a karmic one. What we have been given, we must accept." She glanced at herself in the mirror. Her adornment seemed to have little to do with vanity. Her beauty was just one of those things she accepted as part of her being. It was a way of esteeming that with which she had been blessed.

Perhaps, Cornelia thought to herself, if she could have had that same attitude about modeling, she might not have hated it so much. Perhaps if she could have maintained her center, her composure if you will, the endless fawning, competing, back-biting and comparing that went on in the industry would not have so exhausted and disgusted her.

Anasuya perched on the divan next to her. "Are you not going to get ready at all?" she asked. Her head cocked to one side with an expression of perplexity.

"Oh, I'll throw something on," Cornelia said. "I was just wondering. Why don't you wear a bindi? I should think it would look good on you."

Many women in India marked a red circle just above and between their eyebrows. She had been told it signified the position of the third eye of consciousness, which intrigued her.

Anasuya blushed and her eyes looked down and away. "Perhaps I shall never wear a bindi."

"Why not? I bet it would look beautiful on you. Ridiculous on me, but gorgeous on you."

"Are you Americans always so brash?" Her eyes flashed, signifying that Cornelia had once more offended her in some way.

"I'm sorry," she said. "Did I say something wrong?"

Anasuya looked astonished. "Did you not know that the bindi is usually worn only by married women?"

"I'm sorry, I did not." She closed her book, went over to the foot of the bed where she pulled herself into a cross-legged position. "Anasuya, you must forgive me. I *am* sorry for everything you know. I truly don't mean to hurt you. Honestly."

They were silent for a long moment as the unspoken truth of Hadji vibrated between them.

"It is perhaps karma that it was not meant to be. I must accept that." Anasuya rose from the pillow and pulled her feet up into a cross-legged position that mirrored Cornelia's. They faced each other, but Anasuya's fingers picked nervously at the fraying gold embroidery on her sari. Cornelia wondered how old the sari was, and whether it had belonged to her mother or even, perhaps, a grandmother. Zaina had told her that though Anasuya's family was Brahmin, which was a high caste, in fact they were as poor as temple mice. Anasuya sighed. But then, with that flash of bad temper that surfaced quite often in the last few days, her chin rose in defiance, and she snapped at Cornelia. "But how can it be? It is not as if you two can actually marry, you know."

"Why not?"

"His mother would never allow it. That's why. It could never happen. You are not one of us."

Fear nibbled at her heart. "Perhaps not." Her lips tightened.

"But what am I thinking?" Anasuya danced her shoulders and a cloak of brightness fell over her. She clapped her hands and hopped off the bed. "You *must* look pretty yourself tonight. I have been so selfish, so caught up in my own misery. And we are meant to be Absolutely unselfish, aren't we? And now look, I have managed to make you feel sad as well." She waggled her head. "We must both do better than that. We must rise to the occasion and do our best. Yes indeed."

She went over to their shared chest of drawers, pulling them open to see what Cornelia had to wear. "Oh no," she said, "this will not do. Your lavender tunic is all stained. Your green one should have gone out in the wash this morning. This *will not do.*" Without another word, she left the room.

Cornelia sighed, rolled off the bed and went into the bathroom to slap on some blush, mascara, and lip-gloss. She scrutinized her reflection. Her weeks in the hills with little sunshine had made her complexion very pale. The blush popped on her cheeks like a clown's, so she rubbed it off. And the pink lip-gloss looked fake and too bright, so she rubbed that off as well. There was nothing she could do to change her too-large mouth, severely slanted cheekbones, and prominent jawbone. Only the mascara worked to help her feel pretty, defining her almond-shaped black eyes in the ivory hexagon of her face.

When she came out a few minutes later, the bed was arrayed with a wild selection of bright silk saris and a pleased Anasuya stood proudly next to the bed. "You should feel honored. His mother has offered these for your use."

Cornelia took hold of her hand, willing herself to be gentle. "Listen to me. I appreciate your thought but honestly, saris just won't work for me. I'm afraid of all the pleats. I'd just stumble and feel an awkward mess."

"Truly?" Anasuya asked, looking hurt. "For us it is second nature."

Cornelia tried to make it better, "Are there any kurtas in here?" She waved her hand at all the silks on the bed.

Anasuya shook her head, "His mother is too traditional to wear the salwar kameez. That form of dress is considered Punjabi, you know. Not at all the thing for a proper South Indian lady."

"Oh, I see." As if she were sinking ever deeper into mud, she realized that if she didn't wear the proffered saris, she would probably offend Hadji's mother. So she shuffled through the pile once more. She chose a simple pale pink silk, but the blouse top was too narrow to fit around her, and the tailored area for the breasts was way too big. She held one up against her and then, to her immense relief, Anasuya giggled.

"That wouldn't do, would it?"

"No," she shook her head, "not at all."

And so, a few minutes later, when they made their entrance into the elegant formal parlor where Hadji, his mother and a score of guests were chattering, the contrast between the two young women was stark.

There was Anasuya, resplendent in red and gold silk, tiny and perfect, a lush golden idol of a girl, with eyes that tilted up at the corners like those of a goddess. Her mincing steps swung her full hips from side to side. Every part of her was curvy and rounded.

And then there was Cornelia. She wore her favorite white kurta tunic with tight men's leggings. It was freshly starched and pressed and crackled as she took her long steps. Everything about her was sharp angles and edges. But she had washed her hair earlier in the afternoon and let it air dry into long ropy waves that meandered down over her shoulders and across her back, and she knew the tendrils shone like gold in sunshine. It was to her, from across the room, that Hadji's eyes first went and lingered. His mother did not fail to notice.

She crossed over to them, but her greeting was abrupt. "I see, Cornelia, you preferred *not* to wear our more traditional dress. I thought I might tempt you with bright color. Though I do understand you are in mourning. Sadly," she turned to a group of guests standing nearby, "Cornelia has recently lost her father in a terrible car accident." She turned back to her, but whispered loud enough for Anasuya to hear, "I thought a little color perhaps would cheer you up and certainly do something to brighten up your skin." She reached up to pinch her cheek. Cornelia wanted to swat her hand away but restrained herself.

She glanced at Hadji for help, but he had turned back to a conversation with a very large woman reclining on a divan who was stroking his hand as if it were a fine piece of satin. And so Cornelia did her best. She raised her hands into the prayer position and bowed toward his mother, "I do so appreciate the offering. Alas, the saris did not fit. But thank you for thinking of me."

"Of course," she said and turned away, leaving Cornelia standing awkwardly by the entrance while she dragged Anasuya by the hand, taking her across to a group of women dressed in sari colors as bright as parrots. The display of gold jewelry dazzled. "Doesn't she just look exactly like our classical carved goddesses in the Ajanta caves?" Anasuya blushed at the reference, but let the women cluck over her and fondle her hands and face.

Standing alone, Cornelia spied the woman she thought might be the poetess musician who had traveled many long hours from Madras just for the concert this evening. She sat cross-legged on the floor near the main entrance. Her lips moved as if she were quietly reciting poetry. She had a braid so long that it fell down her back then twisted around in front to clasp her waist. Her fingers played with the end strands as if they were frets, and her other hand drummed out a syncopated beat on her thigh. Cornelia felt inspired by her calm self-possession. She took a deep breath and, instead of fretting about what to do, took the opportunity to study the room.

The room was very large, perhaps sixty feet long and twenty feet wide, spreading the whole length of one side of the bungalow, built in the 1920s for Hadji's grandfather. Furnished in an odd amalgamation of British colonial style mixed with more traditional Indian furniture, stiff Victorian settees stood side by side with divans.

As massive as a manatee, the woman with whom Hadji talked lounged on one of these divans. A plate of spiced nuts and chocolate candies sat next to her on a tiny brass table with carved legs. Her hand, as steady as a metronome, kept moving both condiments into her mouth. A white turbaned servant stood nearby, ever ready to replenish the plate. She spied Cornelia looking at her and waved imperiously for her to come over.

Out of her peripheral vision, she was well aware that as Hadji watched her walking toward him, his mother's head snapped in her direction.

"This is my Aunt Reena," Hadji stood up to welcome her. "My mother's younger sister." She crouched down next to the large woman who took her hand, stroked it, then dropped it to pop another chocolate into her mouth. "Hadji was right, you are a wonder, so tall and strong and beautiful, like a triumphant Diana who comes striding out of the woods."

She tried to thank her, but the tirade of words kept coming, "He tells me you're also wonderfully intelligent and reading all the time. We *must* talk books; I have no one to talk books with. I am so lonely for intellectual companionship, you know, you must *promise* to come visit me as soon as you can, and we will have very long talks about Jane Austen and George Eliot," she clapped her hands, then grabbed and swallowed a handful of nuts before continuing. "They are absolutely my favorites – the English novelists – they do so capture drawing room conversation which, as you can see, is also one of our favorite Indian activities. Talk and eat, talk and eat," she laughed heartily. "Two activities I definitely approve of, as you can see." She cheerfully gestured to her corpulent body. "So you will promise to come? Very soon." She patted Cornelia's hand.

Hadji gently pried Cornelia's hand out of Aunt's Reena's grasp. "Aunt Reena, I must take Cornelia to visit others now. I promise we shall come to pay a visit. Very soon."

Aunt Reena grabbed both his hands in hers and implored him. "You must promise to come. I am so alone, you know. No husband, no children, only my sisters for company and they ignore me as much as possible. Speaking of my sister," and suddenly her tone was sharp, "children, you must also promise me, both of you, not to take her disapproval too seriously. She counts too much on Hadji, don't you see, it would be good for her to have to share him with a wife. You listen to me now, you hear?" She shook her finger at them. Cornelia saw a drool of chocolate fall down to stain the rich brocade of her sari.

Hadji led her across the large salon, where an elderly man dressed in white with a Nehru cap nestled on his bald head huddled next to a tiny porcelain stove. He was an esteemed politician, retired now, Hadji said, but a wonderful reader of books. Hadji pulled up a tufted ottoman so she could sit close to the man then, with a gentle pat on her shoulder, Hadji moved off to a group of men who greeted him with great shouts of laughter. One of them called out they had just "bagged" a leopard that very afternoon.

The old man studied her. She half expected him to pull out a magnifying glass. He asked whether she minded the fire. She said she did not. He said his bones were so old that they needed fire to keep them moving. She laughed. He asked what she was reading. She mentioned R.K. Narayan, a South Indian novelist whose books she had just discovered in Hadji's library. He clapped his hands. "He was the very best at depicting South Indian life."

Minutes later, Hadji's mother tapped her on the shoulder with a fan, "You are monopolizing our most honored guest, that is not allowed. Go now and let someone else take your place." She tinkled with laughter, but it was clear her desires were not to be crossed. Cornelia dutifully went across the room and studied the portraits of Hadji's ancestors.

She fast moved on from endless numbers of dour looking couples posed stiffly against black backgrounds to a colorful portrait of a smiling gentleman dressed all in golden brocade with a giant turban encrusted with huge rubies and emeralds. At his feet curled a tiger, behind him stood a painted elephant and in the mid-distance shone a lake lined with willow trees. Hadji came up beside her.

"What do you think?"

She clapped her hands, "I love this. The landscape is a perfect miniature. It's like the wonderful Italian hills you see in the background of da Vinci's paintings. Not the main focal point, but delightful nonetheless."

"Typical," his mother trilled from across the room. "Why is it Americans always go for the one of the Maharajah?"

Hadji held his finger up to his lips and shook his head ever so slightly. "Doesn't matter," he whispered, "let it run off you like water off a duck. What matters is what I think, and I think you are as perfect as can be, a Renaissance maiden indeed, but perhaps, with your golden tresses, more a Titian than a da Vinci I would say."

She smiled up at him and let the barbs roll off her without sticking.

A turbaned servant came in with a dinner gong. They trailed into the high-ceilinged dining room where more portraits lined the walls and the long narrow table was covered with white linen, heavy silver polished to a sheen, and fine Limoges porcelain. Behind each chair was a turbaned footman. Cornelia was embarrassed to realize that, with their long starched-white tunics and leggings, she was dressed more like a man and a servant than anything resembling a lady.

In the last few days, she had been amazed at how many people there were in the house to cater to just the few of them. No matter how often she counted, there always seemed to be a new servant popping up in every corner.

The sweepers came in at dawn, crouching down onto their haunches and using tiny brooms to pick up every bit of dust that had fallen overnight. Then there was the wallah, who dropped a tea tray just outside their door as the grandfather clock in the hall struck half-past six. The kitchen held several cooks; one squatted next to the charcoal braziers on the floors; others chopped vegetables on the steps leading out to the garden. And there were at least three women who did the laundry and made the beds. But none of them spoke to her, only nodding their heads when she greeted them. Hadji had explained that they all only spoke the local dialect.

"You must be rich," she had said to Hadji.

"Hardly," he smiled, "Every house in India comes with its resident servants. They would be bereft if we asked them to leave. They've been with us for generations." To him, his explanation seemed obvious, but for her it had raised more questions than it had answered. She had much to learn about Hadji's world.

When she leaned over her shoulder to thank the man who had pushed in her chair, she noted that the man seated next to her at the dinner table appeared shocked as if it were improper for her to even notice the servants at all.

The dinner went by with an endless array of curries, all of them delicious. She chatted with the man to her left and found out he was the local pharmacist for the family. The man to her right was a clerk in an attorney's office. "Quite obviously," he stuttered, "I am thrilled to be invited to such an elegant gathering as this."

It seemed she had been placed between two family retainers, not between anyone important, which was fine by her because at least they were friendly. Hadji had been seated at one end of the table, between his Aunt Reena and an unknown matron with silver hair and an extraordinary array of jewels glittering her neck, every finger, and up her forearms. His mother presided over the other end of the table, surrounded by dignitaries.

The dinner went along without incident until suddenly, with her voice ringing out like a bell from her far end of the table, Hadji's mother said brightly to her neighbor, "Of course it *is* lovely, but honestly don't you think the color must be from a bottle? They say all American girls use Clairol. In fact. doesn't their ad campaign say, 'Does she or doesn't she? Only she herself knows for sure?'" She called out to her, "Cornelia darling, do tell us, do you actually dye your hair to get that wonderful brass color? We promise not to tell if you divulge your secret."

Cornelia forced herself to smile then turned her head away, pretending that the man to her left had said something, hoping to hide the flare of outrage that crimsoned her face and ears.

After dinner, they convened out on the veranda for tea, plates of sweets and music. The poetess musician had piled up pillows on the shining concrete floor to make a cushion for herself. Her traditional instrument, called a veena, Anasuya told her, was cradled in her lap, one giant gourd stretched beyond her crossed legs, the long-fretted neck lay across her lap, and, at the other end, a decorative silver gourd with feet kept the five-foot-long instrument grounded. Her fingers flew over the frets, her other hand plucked at the strings and her voice whined high, as she spun endless ragas, all in Hindi.

The elderly lounged on divans, those who were more youthful, like Cornelia, sat on cushions on the floor around the musician. Those on the far reaches of the veranda never stopped chattering. Others listened for a while then moved off, but Cornelia chose to stay close to the source of music. She wished Hadji would come sit next to her, but he was again deep in conversation with another group of men.

The haunting sound of the musician's lilting voice rising and falling to the counterpoint of the howling drone of the veena was mesmerizing but alien. The sound whirled around in her brain, tingling so deep into her inner ear, and resonating inside her in such a deeply strange way that finally, she closed her eyes to listen better.

The sharp rap of a fan on her shoulder startled her eyes open. Hadji's mother was leaning down over her, and it was not a pretty sight. Gravity pulled her face down into an angry mask. Cornelia felt frightened. There was no longer any music. Had she fallen asleep?

His mother tittered then stood back up and her face slid back into its more genial expression. She smiled around at her guests. "Would it be fair to say that our young visitor from the West was so bored by our ancient Carnatic music that she fell sound asleep? Is that a fair assessment?" She looked around to the others for approval.

Sitting quite near her, Anasuya smiled and shrugged her shoulders. "Perhaps so."

Cornelia sprang to her feet. "No indeed, I was fascinated. Truly. I've never heard anything like it. It was just that ..." She trailed off.

"It put you to sleep."

"You're not being fair now, mother. You can't expect her to understand all our ways." Hadji had come to quietly stand next to her. "She's more familiar with Western music."

His mother drew her tiny body up as if his gentle chastisement had injured her. Her sari was richly embroidered, but the purple silk matched the circles beneath her eyes, and the egg-sized amethyst that hung down into her cleavage only exaggerated the pleated skin.

Insight bolted into Cornelia. His mother was jealous of her, of her youth, of Hadji's obvious attachment; all her acting out just proved it rather than otherwise. "Certainly, our Western culture has little to offer compared to the vast depth of the history here in this continent."

His mother tinkled. "Yes, you are certainly right." She held out her hands as if she held scales, "Let's see, three thousand years of a musical culture emanating from the divine. Compared to what? Three hundred years of your Western classical music."

"Well, there are Gregorian chants," Cornelia said. "They're very old."

His mother snorted, "Oh the monks, our monks have been around millenniums longer."

The barb stuck. "Well, how about jazz and blues and calypso and all sorts of wonderful music? You can't think all of that amounts to nothing?" To her horror her voice had turned shrill. She hated that she had been goaded into an argument.

"Oh, jazz. Blues. Negro music," his mother sniffed, looking victorious. "I don't suppose you'd be willing to share some of that with us, now would you?" Her eyes narrowed.

"Nee Nee," said Hadji, "You don't have to do this."

"Yes, I do!" She wheeled away from his sheltering hand. "Here, *this* is a song from where I grew up. They used to sing it when they were pulling in their nets far out to sea, and they were missing their wives and children. It may not have three thousand years of history behind it, but it has heart and soul." And she spread her feet apart, took a deep breath and launched into a wailing ditty that she had learned from the fishermen in the Bahamas.

The song had the slow rhythm of an ocean swell and it had to be sung at a lower range to replicate the mournful howl of the west wind in the riggings. She let the notes start low, thrumming them in her chest and then sliding them up into her throat until they came out rich and strong and perhaps, in hindsight, quite loud and startling.

Years later, she would come to understand just how outlandish her voice must have sounded. Most female singing voices in Asia are vaulted up into the higher octaves and have a high-pitched nasally whine. Her own low contralto must have sounded, to them, like a bellowing cow.

Anasuya covered her mouth; but the sound of her stifled giggle evoked a snort from the woman next to her. A man guffawed then coughed. Eyes glittering with triumph, Hadji's mother was the first to throw back her head and openly laugh.

Cornelia stopped singing. She squared her shoulders. When the laughter died down, an awkward silence filled the room. Cornelia waited for a beat, then spoke, carefully measuring her words out. "We may not have the thousands of years of history behind us that you have. But my mother taught me to believe in common courtesy to strangers. And my father taught me to believe that all people are absolutely deserving of love. Tonight, you have showed no evidence of either."

She heard a few gasps. His mother quivered as if she'd been struck. And then everyone was again horribly silent, except for a mild clapping from one corner of the porch.

Without meeting anyone's eye, Cornelia stalked from the room.

| 16 |

Cornelia charged down the steps and into the garden, striding down the long lawn toward the river where the moon rolled out a glittering pathway across the water. She wished she could walk out across its shining spangles and up into the sky. As soon as the chastising words to his mother had come out of her mouth, she had regretted them. Did one sting deserve another? No, she did not think so. She had been provoked, to be sure. But hadn't she acted in an equally reprehensible manner? Hadn't her father and Horace Baker taught her to turn the other cheek, to bear insult with dignity? She felt ashamed.

It helped to keep walking, deeper and deeper into the garden, until she reached that mossy cavernous cliff where orchids trailed, and butterflies danced in the day. But it was night, and the moonshine only flickered weakly down through the thick canopy of blooming camellias. Though, as she looked above, the white flowers glowed like pearls in dark water. She fumbled her way to the concrete bench, sat down and folded her knees into her chest, hugging herself close, rocking ever so slightly.

She must have finally nodded off because the sound of approaching footsteps startled her. She was curled up on her side and, though the night was warm, she was stiff and achy from the damp air. The moon had set, and the dark was dense.

He stood quietly some feet away. His white shirt glowed in the starlight and so did the whites of his eyes. The rest of him was shadowed and she could not read his expression.

The silence vibrated.

She knew it was Hadji because, in the thick humidity, his scent floated across to her. She loved the way he smelled: spicy and citrusy with a slight underlying musk. But tonight, there was a new aroma. Something acrid. It reminded her of the scent on a dog who had just survived an attack from a much larger animal.

Finally, she spoke first. "It's not going to work, is it?" her voice trembled.

"If you say so."

"Oh, don't be mean. I know I was horrible. I should have turned my cheek. But how can this work, Hadji? I just don't fit in."

"I don't want you to fit in. I want you to glory in your individuality. I just don't want you to crush my mother in the process."

"I've crushed her?"

"She is devastated. You wouldn't recognize her. You have to understand that beneath that façade of superiority is a weak and frightened woman. She feels terrible about what happened. She has admitted that she has behaved most abominably. And indeed, I found her behavior toward you despicable. But she has promised to apologize tomorrow if you will let her. And I have booked a noon railway journey for all of us to go to Madurai. It's a six-hour train ride. The three of you women will sit together in one compartment. And perhaps that enforced intimacy will allow some kind of rapprochement to develop."

She was dubious but kept silent, waiting for him to go on.

"And I am glad you are ready to acknowledge that your response to her provocation was also not right." His voice lowered from his original high-pitched tone that held a note of censure into a lower-register growl that sent shock waves through her.

Without thinking, she stood and crossed the distance between them. "You don't hate me?"

He groaned and pulled her close. "When you walked out, I thought you were never coming back. And my heart broke."

"You are part of me, Hadji," she whispered.

His mouth came down on hers and there was hunger and need in his kiss. Her heart raced, and her mind shut down and, as always, the rest of the world melted away. Then, as always, he gently pushed her away, holding her at arm's length, combing his fingers through her hair, trying to take away the sting of keeping her at a distance.

But this time, instead of humbly allowing him to maintain their separateness, she reached down and pulled her tunic up over her head, then stood, tall and proud. She never wore a bra and so her exposed breasts glowed in the starlight.

He sucked in his breath. "Nee Nee, we can't."

"We can and will," she said. "You know I am fierce. And this time I will not be denied."

He laughed, and the sound was croaky. He was silhouetted against the shining river behind him, and she had a hard time making out his expression. But he groaned and, as his lips pulled back, his teeth shone like pearls in dark water. As he stepped back toward her, the scent of night blooming flowers dizzied her, but intertwined in that heady fragrance was the sudden musk of him, spicy and warm. As if pepper blasted up into her nose, her senses sharpened.

Her blood raced, throbbing so hard in her lower belly that her knees buckled. With a sure swift movement, he scooped her up and her legs snapped around his waist. They settled each part against each other until they were joined, locked together. The cool night air crawled across her back but where their flesh touched it burned.

Fingers trembling, she fumbled at the buttons on his shirt, then with a grunt of frustration ripped at them and saw the mother of pearl buttons go flying like shooting stars into the dark. She pressed herself against him, melting into him until she knew not what part of her was hers and what was his. The world dropped away, and it was just the two of them joined together.

Then her spirit vaulted up through the sheltering trees, out into the nighttime skies, exploding into stars. Her head slumped down onto his chest as her racing heart skipped, then settled back down to a steady beat. She could feel his heart thudding against her, then stilling to her beat. She tucked her head under his head and clung to him.

Sound came slowly back.

Water lapping at the edge of the river.

A cricket, timid at first, then resoundingly loud just above their heads, which made them laugh.

Still holding her aloft he walked them over to the bench and lay down, bringing her on top of him. He stroked the length of her back. "You darling, you little darling." He kept saying it over and over until the litany changed to, "what have we done, you little darling. We shouldn't have done this."

"We should and did."

"That we did." And he laughed and the rumble in his chest was a delight to feel against her skin. And then his strokes deepened, and he kneaded at her flesh, running his hands up and down her body, finding the pulse points, splaying his hands out over the swell of her hips, as if he were both memorizing her and molding her all at the same time, grinding her against him. This time, as they came, they roared into each other's ears.

Three times more they joined and three times more they panted and recovered afterward, whispering sweet nothings, reassuring each other that all was well, that something so good could not be so bad after all. Finally, she dozed off in his arms. But she awoke a few minutes later when he carefully extricated himself and stood up, pulling her up toward him and whispering into her ear.

"My dear girl, we must go back. It is going on toward dawn. I hear the piping of early morning birds. We must go before we are found. I will not have you chastised further. Not at my expense."

And so they walked back, their arms wrapped around each other's waists until they came to the lawn, and they kissed one last time. His mouth was salty with tears. She reached up through the dark to find him crying. "What is it, my love?" she whispered.

"You are so beautiful to me, so very precious. I fear I have hurt us. Damaged us in some way."

"Never think that," she shook her head. "Please don't think that. Don't forget, I wanted you."

He chuckled then, "That you did. And now you have me."

"Yes," she said, and her tone was stern.

He touched his fingers to his lips and then to hers. "My fingers smell of you," he said. "I will lie in bed and think of you, my darling. Let us both go sleep now. Go ahead." He gave her a slight push toward the stairs leading up to the veranda. "Go now. And know that, in a few hours, we will see each other again."

She tiptoed up the stairs, blowing him one last kiss, then slinking down the hall to the room she shared with Anasuya, who mewed once when she pulled back the covers but did not awaken. Cornelia curled up with her back to her, putting as much space between them as she could. She hoped Anasuya would not recognize the smell of Hadji on her.

An emerald landscape swept by outside the train windows. Rows of bent-over women, their bright saris tucked up like billowing diapers, stood knee-deep in the silver waters of rice paddies. Off in the distance, a row of blue mountains hovered over a long, sloping alluvial plain across which the coal-burning train chugged.

Cornelia half hung out the window until a bit of coal dust bit into her eyeball. She jumped back into the compartment, falling back into the seat across from Anasuya and Hadji's mother. As her eye watered and flickered with a stabbing pain, Hadji's mother handed her a wet washcloth. She realized she still hadn't called her anything. She didn't know her first name and calling her Mrs. Nehru seemed more than awkward.

"Your face is as sooty as a chimney sweep," giggled Anasuya. She seemed better now that they had left Hadji's childhood home, less weighed down by a certain passive acceptance. Her natural good spirits were bubbling back up and Cornelia was glad. She wrinkled her nose at her and Anasuya laughed even harder.

Much to her chagrin a great deal of sooty grime came off onto the damp washcloth when she wiped her face. She smiled and nodded her thanks. 'Hadji's mother' it would have to be until someone told her to call her otherwise. From behind the shelter of the washcloth, she surreptitiously studied her.

Indeed, Hadji was right, she seemed shrunken. She had on a navy-
blue gauze cotton sari and wore no eye makeup. Without the bright
camouflage of silks and kohl, she looked a good twenty years older. Her
shoulders were hunched forward, and she was so tiny her feet hung
well off the floor. Although her eyes were closed, by the deep furrowed
look of her forehead, Cornelia didn't think she was asleep.

That morning, back in the house, she had slept in past the usual
teatime rising of 6:30 and was glad for it, because by the time she
dragged herself out of bed, Anasuya was gone. She had the bathroom
to herself to wash off the evening. Her clothes had been whisked away,
and she blushed to think what the washerwomen would make of all the
mud and grass stains on her white tunic and leggings. She hated to wash
off the scent of Hadji, but she needed to be squeaky clean before facing
anyone else. She even washed her hair again.

After she had downed a chapatti and a quick cup of tea for breakfast,
there had been a bustle of leave-taking. It took her no more than five
minutes of packing to be ready, but Hadji's mother fretted over what
seemed like an endless array of baskets of provisions. But now that
they were on the train, Cornelia realized, gratefully, that his mother
had prepared well. There were thermoses of hot tea, carefully wrapped
sandwiches, English tea biscuits, and this lovely warm, wet washcloth.

Every time the train chugged into a station – which was often, since
they were penetrating a part of the Southern plains of India where
there were few roads – they were soon surrounded by barkers, reaching
their hands up to the open windows, shrieking out that they had the
best curries and the "absolutely most ripest sweetest mangoes." Others
sang out the merits of their wares in a language she did not know.

His mother hung out the window, bartering with the sellers. But
most of the time, as the train slowly started back up, she sat back down
empty-handed.

"It's highway robbery what they want for their goods," she complained, shaking her head. "This is why I always try and bring fresh provisions along."

Along the corridor outside their private compartment, a steady stream of people passed, some carrying chickens, others with bunches of bananas and aromatic herbs. It seemed many people used this train to transport goods and animals to the city markets. But by far the largest number of passengers were pilgrims on their way to Madurai, all dressed, both men and women, in brilliant vermilion.

When the far front of the train was visible on a long curve, the splash of bright vermillion in contrast to the brilliant green of the fields made Cornelia gasp with pleasure. She was happy to be once more moving, drinking in the beauty of the world around her. Though she had had no alone time with Hadji yet today, the joy of their union from the night before still throbbed through her, and she was content.

That morning, Hadji had paced through the house in a state of manic energy. There was a problem brewing in Mumbai among the workers hired to print the new magazine, and he was preoccupied and on the phone until the last second before they left. Then he had sat in front next to the driver on the forty-five-minute drive to the train station, yammering away to the man in the local dialect.

His mother shook her head, "Hadji never stops. He must save every soul he sees. He's always been that way. Bringing home beggar children because they were hungry. Fixing the broken wings of birds. Forming a school down in the mango orchard where he taught the servant's children how to read. He cried when there were riots between the Muslims and Hindus in the streets of New Delhi. He has a heart big enough to take on the whole world, it seems."

She didn't look at her as she was saying this, but Cornelia knew the words were meant for her. And, in fact, her words evoked fresh anxiety. Would she be able to share him with the world? She didn't know. Anasuya looked enthralled, but his mother's description sobered her. Was she just another broken bird who needed fixing?

His mother had still not apologized to her as Hadji had said she would. But neither had Cornelia said anything. They were both courteous, even deferential, but the wounds, at least for Cornelia, still gaped, and she wasn't sure the rift could be patched.

"Speaking of Hadji," Cornelia asked, "where is he, do you know?" After making sure the three women were comfortable in their compartment, Hadji had disappeared, and it had now been several hours since they had seen him at all.

While asking the question, Cornelia tried to keep her face bland, but just the sound of his name crossing her lips made her loins quiver and her heart beat faster.

"I believe he's in the lounge car at the back of the train. As you must know by now, he likes to talk to the people." Hadji's mother's lips curled in distaste, "I never can face making my way through the stench of the third-class cars to get there. But if you girls would like to, be my guest."

"Anasuya?" Cornelia cocked her head, hoping she would say no.

"No indeed, I have no desire to face the riff-raff either," Anasuya made a moue as if the very thought were abhorrent. Hadji's mother nodded her approval.

Cornelia leapt to her feet and waved a cheerful goodbye. She loped down the corridor back through several first-class cars, loving the sway of the train, the roaring sound between the cars and the feel of the air rushing all around her. She entered the second-class cars where many rows of backless wooden benches were stacked full of people. Children scrambled across laps and tied up chickens lay next to bags of mangos. Squatting men played cards next to one of the doors. Bands of pilgrims hung out the windows, chanting and praying.

The benchless third-class cars were even more crowded. She pushed her way through throngs of people and Hadji's mother was right, the smells were ripe from unwashed bodies and clothing that was tattered and torn. Many of the women had scores of glass bangles on both arms and stacks of thick brass bangles around their ankles. Some had large, coined rings in their noses and glittering earrings so heavy that the lobes on the older women stretched inches long. She noticed that the skin on most of the people in third class was much darker than second or first class. Many of the men had red-rimmed eyes and seemed stoned. One of the older women smiled at her and her teeth were stained a blackish red from chewing betel berries.

Finally, she came to the entrance to the lounge car where a turbaned Sikh guarded the door. Though he clearly was meant to keep the third-class passengers out, he bowed and opened the door for her. She stood a minute with the door against her back and looked around.

This was a different world. The air swirled with tobacco smoke so thick that it was hard to see to the other end of the car. It took her a moment to realize that the windows were closed, and that this was the only car with air conditioning.

Other than a few matrons dressed in sober blue-grey saris, the car was filled with men. Many of them clustered around oval tables, tapping the ashes of their cigars into heavy cut-glass ashtrays sunk down into holes. Waiters ran back and forth with frosted beers and pots of tea. Several bottles of whiskey stood on one table where a man shuffled and dealt cards to the other men seated around him.

Down at the far end, she saw Hadji crouched down next to a portly gentleman with a high Sikh turban into which his pulled-back beard disappeared. He was tapping his fingers on the table as he listened to Hadji, but his countenance was not showing any evidence of impatience. Evidently whatever Hadji was so seriously imparting held his interest.

As if her gaze touched him on the shoulder, she saw Hadji pause then look back over his shoulder to see her standing at the far end of the car. His black eyes bore into hers and a bolt of fire seemed to dance between them. He stopped talking, jumped to his feet and strode toward her.

"Nee Nee," he said as he drew near. "You found me." He smiled broadly, and her heart leapt to see how pleased he was. "Come, come with me, you must see something wonderful." And he took her hand and drew her back down toward the back of the train. He tapped the portly Sikh on the shoulder as he passed, "Mahatma, we shall certainly at some point continue this discussion as to whether the souls of men or your racehorses are more important. No doubt you are right, the horses are already finer and purer than most men. But that is why I must work so hard to save the men." Hadji waggled his head and the Sikh burst out laughing.

He led the way out of the lounge car and then through an elegant dining room resplendent with silver and crystal laid out on starched white linen. Several richly dressed families picked carefully at their food as they passed. They went out the dining car with a whoosh, then down a corridor past the kitchens, steaming hot and filled with wonderful smells. All the kitchen men nodded and smiled at Hadji as they passed. It appeared they all knew him already. Finally, they came to the end of that car, then crossed over to another. A long corridor ran next to compartments filled with bunks where servants lay sleeping. "The night shift," said Hadji, nodding his head toward them. "And the extra porters for the deluxe sleepers. Each of them has their own crew."

"Where are we going?" she asked.

"You'll see." The train lurched, they bumped thighs and she had to hang onto him to keep from falling. His large hands landed at her waist, and he tightened his grip and looked deeply into her eyes, "I will never forget last night." His voice was low and very intense. "Never. I may live to regret it, but forget it? Never. Come. It's just a little farther."

They entered another air-conditioned car, paneled in marquetry and with beveled-glass windows all along one side. As they walked down the corridor, they passed five closed doors on the right. Through the one open door, she saw a very old woman with her feet up on a stool, looking out the far window. Hadji said this fancy car housed six deluxe sleepers, exclusively for the very proud and very rich.

"God forbid that any foul smell reaches the nostrils of the rich," Hadji said.

She laughed. She marveled at the way he understood so much about the frailty of mankind and yet could make fun of it as well. It was one of the things she most loved about him.

He pulled her by the hand down to the end of that car where there was a door with a window. Hadji carefully opened it and just outside, there was a small terrace with a railing.

"Look," Hadji said grandly, "isn't it wonderful?" His hand swept out to include the entire world. "Birds and animals look ahead to see where they're going. But only humans look behind to see where we've been."

Beneath them the tracks clattered, then stretched away behind, silver parallel strips gradually merging into the far-off distance.

He looked solemn. His fierce eyebrows almost collided. He cupped her chin and lifted it up, gently forcing her to look at him. "Nee Nee, we must not let what happened last night happen again until we are married. God may forgive us one transgression but how can I hold my head up and preach about Absolute purity if all I can think of is your lovely breasts, so beautiful, so round, so perfect for plucking." And then his head went down to her neck, and he groaned, "What am I going to do with my fierce little goddess?"

She laughed, "Fierce maybe, but little and a goddess, hardly."

The next few hours went by in a wonderful whirl. They stayed out on that narrow back terrace of the train, glad to be alone. They talked of nothing and of everything. They discussed where they might have a wedding. Though she assured him she could handle a three-day Indian wedding, Hadji preferred the thought of Switzerland, thinking it might be a good thing for her to have some family and friends of her own attending. She dared to tell him that she didn't have much of a family and few people she counted as friends. He laughed out loud.

"That will change," he said. "You will never be alone again. I can promise you that."

Strangely, these words didn't comfort her. She felt a chill at the thought of never being alone again. But when she looked up at him, such warmth emanated from his eyes that she melted. Words became meaningless because it was the touch that mattered. Not that they kissed or even hugged; it was more her hand alighting quickly on a dark-haired wrist, or her daring to rake back the sweep of his hair, or his carefully extricating a tendril of her hair that had caught in her mouth. The tiny caresses were, in many ways, more reassuring than kisses.

Finally, they realized they must go back to find his mother and Anasuya. And together they made the journey back through the deluxe sleeping car, past the kitchen cars, through the dining and lounge cars and all the way back up through all the various classes to where his mother was.

The way back took a long time because Hadji kept stopping to call out a hello, to pat a shoulder, to chuck a baby under its chin, to join in a chant, to grab a mango from a pile and feign astonishment that the man wanted to be paid while slipping his wife a bank note. And she loved him all the more for all of it.

As soon as they reached the compartment, it became apparent that something terrible had happened. Hadji's mother's face was pinched, and she was literally wringing her hands. Anasuya was curled up in a corner, her eyes all swollen. Before they could ask what was wrong, his mother assaulted Hadji.

"What is wrong with you?" The venom in her attack made the hairs on the back of Cornelia's neck bristle. Unpleasant goose bumps prickled her arms.

"Calm yourself, Mother, just exactly what are you talking about?"

"Were you aware that this lovely child's parents think this is a betrothal trip?" She waved her hand at Anasuya who cringed away, sneaking guilty looks toward Hadji.

"What are you talking about?" Hadji's brow was furrowed.

"What were you thinking? Bringing her along with us on this pilgrimage when you knew that her parents had hoped you would be a son-in-law one day? Anasuya has told me about the astrological readings that matched the two of you, and how this has raised the hopes of her impoverished parents. How could you do this to this lovely child? How could you do this to *me?*" She wailed and yanked her hair out of its prim bun until it hung lank and oily around her face. She shrieked, "What is the matter with you? What were you thinking?"

"Mother, calm down, please," Hadji held out his hands in a calming gesture. She slapped at them, and Cornelia saw the rise of color in Hadji's cheeks. He cleared his throat and spoke clearly and deliberately.

"What was I thinking? I was thinking that Nee needed a chaperone so that all would know that everything was aboveboard."

"Cornelia needs a chaperone?" Her voice was shrill with scorn. "Here's a woman who travels alone without her family, who has already lost a baby, and you care about her reputation? Really and truly?" Her tone was withering.

"I am so sorry," whispered Anasuya. "I told her about the baby."

Cornelia felt her head spinning and the words swirled around in her head as if bees were buzzing near her ears and threatening to sting her multiple times at any second. She slumped down onto the seat and thought she might vomit.

"Get her out of here," his mother screeched, waving her hand at Cornelia, "get her out of my sight. To think that you would have let this poor lovely girl Anasuya be so humiliated when she arrived in Madurai. It's beyond me how you could have been so callous."

"What do you mean 'so humiliated' when she arrives in Madurai?" Hadji looked startled.

"You didn't think I would take this sitting down, did you? No indeed, I have not waited so long for grandchildren to have both myself and a lovely virgin publicly humiliated. No indeed. At the last station stop, I slipped out and made a few phone calls in the office there. Anasuya's parents and others have been alerted. They will be in Madurai to greet us." She raised her head and the bereft woman disappeared as she raised her hands and swiftly coiled her hair back into a tight bun. She slapped her hands together. "We shall see what happens now."

"Come, Cornelia. This is your bag, is it not?" Hadji's words were clipped. She could tell by the tight line of his lips and his stiffly held posture that he was furious but refusing to make a scene. He held out one hand to her and then reached the other up to where her leather satchel sat on a shelf. She allowed him to lead her outside.

They went and stood together down at one end of the car. Cornelia felt as if she couldn't breathe. He stood over her, his body trembling ever so slightly, his fingers stroked back her hair and his thumbs went into the corners of her eyes where he wiped away the tears. She panted as her heart raced. Black spots swirled in front of her eyes.

"Listen to me: this doesn't matter. Truly it does not. We can shake the dust off our sandals and face the future together. Alone, if need be. If they are not with us, then they are against us. I am not frightened. And I don't want you to be."

"But it's your mother." Her voice trembled.

"She's sad and lonely and jealous and her powers are fading. Once, this might have worked with me. But her tantrums no longer control me, Nee. My higher power is the one I answer to, not her. Have no fear, my love, I am with you."

She reached up and curled her hands up under his chin and let him pull her in close and they stood for long moments together, letting their hearts settle down, until they both stopped trembling and their breathing slowed. Their hearts began to beat as one. She could feel the boundaries blur between them. He was the missing puzzle piece of her. She let much of her body weight lean into him and felt at peace.

"My love," he whispered. "My little love. I have loved you from the moment you ran past me so many years ago."

She looked up into his shining eyes and sighed. "We belong to each other."

"We do."

They held each other close and laughed and wept. "We will never be apart again," he promised. And they both thought, at that wonderful moment, that all would be well.

Yet, an hour later, when their train chugged into the train station in Madurai, they were literally torn apart.

As with all Indian train platforms, thousands of people waited on the platform. Cornelia felt a chill creep over her as she saw broad smiles on the waiting faces and hands raised in greeting as the train slowly moved past them. At first it didn't compute, but then she realized they were chanting her lover's name. The chill ran cold, and she started to shake.

"Hadji! Hadji!" the thousands chanted. Even before the train came to a complete stop, men were rushing up the stairs toward them. A frisson of adrenaline went through Cornelia as she turned and saw a horde of smiling men charging toward them from the other end of the corridor.

| 17 |

The year before, Hadji had walked across the entire width of southern India from the silver shores of Cochin, up over the mountains, through the tea plantations, past elephants clearing fields and down across the fertile plains to Madurai. Along the way, he had collected thousands of followers. And when he had arrived in Madurai with this raggedy band behind him, the city elders had sat up and noticed, asking him to speak to the populace from a podium set up in the soccer stadium. His face appeared on billboards. Women swooned as he spoke. Thousands lined up to have just a few words with him. And now the word had spread quickly through his followers that not only was Hadji returning to their city, but that he was making a pilgrimage to the temple with his bride to be.

Cornelia knew none of this when his followers charged onto the train. She saw only what looked to be a mob running at full speed down the corridor toward them. Frightened, she turned back toward Hadji, but he was smiling broadly at the approaching men. More unsettling, his eyes glowed with that same warmth that, just moments before, she had foolishly, it seemed, thought that only she evoked.

A corpulent man, his dark skin glossy with sweat, bumped her aside and embraced Hadji. "This is wonderful news, Hadjisan! You are to be married. Where is the beautiful bride to be?" He waggled his head from side to side. He bared large yellow teeth. Hadji lifted his eyebrows and cocked his head in Cornelia's direction but, as the man turned, he looked past her and beamed even wider at the sight of several middle-aged matrons pulling a blushing and protesting Anasuya out of the compartment at the other end of the car. Hadji's mother was smiling and beaming.

Cornelia had time to see her send one triumphant look down her way before a group of pushing men and women stampeded in from the other end of the car, behind where Hadji was standing. They swept him off his feet and surrounded him, pushing her aside.

As the crowd pressed in from both sides, Cornelia was lifted off her feet, not by embracing arms, but by the sheer press of bodies smashing into each other from opposite directions.

First the mob surged in one direction. Then abruptly back in the other. She felt herself slipping down and feared she would be trampled, but then the momentum squeezed her back up again and past an open train compartment.

She grabbed at the doorjamb. Her shoulder yanked, and she almost let go. But then, just as suddenly as it had come, the mob flowed past and she was ejected onto the floor, still holding on to the doorjamb. She slowly drew herself up to a standing position. And stood there, trembling, panting, trying to catch her breath and slow the beating of her heart.

"That's it. Calm yourself," said a cultivated voice from inside the compartment. An elderly Indian gentleman looked over his spectacles at her. He was reading a newspaper. His eyes slipped from her face down to her feet. "You look like you've had quite a time of it. And don't mind my fellow Indians. The general populace always tends to get a bit hysterical when one of these religious fellows comes into town." He shook his head in disapproval. "But most likely it should quiet down in a bit, and we'll be able to disembark in peace. There he goes now."

She looked in the direction of his gaze and out the window saw Hadji being carried off on the shoulders of a clutch of men. She saw him cast one wild look back toward the train, but she could tell he couldn't see into the shadows of the train where she was standing.

Beyond him, farther down the platform, Anasuya was being carried aloft as well. Cornelia looked down at herself and snorted with rueful laughter. Her white tunic was an ashy grey from all the coal dust. Only now did she realize why all the women knew to wear navy blue saris on the train. Her hair was a wild tangle of wind snarls. And no doubt her face was smudged with ash, sweat, and tears.

It was no wonder no one had thought her a bride. Anasuya, with her carefully combed and oiled hair, her stunning classical beauty, and dressed tastefully in a traditional sari seemed a much more likely candidate for the job than this wild harridan of a westerner. Thank goodness she still had her leather satchel slung across her body. If that had been snatched away by the crowd, she would be without passport or credit cards.

She waited a minute for the corridor to clear of people, thanked her erstwhile companion for his "hospitality" then slipped out and trotted down the aisle toward the exit. She wasn't sure what she was going to do, but she knew she must follow Hadji. He had said their first stop was to pay a visit to the famed Menakshi temple, so that is where she would go.

There was pandemonium at the train station. People scrambled in all directions. Huge families carrying even larger bundles of textiles lumbered slowly toward the exits. Scattered throughout the crowd were bands of pilgrims dressed in vermilion. By the time she managed to make her way through the thousands of people walking every which way, Hadji and his followers were nowhere to be seen. They had dispersed seamlessly into the mass of people, like pouring water into a sink already full of water.

Outside the train station, a shallow staircase led down to a large plaza, packed with bullock carts carrying textiles, rickshaw drivers and a row of beggars who held out their hands in supplication. She hailed a rickshaw driver. He handed her up onto a platform built above his bicycle and they set off through the thronging streets. Anxiety threaded her veins with an unpleasant metallic sensation. Her heart beat so fast that she felt dizzy. Part of her was exhilarated at being alone in such an exotic place, and part of her was terrified she'd never find Hadji.

After ten minutes of being pedaled through the crowded streets, the temple loomed ahead. Several conical towers, hundreds of feet high, faced the street, their facades a wild cornucopia of orange and purple gods and goddesses intertwined with mythical animals in such a riotous profusion of limbs and color that her head spun.

She paid the rickshaw driver, then made her way through the throngs of pilgrims to the main entrance of the temple. An anteroom had shelves reaching to the ceilings all filled with shoes. A sign in English said no one was allowed to go into the temple with shoes on. As she sat down on a wooden bench to unstrap her leather sandals, a thin young man with thick glasses approached her.

"Cornelia?" His tone was tentative.

She looked up at him, nodding yes.

"Hadji has absolutely sent me to come find you. He has gone into the inner sanctum of the shrine with the priest, and he told me to come find you and bring you to where he is."

"Thank God," she whispered. She stood, took the ticket for her shoes then followed the young man, who said his name was Raj, into the first circle of the vast temple complex.

It took her breath away. At the foot of the twenty-foot-high walls that surrounded the entire compound, steps led down to a large sunken pool filled with swampy green water. Hundreds of people sat on the lowest steps, bathing their feet and bodies. In the pea green water, several women bobbed up and down, almost submerged, their saris floating up around them like giant flower petals blown off a tree. Old men with saggy bellies sloshed water up into their armpits and over their heads. At the far end of the pool, a group of chanting pilgrims waved their arms in jubilation. One woman danced. The sound of the bells on her ankles and fingers jingled through the air.

Around the compound, the three largest towers soared up several hundred feet, profusely encrusted with writhing gods and animals. The bottoms of the structure spread out like skirts, sheltering corridors that encircled the sacred inner shrines.

Raj beckoned to her, and they plunged into the darkened bottom of one of the towers. Each tower housed a sacred god. Raj led her into a shell-like whorl, each circle taking them ever deeper into the bowels of the temple. And all the while, a cacophony of color and people swirled around them.

The first circle was all about elephants: rows of stone elephants, many painted wooden elephants, and one real elephant, painted in gaudy colors with her eyelashes curled and her toenails done up in gold. The gentle sway of her body from side to side seemed to indicate a drugged state, but as Cornelia passed, the elephant's trunk snaked out and quickly touched Cornelia's forehead in blessing. She flashed a quick *namaste* to his mahout, who waggled his head in disapproval that she wasn't offering money.

A dark passageway led to another tower, and there it was all about flowers: stacks and stacks of marigolds braided into garlands that everyone was buying. Other stands sold long sticks of incense. The smoke swirled in great parabolas up into the gloomy depths of the towers.

Another tunnel corridor, lined with yard-high lingams, led them ever deeper into the inner sanctums. Bas-relief statues writhed on all the columns. Nearly naked priests sat cross-legged in a row of miniature temples. Giant painted animals, decorated with jewels and flowers, sat waiting to be carried through the streets at night where they would gather up the local gods to bring them back to the main temple to sleep.

As they went deeper, around and around, the air grew darker and ever thicker with potent incense. The chanting, which had been pleasing in the outer circles, drummed through the temple as if she were literally inside the heart of a giant.

"Ommmmm…namashivaya……ommmmm……namaaaashiv-aaaaya……Ommmmm…..namashivayaaaaaaa."

Pounding, thrumming, over and over, louder and louder, until her chest bone and heart pulsed in time with the chant.

Suddenly, dizzy, and nauseous, she came to a stop. She put her hand to her head and tried to breathe, but the chanting kept throbbing and she couldn't bring herself to think clearly.

Pointing toward a smoke-blackened arch, Raj said, "Just inside there is the *very* most inner sanctum, the most sacred place of all, the house of the *most* divine goddess. Hadji is *no* doubt there, consulting with the priest."

She lurched forward, determined to find Hadji as soon as she could. But Raj put up his hand and blocked her way. He waggled his head at her. "Perhaps it would be best to wait right here. You cannot join Hadji at this time."

"Why not?" She swallowed hard. "You said you came to fetch me."

"Well of course, indeed, you see," he hemmed and hawed, clearing his throat before blurting out, "you see, it is because you are indeed *not* a Hindu. Unless you are a Hindu, you see, you are not allowed into this innermost circle. *Only* Hindus can enter there. And *that* is where Hadji is right now."

"But you *said* he wanted me brought to him."

"Yes, indeed. But I myself cannot take you where he is. Indeed, I cannot." Sweat broke out in beads along his furrowed brow. "You will just have to wait, that is *all* you can do. I am so sorry." He waved his hand at her as if she might sting him.

A steady stream of pilgrims shuffled past, their hands held up in worship. Many of them threw back their heads with joy as they disappeared into the innermost sanctum. Others wept. She watched them pass by and then get snuffed up by the dark.

But she was not allowed to go.

She was on the outside.

On and on, all around her, chanting throbbed, filling every molecule of air until she felt suffocated. Thousands of people, all chanting the same thing at the same time. Each ommmmm thunked into her chest, piercing her with pain. She looked down at her chest wall, surprised there was no arrow deeply embedded there. The pain was so intense that finally it exploded out, and she opened up her mouth and howled. Then, ashamed at her outburst, she hung her head and sobbed.

"Oh no, now you are perturbed, and I am so sorry." Raj wrung his hands. "But I cannot do anything about it. I am not the one to make the rules. It is not allowed you see; you cannot go inside the final chamber. Only Hindus can go in."

"You already said that!" she snapped, jabbing at her tears. The sudden irritation allowed clarity to flood back into her. She could not see Hadji, but she knew what she would see: a man intensely worshipping, surrounded by his followers. He was just where he was supposed to be, and so was she.

She knew now what she had to do. She turned and began to stride back the way they had come.

"But where are you going?" Raj wailed. "Hadji will be furious with me when he finds out you have left. Where will he find you?"

She didn't bother to answer.

She strode back out the ever-widening circles, back to the fresh air, past the pools where a never-ending stream of pilgrims were bathing, past the room where young girls allowed priests to cut off their long plaits. She shook her wild mane out of its topknot to swing loose and wild and free.

Despite the wild cacophony of sound and sight all around her, the quiet voice inside sang loud and clear. *Hadji is not to be for you, and you are not to be for him. If you Absolutely love him, then you must let him go.*

She strode back past the long rows of lingams. Past the incense stands. Past the row of nearly naked priests. Past the stoned elephant. Past the flower stands. And as the chanting faded, pain no longer pierced her. And the quiet voice inside her sang its song. If she were absolutely honest, there was even a certain relief to letting go.

She found her way back to the entrance, where she retrieved her shoes before launching herself out into the heaving streets where she hailed a rickshaw.

Half an hour later, as the sun set behind green hills, she was around four kilometers out of town, winding up a sloping street lined with jacaranda trees. At the top of the hill sat an old colonial mansion, now a small luxury hotel. As she checked in, she slipped the desk clerk a twenty, then told him she was not to be disturbed, no matter what.

She followed the porter to a small cottage with a view of the city, humming with life even at this distance. She could see the towers of the temples rising above the smoky streets. She ripped off her sooty clothes and jammed them into the wastebasket. She took her wrinkled mauve salwar kameez out of her satchel, washed it out with shampoo and hung it up to dry. She climbed into the huge claw-foot bathtub, filled with steaming hot water, and scrubbed herself clean of soot and of the smell of incense. As she doused her hair underwater, one last scent of patchouli wafted up off the water and into the air where the ceiling fan dashed it away.

As the soot swirled down the drain, she thought of her father's ashes, and of her baby, and then finally, of Hadji. *I release them to thy spirit*, she prayed.

Afterward, bittersweet that it still smelled of jasmine and the musk of Hadji, she wrapped herself in her lavender pashmina shawl, then sat cross-legged on the bed and pulled the telephone toward her. She had the operator put through a long-distance call to New York.

"Darling," Geraldine drawled, "where have you been, you naughty child? I've been calling everywhere, and no one knew where to find you. Aren't you the clever little monkey? That picture of you jumping in front of golden clouds and then being fondled by some Indian religious leader has created an *absolute frenzy* of magazine offers ..."

She cut her off. "Don't say 'absolute.' Whatever you say, do *not* say that word."

"Did I say 'absolute' when I meant to say *Vogue*? Darling, do tell me I can say *Vogue*."

"You can say *Vogue* as long as you want. Just so you understand that I make the decisions now. No more telling me where to go and what to do, do you understand?"

There was silence. Cornelia launched in even deeper, "I will pick and choose my assignments. Is this agreed?"

"Don't be such a fierce little monkey now darling, honestly..."

Cornelia cut her off. "Don't you get it? Do I have to choose someone else to represent me? Listen and listen well. I am not anyone's fierce little monkey anymore."

"Well, then who *are* you, darling?" But her voice was more subdued than usual.

"Cornelia," she smiled, "Just plain old Cornelia. That's who I am."

"I see. Cornelia. Well, Cornelia it is then. And can I presume that Cornelia will accept a *Vogue* cover?"

"Yes," she said, as confidence flooded in. To her vast relief, for the first time ever she had spoken to Geraldine with no hint of petulance. "Yes! You can say yes. And while we're at it, will you call my mother please and tell her I'm coming back? That would be very nice. But not to live with her. I think it's time I got my own place. And by the way, time for me to handle my own money. You'll send the checks to me now that I'm of age. Tell Nevin not to worry, I'll make sure she's taken care of." And somehow, for the first time ever, she seemed capable of talking in that clear quiet voice that somehow had always been there. "Time for me perhaps to go to art school and study painting." And as she said it, a surge of joy flooded through her. She thought of the pilgrims worshipping, and of Hadji's glow of love when he looked at his followers, and she thought, yes, this is how it feels to be sure of something.

But then Geraldine pushed back. "Well, that's all very well, but what about *Harper's Bazaar*? They'll be annoyed if you just take *Vogue*. *Bazaar* wants to do an entire six-page spread. Something about religious costumes. I imagine they want to take advantage of your recent notoriety. I think there should be *no* question you should do them as well." Her tone had that old disapproving cadence that had so often caved in Cornelia's confidence.

Anxiety nibbled at the edge of her newly forged self. But she found herself saying, still in that quiet clear voice, "I'd like to wait until I get back to make that decision if you don't mind. I'll want to see where they plan on going with that." She could almost hear a quiet "Hear! Hear!" from her father and Horace and even Hadji, though thinking of Hadji made the pain throb back through her. She pushed the thought of him aside.

"But," Geraldine's tone was querulous.

"As I said, I'll think about it and let you know. Bye!" she said, hanging up before another onslaught came her way.

The next morning, she was on a plane to Mumbai. The following day she flew to Paris, then on to New York where she checked into the Gramercy Park Hotel, which was near art schools and would do until she found a place to rent.

Once in her hotel room, her first phone call was to the DA's office in Michigan. She asked about the statute of limitations. She asked about the whereabouts of old evidence. Yes, she answered, she was now an adult and able to pursue prosecution on her own. When she got the answers she was looking for, she took a deep breath then told them she said she would like to reinstate the charges. Yes, she was very sure. Yes, she knew it would be hard. Yes, she was ready to stand up and witness against Hall Hamden.

No, she was not afraid.